THE DARK BEFORE DAWN

JAIMA FIXSEN

Big E, little e, what begins with E?
A sweet, small boy who is dear to me.

This is also for Blake, who does not want a book dedicated to him, but gets one anyway.

CHAPTER 1

Vienna, 1814

Night was better for keeping secrets, but cold, even in the middle of September. Kasper shoved his hands deeper into his coat pockets and hunched his shoulders. He was late.

Over cobbles slick with evening rain, he crossed the plaza to St. Stephen's. Though the rain had stopped, thick clouds blanketed Vienna, muffling sound and blotting out the moon. In the dark, the great doors of the towering cathedral frowned as he passed. A stone lion, carved into a corner and worn smooth by time, watched with legs bent, ready to pounce.

This isn't a time for fancies, Kasper reminded himself. Though unpleasant, tonight's errand was unavoidable. If Theresa didn't have money soon, there was no knowing what she'd try next—stealing watches and stickpins from her gentlemen, perhaps. Tonight's scheme was enough trouble. Kasper didn't need more.

Past the south tower, a small door hid on the quietest side of the square. This entrance also lurked behind a gate of wrought iron, but—Kasper let out a sigh of relief—the gate was open, and only Gunter was about, waiting just inside, leaning against the short stone pillars. A large black key swung from his callused hand.

"You're late," Gunter said, unperturbed.

"There's still time."

"Not much."

"It will be enough." Kasper had planned for a half hour, but the ten minutes he had would suffice. "Let's hurry." Olsberg would be here soon.

Gunter separated himself from the pillar and unlocked the door. When he moved, a fusty smell of decay swung around him like a cloak. "You've a light?"

"Here." The empty lantern hung from Kasper's arm. He set it on the step to grapple with flint and tinder, balancing his walking stick under his arm. He dropped the tinder twice but finally conjured a wavering flame. "Take me below." Shifting his stick and lamp to one hand, Kasper fumbled in his pocket for the rest of the money and laid it in Gunter's open hand. The instant the silver touched his dirt-creased palm, it vanished.

"This way."

Down the worn-edged stairs they went, into numbing cold, the lantern's glow bobbing along the brick walls. It was too dark in the crypt to see more than a few yards ahead, but the bones of St. Stephen's didn't require light or comfort, and the men who toiled here scraping and stacking were gone to their homes—save Gunter. He nudged Kasper's arm, directing him down a smaller passage, past shadowed vaults that mocked the puny lamplight. The sandy floor whispered as they went.

At the next turning, Gunter stopped, motioning with a blunt forefinger. "Just down there. On your left. Better air, if you'll be doing much waiting. No flesh on the bones, and they're stacked, tidy-like." He folded his arms, his hands disappearing into the tattered sleeves of a worn coat that couldn't do much against this cold.

"My friend should be here before long. Go back above. Just bring him once he comes," Kasper said.

Gunter made an indecipherable sound that might have signified skepticism or assent. Friends didn't meet in places like this, but he'd been paid for silence and the use of his key. He melted into the dark.

"You don't need a light?" Kasper called after him.

A laugh echoed down the tunnel. "I know my way out." Within seconds, all sound of him was gone. Kasper took a steadying breath but repented quickly. This sour air was best taken in shallow sips.

At least he wouldn't have to wait long. Kasper raised the light to cut a path through the shadows. On his right, a wide arch yawned over a tumbled heap of bones. Staring at the gray, broken pieces, Kasper nearly stumbled on a spade left behind by Gunter's crew.

Steadying himself on the brick wall, Kasper turned from the gruesome sight, heading for the tidier vault Gunter had indicated. Light spilled ahead of Kasper's advancing feet, lapping against the far wall. It was stacked high with skulls, neat as a tray of baker's buns, except these were gray and pale. Kasper shivered, unable to look away.

Something moved behind him.

He swung his lantern but only discovered the source of the sound when heavy arms wrenched him backward, forcing the air from his lungs. A sharp point nestled against his belly. Kasper went dead still.

"Do you have it?" Count von Olsberg whispered.

"You're early," Kasper said. "I didn't expect you this soon." His stick with the hidden blade was gone, dropped in the surprise of the attack. The lantern, swinging in his outstretched hand, cast its erratic beam over the wall of leering skulls.

"My papers," Olsberg said. "Give them here."

"You have the money?" Kasper shifted, his boots crumbling

the gravel—or bone dust—beneath. Olsberg's blade slid closer, stopping Kasper's breath. "I must reach inside my coat," he managed.

Olsberg's grip slackened. "Slowly."

Seconds stretched as Kasper's fingers crept into an inner pocket. He had a knife too, thin as a playing card. It would be invisible behind curved fingers, but with Olsberg's knife ready to slide beneath his ribs…

Quickly, before he could think himself out of it, Kasper whipped his blade down, tearing at Olsberg's thigh. His other hand hurled the lantern at the wall, killing the light. A hand raked down his back, seizing his coat. Kasper lurched and pulled away, pitching headlong to the ground. Something struck him as he clambered to his feet; he tried to evade a flailing arm and collided with a heavy shoulder. With a grunt, he shoved once more and was free, spinning in the blackness, unable to remember the way to the door. He moved left, heard an answering footfall, and stopped breathing. The silence was absolute. Olsberg had stopped breathing too.

Feet still, Kasper swept a hand in front of him, afraid of what he might touch. Instead of cloth and outraged muscle, he grazed brick, shaving skin from his knuckles. Something clattered—Olsberg blundering into the bones—so Kasper ran, his hand trailing against the wall until, without warning, it vanished beneath his fingers. He'd found the door of the vault.

Like a fish loosed from the line, Kasper fled down the passage as fast as he could go.

"Gravedigger! I need a light!" Olsberg's shouts reverberated down the low tunnel but faded quickly. Kasper paused at the sound of a crash and a sharp curse. Olsberg had probably knocked over the spade left in the tunnel. Kasper had taken the wrong way. Olsberg and Gunter were between him and the only way out.

"Bring me a light!" Olsberg roared, summoning a shuffle of

footsteps and a glow that forced Kasper to shrink deeper into the tunnels. There was, he knew, another set of stairs that went up into the cathedral, but he might wander all night in this black labyrinth without finding it, and the door was surely locked. Evading Olsberg and the gravedigger long enough to creep past them was his only chance of escape. He must find somewhere to hide and remember the way out.

Kasper ran, counting turns, clutching his burning side. His coat was wet and sticky. He was bleeding, but there was no time to tend it now. He hadn't expected betrayal. Olsberg must have offered the gravedigger more money. Kasper should have thought of that—if a secret was worth paying for, it was worth spilling blood for too. He walked on until, unexpectedly, blessedly, the air tasted sweet again. *Another door?*

Pulse quickening, he rounded a corner, following the clean air into a high vault. Deep within was a grating, small and remote, set in the ceiling, a black fretwork against the lighter dark of the sky. Beneath lay a pile of dry bones—plague victims, dropped from the street because there were too many to bury. Kasper scaled the pile, slipping this way and that, but the bars were impossible to reach, and climbing was noisy. The network of passages and vaults was vast, but they'd find him if he kept making a racket.

He needed a place to hide. Kasper felt his way back to the passage, heard voices, and broke into a run, counting strides so he wouldn't lose his way. The wall beneath his left hand stopped, and he plunged into this newfound void. It too had bones, judging from the smell. Newer ones.

No sound of Olsberg or Gunter, so Kasper risked bringing a spark to tinder. The lint in his fingers flared, revealing a tangle of greasy, blackened limbs. Kasper recoiled, stumbling over something on the ground and dropping the light. It winked out before reaching the ground, stranding him in the dark—hands splayed, too afraid to move because of what he might touch.

Kasper edged sideways, striking a hard corner with his shin. Not bones, clearly, but with his flint gone, the only way to identify it was with his hands. He swept his fingers over it, tracing a smooth surface beneath a fuzzing of dust. It was a coffin, long and low and splitting at the sides, the hinges of the metal handles rusted fast. Kasper considered only a moment, his hand resting on the lid, then felt his way to the corner. The lid shifted a mere inch when he pulled, but the short side, where the head should be, gave way with a splintering crack.

A hard tug pulled the nails loose; a second pried the broken board off. No time for squeamishness. Feeling his way to the other end, Kasper raised the coffin, spilling the contents to the sandy floor, kicking them in the direction of the gruesome pile. The new body wouldn't be so different from the others, merely adding to the general horror of the place. He pointed the intact end of the coffin toward the door, then knelt at the opening and crawled in.

The box closed in on him, brittle wood creaking every time he moved, the silk lining shredding and clinging like cobwebs. Kasper quivered, gasping for air—there wasn't enough, not with the silk and the stink. Every breath he took, the space shrank, until it was all he could do not to scream and kick his way out.

Count your breaths. Think of ordinary things. There was no way to see, but he kept his eyes squeezed shut. The only way to measure time was by his growing aches—no matter how he shifted, he couldn't escape the lump boring into his back. The blood seeping from the cut on his side grew stickier, then stiff and tight. Then he heard voices.

"This way."

A pause, some shuffling.

"You must have wounded him."

Fear pierced Kasper, sharp and cold. Hiding was no good, not when you left a trail. He was trapped. It was too late to run.

"Might be mine. Look at the way I'm dripping."

Olsberg was bleeding too. Kasper had forgotten.

"Can't be yours. We never came this way."

"Are you sure?"

"I know this place," Gunter told him. "We'll find him. You'll see."

"We'd have him by now, if it hadn't taken you such an age to bring a lantern."

Gunter said nothing. The sound of their footsteps came closer.

Kasper braced one hand on the lid, the other tightening around his knife. Light lanced onto him through a crack in the wood.

Someone retched. "Disgusting! I don't know how you stand this."

"We can't all be born to the purple." Gunter spoke evenly.

"No one would stay here," Olsberg said. "Come on."

"Do you see more blood?" The light flickered over Kasper again.

"No. Even if there were, how'd we see it in this mess?"

Kasper listened to their footsteps fade deeper into the tunnels. He counted to thirty, the muscles of his limbs coiling tight.

Unable to keep still a moment longer, he heaved against the lid. It splintered with a tremendous crack, but Kasper was already sprinting from the vault. With a hand on the wall to guide him, he raced down the passage, counting each stride, marking each turn. Shouts echoed behind him.

Faster.

He passed the first vault. Nearly there—but his foot struck something, and he stumbled, crashing to the gritty floor. The cut on his side burned. Pushing up on scuffed palms, he bumped against the wooden shaft that had tripped him, hefted it, and discovered it bore a handle and a weight on one end. The spade. Kasper grinned. He was almost to the door, and this was a better weapon than a knife.

Pocketing his blade, Kasper raced on, gripping the shovel, slowing only when he came to the steps. They were uneven, shallow, and worn low in the middle. It would be easy to trip again, and the count and Gunter were drawing close. He couldn't see their light, but he could hear them, louder and louder.

Surfacing at last in clean air, Kasper threw himself at the iron gate—and fell back, bruised. The bars didn't budge. Desperate, fumbling for the latch, he let out a choked sob as his fingers closed around a heavy lock. No wonder Gunter hadn't worried about losing him.

Shouts floated up the stairs. They were coming. Olsberg would kill him, then comb his pockets for the papers. They'd strip his body and hide him with the bones. No one would ever find him.

Raising the spade, Kasper slammed it against the lock—once, twice, and again. He must get out. Behind him, he could see a glow at the bottom of the stairs. He was raising the spade for a final, frantic blow when he heard the ring of metal on stone. The lock was broken.

With a monumental clanging, Kasper pushed through the gate and threw aside the shovel, before even his thoughts caught up with him. He shot across the plaza and into the sanctuary of the nearest alley, free as a fledgling who'd discovered his wings—but blind to the hooded shape untangling from the cathedral's thick shadows and following him out of the square.

KASPER RAN, darting in and out of passages at speeds that scattered the flimsily gowned grabennymphen loitering in the street. They flew away from him like startled birds, petticoats flapping. Veering west, Kasper ran past the battered city walls all the way to the Rathaus and collapsed in the shelter of the arched stone colonnade. There were lights inside the town hall and in the nearby houses. He wanted lights and their warm comfort, but they were dangerous to him now.

With stumbling steps, Kasper aimed for a slimmer, blacker street, steadying his breath and probing tentatively at his side. The touch did nothing to tighten or loosen the pain; it throbbed just the same, a hot pulse every time his lungs moved. In this dark, all he could tell for certain was that the bloodstained patch of his coat was bigger than his hand.

He heard singing, warning him that there were drunks ahead, just around the corner. Four of them came into view—students who slowed instead of walking past. It might be wise to draw his knife.

"What's that stench?" the closest asked, grimacing.

"Filth. Must be French," the tallest suggested. "Not the kind we want here."

Kasper had seen reports of lone foreigners beaten by student gangs. Mumbling apologies in German, he backed away, escaping down a side street. He was exhausted, bleeding, and stinking, but there was no sign of Olsberg or Gunter. He'd best take himself home, or who knew what new trouble would find him? He'd run so far that he now had a long walk ahead of him. He glanced over his shoulder at every corner all the way back.

Kasper's rooms were in a house off the Fleischmarkt, in a street so narrow the entrance was almost invisible. Shouldering his way into the passage, he winced as he took out his key. Shaking hands forced him to spend more time coaxing open the lock. It was a relief to bolt the door behind him. He tiptoed up the stairs. His landlady, though long abed, was a light sleeper.

The lock on the door to his rooms gave less trouble than the one to the house, and no lights were burning inside. Good. Levi hadn't outlasted the candle, though it looked like he'd tried, judging from the long shape stretched out in the one good chair. Kasper stepped over Levi's sprawled legs, listening to his breathing. It was easy to forget he was old, except when you watched him sleep.

It would be better to deal with this injury on his own, if he could, so Kasper closed himself in the bedchamber without making a sound. Easing out of his coat, he struck a light. The sight in the mirror made him grimace. Pale and shadowed with dirt—or worse—his waistcoat defaced with a broad, dark stain, it hurt just to move. Stripping away the waistcoat was agonizing, for it stuck to his shirt, which was glued fast to his skin. Kasper tackled the buttons one-handed, pressing the other against his side, hissing with pain. By the time he tossed the waistcoat to the floor, he was white, sticky with sweat, and panting. The shirt would be even worse. He wouldn't attempt removal without dampening it first.

Unfastening cravat and cuff buttons, Kasper rolled up the sleeves, baring his arms. The water on the washstand was so cold that when Kasper held a wet cloth to his side, it temporarily overpowered the pain. He soaked the shirt, softening the crust that held it to his skin until it gently peeled away.

Time to see how bad the cut was. Kasper mopped away the blood-pinked drips, gathered his shirttail, and hoisted the garment overhead—and stood in front of the looking glass, examining a slice that would have been so much worse had it not been for the tight corset that hid and held in her breasts.

CHAPTER 2

Used to having his way, Count Marius von Olsberg did not take well to his blackmailer's escape. Berating the gravedigger with curses that echoed through the square, he broke off only when a tall figure trespassed into their circle of lamplight. Marius's hand twitched, ready to go for the knife in his boot, until he saw it was only Lennard, his younger brother.

"What are you doing here?" Marius asked.

"I need to talk to you."

"You followed me?" Marius's mouth twisted. Lennard never could keep quiet. Wishing his brother miles away, Marius spoke more harshly than usual. "What did you see?"

Lennard cleared his throat. "Someone came to meet you, but he ran from here just moments ago. I followed as far as I could but lost him in the side streets near St. Peter's."

Marius grimaced. The one time his brother might have been of use… "Did you get a look at him?" Any clue to the blackmailer's identity would help.

"He was too fast for me. In this dark…"

Marius owned many secrets, but this one couldn't be shared, not with Lennard. He had to find this blackmailer, get rid of him, and keep his brother from nosing around too. "Go home. You've wasted your time. I told you before I'm not speaking to Hardenberg for you. I meant it." Turning away, he dismissed the gravedigger. No need for him anymore.

The ragged man whined he was owed money. Lennard protested too, but for the moment, Marius gave his attention to the cringing gravedigger. "I don't have what I came for, do I?" Marius spoke softly, scarcely above a whisper. Now the blackmailer would contact him again, angry and demanding even more money.

"I don't know how he slipped past us, my lord."

"You should have been more careful. I don't reward fools."

Swallowing his grumbles, the gravedigger bowed, edging his way out of the lantern light. Marius frowned at Lennard, who was pleading again.

"Anna's parents are insisting she announce her engagement to that banker. If you would just—"

"Marrying him needn't stop you from having her," Marius said. "Better that way. You won't be responsible for any bills." He went to walk past, but Lennard grabbed his coat.

"Listen to me!"

Marius stopped, surprised. Lennard—melancholy poet, butterfly collector, perennial bungler who inspired no obedience from the men in his brigade—was laying hands on him and proving unexpectedly strong. Marius leaned forward, laughing derisively. He wasn't afraid. Though an accomplished swordsman, Lennard wasn't the kind of man who could fight with his hands. Marius was. "Do you want me to school you?"

"You can try." Lennard swore and threw a punch, easily dodged. Marius let him swing again, waiting until his brother was off balance. Then he jabbed twice with the precision of a ticking clock, aiming at the face, then at the gut. Lennard wobbled at the first impact and staggered with the second, buckling like a stage clown.

Marius turned him faceup with a booted foot, which he planted in his brother's shoulder, making him groan. "Don't ever raise your hands against me." He was reasonably sure Lennard was conscious but walked away without making sure. Lennard knew better than to challenge him.

Marius's fight-fury dwindled as he limped from the square, cursing the wound in his thigh. His leg was covered in blood, and the handkerchief he'd used earlier to shield his nose had been dropped somewhere in the crypt. On the next street, Marius hailed a run-down fiaker, careful to conceal the stains behind his cloak. The driver wouldn't take him if he thought he'd get blood on the worn cushions. Safe inside the coach, Marius prodded the gash. Normally, it felt good, being the man who walked away from a fight, but though he'd beaten Lennard, the contest he'd lost was more important. He was worse off now than before.

He must learn who this blackmailer was, but his only clue was an anonymous letter offering to sell him proof of something no one could know. True, he'd wounded the man but not badly enough to kill him, unless the cut festered. Marius doubted his luck would stretch that far.

The driver made slow progress through the dimly lit streets. If not for his wound, Marius would have walked. His apartments weren't far from the cathedral. The house was older than he liked, but the neighborhood was good, and one was lucky to rent lodgings anywhere in Vienna just now, never mind the price. Still, as the carriage stopped, he felt again how humiliating it was, living in what must surely be the smallest house on the square. He hadn't even been able to afford the more expensive suite of rooms on the first floor, which were leased to a member of the Russian delegation, here in Vienna for the peace congress.

He paid the driver. It was late and Marius was filthy, but even when he wasn't, he used the private back stairs, accessed from the small courtyard behind the house. They kept him out of sight of the neighbors or anyone else who might be watching. Marius fitted his key into the lock but found it already open, though the heavy door didn't move at his touch.

He frowned, sure the unlocked door was the fault of that Russian sneaking in prostitutes again. Marius sighed. He could lock the door behind him, which would spare him the angry mutterings of the landlady, but if the Russian's woman was still with him, she might not be able to get out, and that was the kind of thing Marius's wife would complain about. She'd sigh, look grave, say how unfortunate it was they were forced to make do, then watch him with narrowed eyes for a couple of days, wondering how often *he* brought women in and out using the same stairs.

Still deciding, Marius pocketed his key, causing a sharp twinge in his leg. Cursing, he reached for the door with his other arm but never touched the handle. Something flew over his head, tightening around his throat. For an instant, he was too stunned to move, but when he gulped for air and got nothing, panic flung him into action. He jerked, clawing at the cord, then remembered there were better ways and hurled himself against the wall. His assailant's breath escaped in a low groan, but the grip at his throat didn't slacken. Struggling, Marius threw himself back again, his face contorted in a soundless snarl as he twisted and heaved in a swirl of pulsing lights. His boots slipped on the threshold. Like a landed trout, his flailing grew weaker, but then the tension in the cord at his neck eased, and he sucked in a thread of air.

A whisper rasped against his ears, coalescing sluggishly into words. A question. Marius jerked a negative, and the cord tightened again. He would have whimpered, but he couldn't make a sound. Unable to read the answer trickling from his eyes, the figure behind him once more gave him air—and asked again.

This time, Marius gave up everything, the words scraping his throat.

"Pity," his attacker whispered.

The flow of silken air dwindled and was gone, dissolving him in a scintillating field of stars. They rushed at him now, glittering, intense, white.

But the night, as every living soul in Vienna knew, was cloudy.

CHAPTER 3

She was bleeding again. Removing her shirt and corset had opened the wound. Now blood ran down her middle and dripped onto the carpet. Clamping a towel to her side, she dropped to her knees and blotted the dingy rug with the wet rag. Scrubbing furiously and ignoring the pain along her ribs, she didn't hear the door open.

"Klara!"

She looked up. Levi never forgot himself enough to use her real name. She shrank guiltily but didn't try to cover herself. He knew her secret. Without Levi's help, she'd never have created the identity of Kasper Stark. At the beginning, he'd posed as her tutor and now as her valet. She couldn't live without him.

Klara picked herself up from the floor. "I ran into some trouble." Her apologetic smile only deepened his frown.

"How badly are you cut?"

"I may need stitching."

"Weren't you going to tell me?"

She hoped he meant about the wound but feared otherwise. She'd held back much more, like the fact she was meeting Olsberg tonight. "I knew you didn't approve."

He snorted. As he crossed the room, he picked up her unused nightshirt. "Let me see it."

Klara took the shirt and held it to her front, turning sideways so Levi could see. He knelt beside her, as grim as if he'd been carved from ironwood. "I've told you again and again to never let an armed man surprise you. Why wasn't your knife ready?"

"I did strike him in the thigh."

Levi shook his head. He was old but, in his renegade youth, he'd never been beaten in contests with fists, knives, or genteel swords. Once, Levi had been a reckless, flamboyant playwright, whose works never failed to provoke the censors. He wasn't nearly as mild as he made himself look. When he had a mind to be, he was a stern teacher, and he looked stern now, lips pressed together, probing her side. Klara shut her eyes and recited Latin under her breath.

"I understand now why you've come back to me all torn," he said grimly. "Explain this smell."

They might have to get rid of everything she'd worn. Klara made a wry face. "I lost my walking stick. And my hat." She'd worn older clothes, but hats and weapons were expensive.

"You smell like a charnel house," Levi said.

"That's because I met Olsberg at the crypt of St. Stephen's." She gave him the briefest summary she thought he'd accept and finished with a confession: "I should have guessed Olsberg might outbid me for Gunter, but I never imagined he'd have time to find him. The boy at the opera house only delivered my demand this evening. Olsberg only had a few hours' notice, no more."

"It's enough time for a man like him," Levi said. "That's why I objected. He's dangerous."

Klara huffed. "I was nearly late for the meeting myself, which accounts for half the trouble."

"The baron kept you late?"

"Reports," she explained succinctly.

Levi shook his head. "If you insist on blackmail, do it properly, and don't let Theresa tell you what to do. She never considers all the angles."

In spite of herself, Klara smiled. She'd heard this before. "Not like you."

Levi was meticulous and not finished with his lecture. "You shouldn't do this at all. Your life is dangerous enough as it is."

They'd argued this many times. Klara sighed. "If I don't help her, she'll start stealing. Or go back to the moneylenders." Men like that would grind Theresa to powder. In a quieter voice, Klara repeated the most important point, the one that clinched it for her and should for Levi. "Her debts were for me."

Levi sniffed. "Rubbish. And she's stealing already. She didn't come by this secret honestly."

Klara flinched, only partly because of the pressure of his hands patting her side dry. "I owe her, Levi. Just like I owe you." Seeing his pained look, her shoulders fell. "You used to be friends with her. Can't you—"

Levi shook his head. "Not until she starts considering your safety. I told her this was too dangerous. I was right."

"I'll talk to her." If she was careful, she could meet Theresa's most pressing needs from her salary. That would give them more time.

Levi shook his head. "*I'm* talking to her this time. You won't even tell her you were wounded."

"I don't want her to know." Klara looked down. "Does it need stitching?"

"No. Only a plaster." He got up and washed his hands, leaving the room with a frowning admonition. "You were lucky."

She knew that well enough. The hairs on her back prickled, remembering the bite of Olsberg's knife. She'd have to think of something else. Blackmail wasn't a good business.

When Levi returned, his hands were full of ointment and plaster. Klara submitted to the bandaging and the bitter reprimand, knowing she needed both as much as Levi needed to give them. Then she gathered her discarded clothes while he inspected the stains on her modified corset.

"They won't come out," he said.

"I don't mind, so long as the smell does."

"It's not as bad as on your other things," Levi said. "I think we can save it. The rest I'll drop in the river. Burning's too messy, and there's still time before it's light."

Klara nodded tiredly. "I'm sorry." He gave her a glance. "Truly."

"Good." He sighed. "You're all I have, Kasper. Try to remember."

Her eyes dropped to the floor, but he wasn't leaving without an answer. "I'll be more careful. I promise."

He left her and she climbed into bed, sliding gingerly beneath the covers. Her hair, wet from washing, surrounded her with the smell of soap and safety. She didn't dream, and it never crossed her mind, asleep or awake, that some promises are impossible to keep.

WHEN LEVI WOKE HER, it felt like she'd slept only minutes—or else a hundred years. Everything ached, and her right side burned. She sat up, discovered she was too sore to progress any farther on her own, and let Levi help her out of bed, to the wash-stand where he handed her a glass of bitter-smelling liquor.

"This will blunt the pain, but it will make you bleary. We'll follow it with coffee."

She drained the glass, then buried her hands in the hot wash water. She sighed with pleasure. "Thank you."

He nearly smiled. "I got rid of yesterday's coat, so you'll have to wear the brown one today."

"I'll need to buy another." Klara frowned. Between replacing coats and hats and helping Theresa from her salary...

Levi must have read some of her thoughts. "We'll make Theresa pay for it."

"No."

"It's her fault—"

Klara interrupted, "No, Levi. I'll let you talk to her, but I won't let you do that."

Expecting argument, she was surprised when he conceded, muttering that she looked too pale. "And we've no time. Not if we're to get you dressed and to the Hofburg before Hagen is there."

To succeed at her post, it was essential that Klara arrive early. Dressing was a complicated procedure, but they'd had years of practice. They moved smoothly and swiftly as machinery, tightening her corset, adjusting the padding in her drawers and on her shoulders. Her shirts were worn by Levi first to collect an appropriate odor, which was then hidden beneath a spicy scent—not too heavy, lest she appear effeminate. As Klara glued on her mustache, Levi brushed a light stubble onto her cheeks, which she'd darken later in the day using the cosmetics in a secret compartment of her snuffbox. Her cropped hair was pomaded into fashionable disorder, her eyebrows thickened with kohl. While she drank a cup of coffee, Levi filed her nails flat, accentuating the bluntness of her fingers.

When they finished, she was a lean young man with a face dominated by heavy brows and a sulky mouth. The nose that was too wide for womanly beauty sat right on Kasper Stark, as did the grave intelligence of the eyes. She looked drawn and tired today, but as she studied herself in the looking glass, she found no mistakes and turned away from her reflection just in time to see Levi raising his arm to fell her with a blow.

With the instincts of long practice, she swerved and blocked it. Levi's face relaxed into a smile. "Good. I was just—"

"Testing. I know." After last night, she was grateful Levi was an exacting teacher. "I won't let my guard down again."

Levi nodded, donning his valet manner, his face becoming blank and impersonal as he bowed. "I wish you a good day, sir." On this, the usual benediction, he sailed away with her empty coffee cup. Klara went out the door. It was early still, but not so early she troubled to step softly on the stairs.

Outside there was light, the pale golden kind that is so good to Vienna, but she was in a hurry and didn't notice this delicate loveliness. Today was a day like any other, and she was expected at the offices of Austria's secret police.

THE HOFBURG PALACE stretched along Michaelerplatz, acres of pale stone adorned with baroque statues. Two of these heroically muscled groups flanked the massive gate. Instead of walking beneath their outflung arms, Klara went past the winter riding school, turning onto a narrow passage between the old castle and the hall of state. At the Swiss gate—older, smaller, striped in red and black stone—the guards allowed her to pass. She never entered the palace without her skin prickling, but fear was a helpful habit according to Levi.

Inside the courtyard, Klara hurried through the crowd of servants carrying messages, ferrying wood for the palace's ceramic stoves, and unloading delicacies for the imperial tables. She was halfway to the unobtrusive door meant for the legion of bureaucrats, clerks, secretaries, and cryptographers when a commotion caught her eye. She peered sideways, then slowed and gave it more attention. Anton Spaller, a fellow secretary, was lumbering as fast as his clubfoot allowed, alongside a pair of guardsmen. Between them, they carried a body on a ladder. For a moment, it looked—

She stopped, waiting for the messenger blocking her view to

bustle past. Her throat seized. She *had* recognized the broad blue coat, the thick brown hair. They were carrying Count von Olsberg. He was dead.

Repressing an instinctive shudder, Klara broke into a trot, drawing even with Anton. "What happened?" she asked, her voice pitched low.

Lurching around—Anton was clumsy even when he wasn't startled—he saw her and swore. "One of my agents, a prostitute who's been watching Prince Stepanovich, found this man in a heap outside the back door. She alerted me at once. Says this man's a Prussian count. Hagen's going to murder someone when he finds out. Even if this isn't related to some plot, it will make the conference delegates nervous. Who knows what kind of rumors...?"

Klara nodded, rubbing her forehead like it would make the corpse in front of her disappear. "Where is he? Baron von Hagen, I mean."

Anton's voice dropped to an appalled whisper. "He's already taken the daily briefing to the emperor."

She had some time then, if only a little. Inhaling slowly, Klara frowned at the corpse's purpling tongue and bulging eyes. He'd been strangled, his stiff limbs locked now in a grotesquely contorted pose that the guardsmen struggled to balance between them. Klara couldn't muster the horror to shrink or the composure to look away. She was paralyzed by two thoughts: *Had they searched him? Was her message still in Olsberg's pocket?*

The note she'd sent him last night was written in her own hand. Anton—and Hagen, for that matter—would instantly recognize it. Against that evidence, nothing would convince them she was innocent of this murder—especially when close questioning would reveal her true identity, proving her a liar. But Anton wasn't motioning for guards to arrest her. He was waving away the servants jostling for a look at the corpse.

"Are you all right?" Anton stepped closer, peering into her face.

"I'm fine." Klara gathered herself. "You're going to have to interrupt Herr Hagen. He'll need to know at once. A murder—"

"While he's with *the emperor*?" Anton shook his head. "My life's not worth it."

"I'll do it, if you haven't the stomach for it," Klara said, praying she'd convince him to go. She must divert him so she could search Olsberg's body alone, while there was still no reason to suspect her. "This is exactly the sort of thing Herr Hagen expects to know. Even if he and the emperor are angry at first, they'll be glad someone has taken the matter in hand. Think how it will look if one of the congress delegates or another monarch learns of it first."

Anton chewed his lower lip.

Klara turned. "I'll go. If they are displeased, I'll keep your name out of it." As she'd hoped, Anton stopped her.

"No. This is my business, at least until Herr Hagen deems otherwise. I'll tell him. You take charge of the corpse." Now she'd pointed it out to him, he wouldn't want to miss this chance. Anton was ambitious.

Klara grunted. "Leaving me with the pleasant work, as usual." Her eyes flicked past Olsberg's bruised face. His breeches were covered in dried blood where she'd slashed his leg. He must have been killed soon after she left him.

"At least you won't get told off by Herr Hagen. You may be right—but he'll be steaming mad first." Anton vanished into the palace, leaving Klara with the bearers and the body.

"Inside. Let's try to keep this quiet." Small chance of that. Dozens of servants had seen the body already.

She led them through the dungeon door and down the stairs. The thick stone walls always held a chill, and the barred windows never let in sufficient light. Just as well. She feared she was unnaturally pale. At the end of a long passage, she found an empty interrogation room. "Lay him out on the table, then fetch me pen, paper and ink. Be quick with it. Herr Hagen will want an immediate report."

They nodded, and Klara watched impassively as they rolled Olsberg onto the bare table. He rocked awkwardly, his frozen elbow pointing at the ceiling. One guard left, and Klara ordered the second to get rid of the ladder. It was tempting to bar the door behind them, but that would look suspicious. She must hurry and find her note before they came back. Heart pounding, she bent over the body.

He had a snuff box and a roll of gold French Napoléons in one pocket. The other held a folded paper Klara opened with trembling fingers, but it was only a crumpled IOU. She laid it next to the coins on the table. With brisk strokes of her knife, she sliced through his coat. It peeled away as easily as cooked fish beneath a fork. She cut open cuffs and seams, tearing out the linen lining. Nothing.

His breeches were soiled and stiff with blood. She cut them away too, only gagging when it came time to remove his socks. This had nothing to do with smells; it was the sight of his toes that upset her. They were unsettlingly human and individual.

Queasy now, she stripped away the shirt. Beneath the stink of death, scents of the man still lingered—sweat and a spicy cologne. Panting, Klara braced herself on the table, pushing away memories of Olsberg holding her prisoner, his knife tickling her side and his whisper burrowing into her ear.

"Herr Stark?"

"Yes?" Klara straightened.

"You've found something?"

Not her note. "Only what you see here." She gestured at the piled contents of his pocket. "I haven't brought myself to remove his rings." The hands were worse to look at than the toes.

The guardsman handed her a writing box. He was lean and weathered, probably in his forties. "Searching the dead isn't easy. Usually, there's little to find. I'm surprised this gold was left behind."

Klara nodded. Thievery was common. Leaving money on bodies was not. "Perhaps you will make a second search in case I missed anything?" she suggested.

The guardsman picked through the remnants of clothing while Klara scribbled, wondering if she was betraying herself with each stroke of her pen. "There's bruising at his neck and a wound on his thigh," she said. It was easier to breathe with words filling the room, even if she had to supply them. "Anything else?"

"Some scratches. Cuts on the right knuckles." The guardsman shook his head. "He didn't give up easy, but he still lost the fight."

Klara penned one more line to include the knuckles, then sprinkled sand on the sheet so the ink wouldn't smudge. "Are there any instructions? Do I send this along to Herr Hagen?"

The guardsman nodded. "He wants it now, before he calls on the widow. Herr Spaller is to search the house."

Klara kept her face still. "Do they leave at once?"

"Almost immediately. Shall I take the report to them, or do you wish to yourself?"

"First, I'll make sure all is in order." Klara reviewed the papers, buying a moment's delay. Olsberg wasn't carrying her note, but had he stopped at home before coming to their meeting? Was the note lying on his desk or lurking in the pocket of another coat?

She had no more time to think. The guardsman was waiting. "Everything seems to be correct. Please deliver this to Herr Hagen. There are other matters I must tend to."

She must search the house first—somehow. She paused at the door.

"When you deliver the report, make sure you bring along Count von Olsberg's ring. Baron von Hagen will wish to give it to the widow." It would take time to twist the heavy band off, but not nearly enough. She might beat Anton and Herr Hagen to the house, but they would catch up with her.

Except they needn't catch Kasper Stark.

CHAPTER 4

Levi Braun knew, theoretically, that valets did not treat their employers like children—or love them like children, at any rate. Though he had sent Klara off with bracing words and admonitions to keep a sharp watch and her head down, he was worried. Threatening Count von Olsberg was a mistake. That man might do anything when cornered, as he had proved. Klara didn't know the half of it.

Theresa did, which was why Levi blamed her. If Olsberg learned the note was from Klara, she'd never be safe. The blackmail had to stop before he could trace her.

Levi did not normally pay calls at the house on Köllnerhofgasse, though it was only a short walk away. He avoided the street entirely, judging that the less he and Klara were seen with Theresa Stark the better—though, of course, Theresa didn't use the same surname. For twenty years, she'd been known as Theresa Vogl and sung opera in the Burgtheater. She'd had more lovers than she could count, but only one child, which was just as well. She was a terrible mother.

Theresa's maid, dubious at Levi's appearance, seemed unlikely to show him upstairs, so Levi brought out a letter from her mistress. It was addressed to Kasper Stark, but the maid would be hard-pressed to put a face to that name or read it at all, as Levi obscured most of it with his thumb. With a self-righteous frown and long-suffering sigh, she ushered Levi into the parlor.

Probably thinks I'm a moneylender, Levi thought. It wasn't a foolish assumption, as he was dressed plainly and carried no flowers.

Theresa was alone, as he knew she would be. It was her habit to reserve this hour for her toilette. Her lovers knew this, and much of Vienna probably did too. She was resting on a sea-green divan with cucumber slices on her eyes, the rest of her face luxuriating under a mixture of crushed strawberries. Age, the relentless enemy, was catching up with her.

She peeled the cucumber off her right eye. "What's the trouble now? I don't need a lecture."

"No." Heaven knew he'd given her plenty of those. "Perhaps a slap, but I'm not the one to give it to you. Your Marius von Olsberg went early to his rendezvous with Kasper. Olsberg would have killed him." It was not hard, after so many years, to speak of Klara with masculine pronouns. "Luck and quick thinking saved him," Levi went on. "But he's wounded."

"Badly?" She sat up, the other cucumber falling onto the sofa.

"Sliced along the ribs. It could have been much worse. You shouldn't have attempted anything so risky. And if you must, leave Kasper out of it."

"Is he all right? Truly?" Her voice trembled. Blinking, she reached for a handkerchief.

"You have fruit on your face," Levi reminded her, provoking a frown. She rang for her maid.

"Get this pulp off me."

While the maid scurried for towels and Theresa twitched impatiently, Levi went to the window and watched the street. There were plenty of comings and goings this close to the Fleischmarkt, but Theresa usually entertained men of significance, and it was possible his visit had been noted. Gossip and intrigue had never been so rife in Vienna. It was naive to think the names of her lovers were not reported to someone. With rising rents gnawing at everyone's pockets, many were willing to sell tidbits to the paymasters wanting 'intelligence.' It was risky coming here, but he'd had to, for Klara's sake.

The maid left. Theresa blew her nose. "You think it's my fault."

"Isn't it?"

"Does she—" Correcting herself in response to his sharp look, she asked instead: "Does Kasper think so?"

Levi wanted to say yes, but Theresa knew her daughter's disposition was forgiving. "You know how seriously Kasper takes his duties to you."

"Thank heaven he escaped."

Levi and Theresa disagreed on nearly everything, but it was undeniable she was upset. He wanted her to be.

Twenty years he'd known Theresa Vogl. Turning piteous eyes on him wasn't going to make him relent, not this time. He'd had a weakness for her once, back when he'd been a forty-three-year-old librettist, and she, the newest golden-haired beauty of the Vienna opera. Her waxen frailty housed a soprano voice of such clarity and tensile strength it made composers giddy. He had loved writing for her. She preferred comedy but brought such pathos to her tragic roles. Performing on stage and in the green room, she could let throat-stopping grief into her eyes, and Levi, who'd also had his heart broken, knew that though she summoned the feeling at will, it came from a hurt that was real.

He'd watched her whirl amid the carnival of success, wrote her words of doomed love and immortal passion, and never once tried to sleep with her. She liked him for that. He knew, of course, about the child she kept in the attic above her apartment. Most women in her place would have abandoned the child or paid to have it fostered in the country. Theresa insisted on keeping her daughter close and guarded her well. The girl was five when Levi finally met her, when he fell in love for the last time.

He'd known he would never have children, but he never felt the loss until he met Klara. A solemn child, she was pale and parsimonious with her smile, a gap-toothed atrocity of wondrous sweetness. Her mind was like quicksilver. He offered to teach her Greek.

Theresa trusted him and thought it a great joke, watching him tutor Klara in the shabby garret upstairs. Klara acquired Greek with lightning rapidity, expanded her French, mastered Latin, and over the inexplicable objections of her mother, gained facility with English. She tunneled, mole-like, into whatever books Levi procured for her, and he, who admired but never appreciated feminine beauty, didn't notice she was plain. It troubled Theresa though, especially when Klara grew so tall.

"Stop going on about it," Levi said. "If you're pinched, let me buy her longer dresses."

"Gladly, if you can. You're months late with your work, and you spend all your money buying the girl books."

It was true he hadn't been writing, but Klara needed him. The dull-witted maid who used to look after her was long gone, and though it was true that at twelve Klara no longer needed minding, she didn't like to be alone. They were working on Aristophanes—

"She must have grown another two inches." Theresa rubbed the frown off her forehead.

"Not so loud," Levi whispered, for Klara was just behind the door, and though she held a new volume of plays, her hearing was excellent. "Nothing's the matter with her. You know how hard she tries to please you, so you might at least fret over matters she can do something about. You're making her unhappy." Twice now, he'd caught Klara staring at the mirror, looking desperate.

Mouth twisting, Theresa jerked her head, motioning him to come to her suite where they could talk privately. He followed her into the elegant, expensive rooms, so different from the Spartan quarters upstairs, ready to rail at her for making insensitive remarks about Klara's height and then telling her slouching was unattractive.

But Theresa spoke first. "Herr Schmidt has a new librettist."

"He hates Jews." Not that Levi was much of one.

"That's not the only reason he replaced you."

"We quarreled," Levi said. "Doesn't matter. He composes nothing but the same three melodies—"

"And your play?"

"Still unfinished. But—"

"I know. You have enough to keep yourself, except you squander everything on Klara," she said.

"When was the last time you bought her something she wanted? Lotion for her spots doesn't count. You made her cry. She thinks she's ugly."

Theresa rubbed her thumbnail. "It doesn't matter what she looks like now, but she won't stay twelve. What am I to do with her?"

"Stop hurting her, for a start. Why are you so worried? You've always sworn your daughter will have nothing to do with the stage, that she's not to be a kept woman, that—"

"I want her to marry a kind man with a good income."

"Who's to say she won't?" Levi asked.

"*I* didn't."

"Just because you couldn't doesn't mean she won't find someone who will value her."

Theresa snorted. "Men don't notice minds."

Levi frowned. "In the main, that's true, but—"

"She's too clever. She won't be happy with an idiot, and though she's bright enough to be any number of things, the best she can do as a woman is work as an underpaid governess."

Levi's frown gouged deeper. Klara was too bright for that.

"Don't you ever think beyond today?" Theresa asked, exasperated.

"She's happy now. Why take that from her?" Life held enough disappointment. "She's young. Let her have what happiness she can."

"One of us must think about the future. Her education—"

"Is better than nine out of ten boys her age," Levi interrupted.

"But it won't fit her to be a wife. For that, I'll have to send her to a girls' school."

The floor couldn't have tilted, but it felt that way. "Where?"

"I don't know. Schools are expensive, and there's no guarantee of finding a husband, not for a plain girl who reads too much." She picked again at her ragged thumbnail. "Be honest with me. If she were a boy, what could she do?"

Levi shrugged. "Physician, notary, priest...but for that, it would help to have connections, which she doesn't. Law, perhaps, though like any course of study, it would be expensive."

"And she could do any of them—if she weren't a girl?" Theresa walked away from him, taking a nail file from the box on the table.

"What are you thinking?" His heart was beating too fast for this circumstance, a low-toned conversation of carefully chosen words.

"Klara would be better off if she stopped wearing skirts." Theresa applied the file to her thumb with unnecessary strength.

"It's more complicated than that. If you're suggesting what I think you are, it's immense. More than a disguise. She would have to lose herself and become someone else."

Theresa looked at him, eyes steady. "That's not impossible. I've done it."

"You didn't become a man."

She ignored him and went on. "There was a woman in

Sweden. Brita Hagberg. She joined the army and fought against the Russians."

"Do you have any idea how hard it would be?"

"Yes. That's why I think she should start now. Listen, you can't keep teaching her forever. Girls learn different things. They don't study Latin with outmoded writers. But there's nothing unusual about a young man living or traveling with his tutor. She could go to university, travel Europe, gain all the benefits of a gentleman's education—"

"Too expensive," Levi said.

"I'd pay for it. I can. I'd rather give her that life than anything she could achieve as a woman."

"It's dangerous," he argued.

"You'd stay with her. When she's grown, you'd pose as her valet."

It was selfish and cowardly, but the band tightening about his ribs loosened. "You'd let her live with me?"

"If she's to succeed in a new life, she must. She will always need help. The only one who can do it is you."

"You're crazy." But he didn't want to lose Klara to a third-rate girls' school, and Theresa knew it.

"Think on it." Then, because she knew it would make it easier for him to relent, she gave her tragic smile. "Please."

It might be a solution of a sort, but it carried a host of problems. Stubbornly, Levi brought out one. "This Brita Hagberg. If you know of her, she must have been found out."

"They say she was wounded. Klara would choose a safer profession."

And she had, until Theresa decided to supplement her income with blackmail.

Levi turned away from the window and his memories. Most of the time, he didn't regret what he'd done. Klara had studied at Heidelberg, toured Greece and Italy, and passed the summers of her youth in the mountains, learning to ride and fence and fish.

She had a good life, in many ways an enviable one. Not in all things, unfortunately, but he did what he could for her.

Theresa was still white, and her fingers shook as she folded her hands together. "Does Kasper need a doctor? How will we find one?"

"The cut wasn't deep. I bandaged it, but you shouldn't have pitted him against that man." She knew Olsberg was dangerous. She'd been sleeping with him for months and understood his character along with the secret he'd inadvertently revealed.

She looked away. "Does Olsberg suspect me?"

"I don't know. I don't mind *you* staking your life, but I won't let you gamble with Kasper's." Levi had tolerated Theresa's schemes long enough, and her anxieties weren't sufficient to summon his pity.

She straightened in her chair. "I'm not a coward."

"Nor is Kasper, but some things are too much to ask." Levi stepped closer. "If you don't stop, I'll tell Olsberg the blackmail's coming from you. If it were me, I'd rather face the moneylenders."

He left her then, for he was too angry to talk. Klara was as much his as Theresa's. He was tired of games. The one they had was enough.

KLARA QUIT the dungeons at a brisk walk, hurrying through the crowded passages hidden inside the palace walls. When these narrow thoroughfares were blocked by wood carriers and maids hauling out the slops, Klara darted through the rooms themselves, blind to the sumptuous luxury. She passed footmen and a daintily dressed lady, but Klara's impeccable clothes and preoccupied look deterred questions. No one stopped her until she reached the attics, when a stout woman wearing the keys of a housekeeper called after her.

"Sir, the maid's quarters are along that corridor." Men were not allowed to trespass here.

Klara gave a tight smile. "Forgive the intrusion. I'm on an errand for Baron von Hagen."

Wordlessly, the woman stepped back, leaving Klara to make her way alone. Even if this housekeeper was not on the spymaster's payroll herself, many of the maids would be.

Klara chose a door at random and shut herself inside, judging that so long as the room housed maids, she would find what she needed. Beneath four narrow cots, next to the rolled pallets for the extra maids brought in to help during the peace conference, were the boxes holding the maids' meager possessions. Klara found a dress in the second box—a faded, cotton print folded up with a clean cap and apron, probably saved for Sundays.

Blocking the door with the lone chair—it was straight-backed, battered, with a split in the seat—Klara tore off her clothes and stumbled into the dress, impatient with the ties and pinning. Too large in the bodice and stopping well above her ankles, it would have to do. With the ribbon at the neck drawn tight, an apron to give her more shape, and a cap concealing her cropped hair, she could pass. At the washstand, she splashed away the stubble and tore off her false mustache. With her man's clothes rolled into a bundle under her arm and her cap pulled down, she set out, a timid maid with dirt on her chin, sent on an errand. Klara crept out of the palace, then broke into a run.

Already, the broad streets branching off Michaelerplatz were filling with carts and carriages, including some of the hundred or more imperial coaches made available by the emperor for his distinguished guests. One of them might be carrying Baron von Hagen and Anton Spaller, on their way to offer sympathy to Olsberg's widow and then take apart his house. Klara dodged a pair of flashing yellow wheels, narrowly missing a steaming puddle, and vanished onto a side street.

The road climbed past a tavern and a bakeshop, edged past a

jutting wall, and jettisoned her into another plaza. Klara hurried across it, weaving between the vendors of the market that sprang up here in the mornings. Shoppers grumbled about the price of bread and traded gossip about the ugly King of Denmark. Perched on the spire in the center of the square, the bronze Virgin Mary smiled, patient with the frustrations and foibles of the mortals below.

Klara spied the house. No imperial carriage was waiting. She stepped out of the way of a uniformed lancer out for his morning ride, then scurried closer. The four-story red stone house was dwarfed by its magnificent baroque-styled neighbors. Anton said a prostitute had found Olsberg's body as she was leaving, probably through a door at the back. Klara delved the surrounding passages until she spied red stone at the end of a dingy courtyard. Tightening her grip on the bundle beneath her arm, she walked closer.

It was a small space, paved, with grass springing up in the gaps between the stones and herbs for the kitchen growing in pots along the south facing wall. A scraggy vine clung to the window frame. Next to the door, a girl bent over a basket of washing. She looked up.

"A coat for my lord," Klara explained, patting her bundle, too flustered to think of anything else. It hardly mattered. The girl wasn't interested.

"Just leave it upstairs."

Klara went for the door. After nearly stumbling on the steep stairs, she remembered to hold up her skirts. They felt clumsy.

Klara knew from Theresa's earlier reconnaissance that the count and his wife had rooms on the second floor. Stowing her bundle on the landing, she waited, scarcely breathing, then edged the door open—just enough to spy a manservant leaving a room at the far end of the corridor. She froze until he turned the corner, then crept into the room he'd left, hoping he was the valet and that this was his master's quarters.

The door squeaked as it closed behind her, making her stomach leap, but no feet rushed to find her. All she heard was someone walking on the floor above and the muted clamor of the square.

Luck had favored her. This was the count's bedchamber, recognizable by the shaving implements waiting on the washstand. Klara glided about the room, turning over scattered oddments: a crumpled letter from a man signing himself "your affectionate brother," an invitation card to an imperial ball. There was a notched deck of cards and a scented note of amorous nothings from Klara's mother. It wouldn't hurt to pocket that. Hagen would learn Theresa was Olsberg's lover eventually, but there was no need to make it easy.

Time was slipping away. Klara rifled the drawers of the desk. She knew the weight and feel of the letter she sought, remembered every inked word.

I have papers in my possession concerning a woman you once knew in Vienna. She lived in Mariahilf parish, in case you do not remember. I'm willing to sell the papers for one hundred and fifty gulden. If you do not wish me to sell them to anyone else, come at midnight to the crypt of St. Stephen's. I will be waiting.

She should have asked Levi to write it—except he'd have refused, just as she should have done.

No sign of the letter. She fanned through the pages of the count's few books, but only an opera ticket fell out. In a lacquered box on the mantel was an untidy bundle of bills, nothing more. Klara glanced about the room.

A smart man wouldn't have left her note in any of the easy places, but it wasn't under the carpet or behind the pictures on the walls. A hand swept beneath the mattress discovered only a crumpled lady's garter in a crimson shade Klara doubted was worn by Olsberg's wife, though it could have belonged to Theresa. Nor was the letter tucked among his clothes, though she hadn't expected it there, where it would easily be found by his servants. Nothing was sewn into any coat linings, and the only thing she found at the back of the clothespress was a dirty handkerchief.

She was about to put it back, when she saw it had writing on it. Two rows of numbers. A cipher. She must leave this out for Anton to find.

Someone hurried down the hall, not troubling to be quiet. Klara went still.

More footsteps. Murmurs. Klara tried to dissolve behind the window curtains, but escape was impossible: there was no ledge below, no nearby gutter pipe. Besides, the window latch looked rusty. It would take time and patience to open.

Drawers opened in the next room, slid shut again. A distant door opened and the sound of footsteps came again, in soft counterpoint to a heavier tread beating up the stairs. Klara heard greetings in a bass rumble, and a door click shut. Hagen was here.

She must keep her head down, her shoulders hunched and calmly walk out of the house. The note was gone. Hopefully, Olsberg had burned it.

Halfway across the room, Klara hesitated, afraid to face the exposure of the open corridor. Suppose the countess offered Hagen refreshment? Or sent for her *sal volatile*? The servants would see her, but perhaps there was another way out. Between this room and the next was a connecting door—into the countess's room, presumably, but hadn't Klara just heard her pass? She was in a sitting room with Hagen now, hearing the news that her husband had been murdered. If all the rooms on this side of the hall were connected, Klara could travel most of the way unseen and dart down the back stairs.

She gave the room one last glance and slipped through the door. The next room was dark, the curtains fully drawn. As she groped her way forward, something struck her on the shin.

Klara stopped, damning all corners and waiting for her eyes to adjust to the gloom. A heavy armoire took shape beside her.

The door had been left open, blocking her way. Klara edged past. If this room followed the pattern of Olsberg's, the door to the next room should be straight in front of her. She tiptoed forward, but before she found the door, she saw the writing desk and a pale packet of letters bound with ribbon. Instinct made her snatch them up—a waste of time, as her letter wouldn't be here. She was putting them back, wondering if she was imagining the rustling beside her, when a creak came from the curtained bed.

She spun around. There was no movement, only opaque shadows. The bedcovers were in a tangle because the countess had left in a hurry, not expecting a call before noon, certainly not from the chief of police. Klara could hear her now, weeping, so there was no need to imagine threats with every sound. The creak she'd heard must have come from the floor above.

In the shadows next to the bed, someone struck a match.

CHAPTER 5

Klara dove for the door, but a hand seized her arm. Fighting would make too much noise. Klara turned, ready to whisper excuses and pleas, and saw it was no good. Pleas wouldn't coax mercy from such calculating eyes.

In no great hurry, the eyes' owner held the match to a candle bracket on the wall, shaking out the flame before it reached his fingers. "And who are *you* working for?" he asked.

He was wearing a sheet—or had been, before he let go of it to grab her. The noise that came from her throat was indecipherable.

He laughed without making a sound. "I'd cover up, but you're standing on my sheet."

"Then let go of me."

He did. She took a long step back. As she moved, he reached past her for the shirt thrown over the back of the desk chair. She retreated farther, positioning the chair between them.

He smiled. "Don't worry. I'm not supposed to be here either." He pushed back his untidy hair. He wasn't holding very tightly to the sheet.

"How long have you been here?" she asked. He'd seen her, obviously, but had he seen or heard anything else?

"Does it matter? Or do you need the number of our couplings for your report?"

Klara flinched. She'd read files with almost as much detail.

"Who sent you? The Russians? The French?" He spoke carelessly, but there was a faint pucker in his forehead. He intended to know, just as surely as she meant not to tell him.

"Please let me go." Klara swallowed, taking another step back. "I can't stay. You shouldn't either." If he called for the countess or her servants, Hagen and Spaller would find them both. "There's going to be trouble."

He cocked an eyebrow. Klara dropped her voice to a thread-like whisper. "The chief of police is with the countess now in the other room."

"Is she in trouble?" He shrugged into his shirt. "I hadn't expected it of her. Lovely as the day is long, but I'd have thought her too careful for that." His head emerged from the shirt, and he caught her again with his eyes. She stopped edging toward the door. "You don't want him to catch you, so you can't be one of his."

Klara said nothing. Let him think she worked for anyone but Hagen. "Didn't you wonder why the countess left?"

"Generally, I interpret waking alone as criticism of my technique. I was deciding what to do about it when you came in. Pass me my trousers?"

He must mean the crumpled bundle beside her feet. Klara stooped and picked them up. "You'll let me go?"

"You're Viennese. What's your name?"

"What's yours?" she countered, every muscle bunched tight.

"Josef." He grinned. "You'll come with me. Given the circumstances, I'd like to know what you know a little better." He held no weapon, but the way he moved was threat enough. Klara backed toward the door, his trousers clutched against her chest.

"Her husband is dead. You make an intriguing candidate for a killer."

"I like mouthy girls." Josef smiled. "I'm not frightened. Herr Hagen won't suspect me."

"Then I'll tell someone who will." It was a weak bluff, and his eyes let her know he knew it. She didn't have his full name, and unless she had powerful masters…

"How unsporting." As he reached for her, Klara hurled the trousers at him. They glanced off his head as they whipped by, giving her the moment she needed to scoop up one of the shoes on the carpet. She grabbed it and ran—to the stairs, to the door, to the courtyard. Josef, whoever he was, might well be bold enough to follow her with his shirt tail flapping, but he wouldn't get far only halfway shod, not in Vienna's dirty streets.

It was difficult to say over her heart's pounding, but she heard no sounds of pursuit. Surely she imagined the laugh.

ANTON AND HERR HAGEN still had to search the house. Hopefully, discovering Josef would delay them even further. Klara didn't believe Josef's claim that Hagen wouldn't suspect him, not when Hagen made it a practice to doubt everyone. But even if Josef managed to slip away unseen in his single shoe, it would take time for Anton to look through Olsberg's rooms. Unless he found her note—Olsberg *must* have burned it—and came looking for Kasper Stark, she was too far away now to be caught. She just needed to change back into herself, then hurry back to the Hofburg.

Levi was at home, watering his plants. To his credit, he did not drop the water jug when he saw her. "What's this? Are you mad?" He hurried past her to bolt the door. "What were you thinking?"

Klara struggled with the ties of the apron. "Help me out of

this. I had to search Count von Olsberg's apartments, and I couldn't be seen."

He set down the jug of water and untied her apron at the back. "You have on the wrong kind of shoes."

Klara looked at her feet. Men's shoes. She swore. For years, she'd been drilled to pay attention to the smallest details. The maid in the courtyard probably hadn't noticed, but what about Josef?

It didn't matter. She'd never see him again. "I forgot about them."

"I trust there was a reason you went there? I thought we were done with blackmail."

Klara tossed the cap on the fading sofa and ruffled her fingers through her hair. "Olsberg's dead. Murdered. They brought his body to the palace this morning. I can't let the police find my note."

Levi stepped from behind her, peering anxiously into her face. "Did you find it?"

"No, and I was seen. When I couldn't find the note in his bedchamber, I tried the next room. I thought it was empty, but the countess left behind a man in her bed. He thinks I was there spying for someone. Not the Austrians."

Levi sighed and started helping her with the ties at the front of the dress. "I suppose that'll misdirect him if he tries to find you, but why speak to him at all? You didn't simply run?"

"Hagen was in the house speaking to the countess. I couldn't risk this man raising an alarm. With any luck, they'll catch him, and he'll take my place as a suspect." This could have been a crime of passion, a jealous lover eliminating the husband who stood in his way. Josef's lazy demeanor and laconic asides didn't quite fit the part, but—

Levi shook his head. "Better not to have been seen at all. You should have sent me to search for you. It's safer that way."

"I had no time. I hadn't even gone up to my desk when I saw Olsberg's corpse in the courtyard."

Levi grunted. "Better him than you. It was close last night."

She couldn't argue. "What do you think he did with the note?" It worried her, not being able to find it, yet so long as it wasn't found on Olsberg's person or among his effects, the letter wouldn't mean much. It was unaddressed and could have been written to anyone. If the count had gone very early to the crypt last night, he wouldn't have had time to leave it at home. Perhaps he'd just dropped it somewhere, and no one would ever find it.

"I doubt we'll know. Unless you missed it in your search, it won't harm us. Were you thorough?" Levi asked.

Klara shrugged. "I thought so. But I also wore the wrong kind of shoes."

She'd dropped her own clothing in a heap just inside the door. Levi lifted her coat, sending Josef's shoe rolling across the floor. He tipped his head at her. "What's this?"

"Belongs to the man from the countess's bed. I didn't want him chasing me. I had a hard enough time convincing him to let go of my arm."

Levi frowned. "How closely did he see you?"

"The room was dark. Just a single candle."

Levi shook out her coat with more force than necessary. "Your clothes are all wrinkled."

"Just be glad I still have them. I was in such a panic as I left I might have forgotten them on the stairs."

"I'll have to press this, and you'll need a new cravat. You can't go back to the palace looking like you rolled out of bed."

Klara gave a relieved smile. "I thought I'd have to persuade you out of packing our bags."

"Why? Is there more you aren't telling me?"

Klara shook her head.

"He won't find you. It was a good idea to wear the dress. Just don't make a habit of it. You'll find yourself unlucky if you try it often."

Levi was probably right. He so often was. "Circumstances aren't ideal," Klara said. "But disappearing now will look suspicious. I didn't kill Count von Olsberg, but I'm well placed to find the one who did. If suspicion turns my way, at least I'll see it coming."

Levi nodded. "Just be—"

Klara sighed. "I know. Careful."

Levi looked slightly offended. He straightened his coat. "I don't like the situation, but so far you've handled it well—and you needn't look suspiciously at me just because I've paid you a compliment."

"I won't let it go to my head." Klara smiled.

"Good. Hurry and dress," Levi said. "We must get you back to the palace before you're missed." He went to fetch the iron.

Left to herself, Klara donned her shirt and found herself remembering Josef doing the same thing. She had a disturbingly exact recollection of the shape of his shoulders. It had to be her imagination; she couldn't have seen so well, not when the room was dark.

Klara climbed into the fraying armchair and pulled her shirt over her knees, waiting for Levi to finish with her clothes. It took time to heat an iron and in this, like all else, he was meticulous. She reached for the abandoned dress and began folding it. There was a place on the elbow where the sleeve had been mended. The cotton was soft beneath her fingers and smelled of roses. The maid who owned the dress must have scrounged petals from discarded palace flowers.

Levi returned, holding out her breeches. "You'd best be quick." He frowned at the dress she'd set neatly on the table. "You can't put it back. Too risky."

"I don't like stealing," Klara said.

Levi sighed. "You lie every day. The way you talk, sit, speak—"

Only because she had to. Doing what she must to create her own place in the world wasn't the same as hurting the weak. "This girl only has one other. She's wearing it now."

"Life is hard," Levi reminded her. "Yours is worth more than a poor maid's faded dress."

Put that way, she supposed he was right.

When Klara left, Levi set out once more for Theresa's apartment. He didn't like repeating his visit, feeling it weakened the force of the threat he had left with her, but the situation had changed, and plans must be adjusted. None of this could be relayed by message. They'd already committed too much to paper.

This time, he found her dressed to go out. She looked like she'd come straight from Vienna's most fashionable modiste, and perhaps she had.

"You can't keep coming here if you want our connection to stay secret." Her voice was cold, and she didn't look at him, busy smoothing her gloves. "I'm leaving almost this minute."

"That's a beautiful riding habit," Levi told her. She'd always liked parading on horseback and did it as well as most of her men, maybe better. She was a commanding presence when she chose.

"What do you want?" she asked.

"I think you should sit down."

Iciness vanished as her eyes went wide. She didn't sit. "The wound is worse than you feared? Is Kasper—"

"He's safe at present. Olsberg is not."

She picked up her riding crop and frowned at it. "But—"

"He was found dead this morning. Fortunately, Kasper learned of it early and has already tried to recover the blackmail note. He wrote it himself, you see."

Their eyes held. She was praying under her breath. "If they find it, they'll convict her," she finally whispered.

Slowly, Levi nodded.

Her face was bone white. "I'll never let it happen."

"How will you prevent it?"

She licked her lips. "I have letters from Olsberg. The usual sordid nonsense, but if I confess to the killing, the police will believe it. No one really trusts a whore. I'll say I was jealous or that he frightened me—easy enough to prove. Sometimes he was rough."

"I hope it won't come to that," Levi said. He meant it. It was strange to be allies with her when just this morning he'd been ready to sell her out. But if things went badly and Klara needed help, Theresa was the one who could save her. Levi had understood this at once and liked Theresa better because she'd seen it too and hadn't hesitated. "This is just a precaution," he reminded her.

She smiled at him. "I'm not as heartless as you think I am."

"I know." He should have remembered that no matter what she said or did, where Klara was concerned, her intentions were good. He remembered too that, frivolities aside, her life wasn't easy. Men often hurt her, bodily or in matters of the heart. She was good at covering both kinds of bruises.

Theresa brushed an invisible speck from her cuff. "Try not to let Kasper worry. I can tell a story. I'm good at that."

She was a magnificent liar, the best he'd ever known. Better than Klara, who hadn't her years, disappointments, or steel-plated heart. When Levi took her hand, her fingers tightened. "This is a precaution," he said again. "I don't think it will be necessary."

Her mouth twitched. "But you feel better having a plan. I do too."

He mustn't stay. Someone was coming for her. Levi freed his

hand and turned for the door, but she stopped him with a light touch on his shoulder.

"Find out for me how he died." Theresa smiled thinly. "I will not miss him."

CHAPTER 6

The rooms housing the machinery of Emperor Francis's government were utilitarian and crowded, nothing like the staterooms gracing other parts of the palace. Desks squeezed against the walls and filled the available space, dividing it into a labyrinth. Tall windows overlooked a busy courtyard with a lone tree and well, but Klara's desk was wedged beside Anton's against an inside wall. Next year, if she lasted that long, she could aspire to a place nearer the window. Her files were stacked and tied neatly with string, but already a snowfall of messages awaited her. She would have to work through luncheon.

Retreating into the intricacies of a staggeringly detailed report from an agent named Chiffon, Klara picked out the likelier bits of gossip. Last night, a game of blindman's buff at a party caused a duel between two German princes. Hardenburg, the Prussian minister, was tiring of his French dancer. If Klara could arrange a suitable replacement, access to Prussian communications would be assured.... Klara left her desk to fetch a file of available personnel.

Anton was back when she returned. He spun in his chair. "Where were you?"

Klara held up the file.

"Before that. I was searching almost half an hour for you."

It had taken longer than she'd planned to change her clothes. "Olsberg isn't the only problem I have to worry about," Klara reminded him.

"I know, I know." Anton sighed. "But you were right. Hagen wants this murder tidied away as soon as possible—before the French minister and the tsar arrive."

"That's less than a fortnight."

"He was pleased with our quick response—"

"My name made it into this?" It was unexpectedly generous of Anton to share credit, but though Klara wanted to keep a close eye on the investigation, she'd prefer to work unseen. The less notice she received, the better.

"I'm not greedy like Fürst." Anton looked offended.

"Of course not." Twice, Georg Fürst had taken credit for other men's reports, and Anton, one of the victims, would never forgive him.

"There's little time," Anton said. "Hagen is trusting me to take care of this, which he'd never have done if I hadn't taken your advice. This is a chance for both of us."

"I'll wait till it ends before I thank you," Klara said. "For now, I'm not sure I should. What did you find at the house?"

He sighed. "I hated bringing such news to the countess."

Klara fiddled with her pen. "How did she take it?"

"She's broken. What do you expect?"

Klara returned a noncommittal grunt. The countess clearly had Anton's sympathies, so she must be pretty. "What is she like?"

"Stunning, even when weeping," Anton admitted. "Next time, I'll bring you along. As a courtesy, Herr Hagen has promised her regular reports." He lowered his voice. "Naturally, I've put watchers on her."

Klara nodded. "You found nothing unusual?" It seemed he'd found nothing to endanger her, but she couldn't believe Josef had gotten away.

"Actually, I did." Anton leaned forward, his eyes bright. "There was a handkerchief in his things with a cipher written on it, just left out on the desk. I already took it to the cryptographers. Olsberg was spying for someone." He motioned at the open files littering his desk. "I checked to see if Olsberg was mentioned in any of our Prussian intelligence. He crops up more than you'd think. This is what I've gathered about him." He passed Klara a page of notes.

Some things Klara already knew from Theresa: Olsberg was an officer in the Prussian army, with a taste for experienced women. But she hadn't known he'd been reprimanded for overzealousness after the allied defeat at Gué-à-Tresmes, or that he'd been promoted—and vindicated, presumably—a week later after a bloody battle at Craonne. A brash and hot-tempered man, he'd been decorated at Freiburg and Kösen. He and his wife had two young sons. That was news too.

"He's not officially attached to the Prussian delegation, but I think I know why he's here." Anton indicated a line farther down the sheet. "His estate was looted by the French. Most of his paintings are in that palace now—"

"The Louvre?"

Anton nodded. "He must have come here to get them back."

The vaguely worded purpose of the Congress of Vienna "to treat the minor arrangements of the rest of Europe" had people flocking to the city. Everyone with grievances and thwarted rights, both real and hoped for, had come to press claims. Powerful delegates were besieged by supplicants looking for people to broker their interests, and favors were traded like cards over the gaming tables.

Anton glanced at Klara's mostly uncluttered desk. "What on earth were you doing all morning?"

"Stealing from the palace maids," Klara retorted, for Anton, with his clubfoot and round face, was sensitive to his failures with women. She'd spoken the truth, knowing he'd misinterpret it and stop asking questions. Trifling with palace servants was frowned on. He looked her over, but as Klara knew, there was no fault with her disguise.

"I should report you."

"At least that will give Fürst something new to joke about. I'm tired of him retelling the story of you and the girl who brings Hagen his cake."

Anton went scarlet, but instead of biting back, he buttoned his lips.

He was too forbearing. She didn't deserve it. "Forgive me," Klara mumbled. "I'm worried, and I had a bad night."

"You look tired," Anton conceded.

Klara pushed away the file of possible mistresses to plant on the Prussian ambassador. "What do you want me to do?"

Anton picked up the report she'd written earlier, the inventory of Olsberg's corpse. He tapped a line halfway down the page. "This troubled me. You said he had a knife wound on his thigh, but there was no blood by the door when I went to the house to collect the body."

"Could he have been wounded somewhere else?" Klara made the suggestion carefully.

"But where? The countess said she never saw him after he left the opera to attend a party hosted by the Duchess of Sagan. No knife fights there." The duchess's parties were notorious, but not for violence.

"We don't know he actually went to the party. Even if he did, he could have gone anywhere afterward. Someone must have seen him." Though she prayed not. "Do you want me to make inquiries?"

"We both will. For now, will you see what Herr Krampitz is making of that cipher?"

"Certainly." Glad to escape the conversation, Klara pushed out of her chair. "Did you find anything else suspicious at the house?" *Or anyone?* She stirred through a box of papers Anton had brought back, but didn't see anything she hadn't seen before.

"Just that handkerchief."

Josef must have slipped away. She wondered how far he'd walked with only one shoe.

"There was this imploring letter from his brother." Anton passed her a folded paper from the box. "The countess said he and Olsberg quarreled yesterday. We'll question him later."

Klara nodded. "Just tell me when." She left with a smile that vanished the instant she was out the door. Keeping herself clear was proving to be a complicated dance.

The code breakers' room was even more crowded than the one she'd left, with shelves and tables cluttered with cipher disks, charts of letters and numbers, worn-out books with random letters underlined, distillations for revealing invisible inks, and scraps of charred paper laid out on felt, where stooped-shouldered men with magnifying glasses labored at putting them back together.

"Herr Krampitz?"

He looked up from a magnifying glass. Krampitz, the senior code breaker, did not usually work at resurrecting papers, but he was helping a younger man with a collection of painfully small fragments.

"Herr Spaller sent me to ask if you'd made any progress with the cipher he gave you."

Krampitz grunted and bent again to the glass. "No, and don't expect any." His whiskered jowls shook. "That cipher's French. Can't make head or tail of it."

They hadn't made any progress with the French codes, no matter how many men Hagen put at the task. All attempts to steal the key had failed, as no one had successfully infiltrated the French embassy. They were running out of time. The French ambassador, Prince Talleyrand, delaying his departure from Paris to magnify his consequence, would have to be in Vienna before Tsar Alexander arrived, and his ceremonial entry was scheduled in twelve days' time. Hagen wanted a spy in the French embassy before Talleyrand was in residence.

Prince Talleyrand was a devious man, who'd served Louis XVI, the revolutionary government, the Directory, Napoleon, and now Louis XVIII. Surviving so many changes was remarkable; Talleyrand knew how to sail the shifting currents of power and when to jump ship. Hagen didn't trust him.

"At least we know who the cipher came from," Klara said. Olsberg had business with the French—his stolen paintings—but possession of this cipher indicated he had additional, deeper ties. What had he been willing to trade to have his treasures back? He wasn't officially attached to the Prussian delegation, but his position in the army would give him access to all kinds of information. "You'll inform me if you make any discoveries?"

Krampitz snorted. "Don't hold your breath. If I learn anything, you'll hear of it, because I'll send word straight to Hagen—or even the emperor himself."

Klara bowed and left. Anton, receiving the news, was disappointed but undefeated. "We'll need to make a list of Olsberg's French contacts. The ciphered message must have come from one of them." It was a bewildering line of inquiry, combing through agent reports to piece together whom he'd been seen with and when, but Klara worked without complaining, glad nothing here could lead to her. They sifted through papers until most of the secretaries left to take afternoon coffee. Klara watched them go, grudging them the respite. Anton was tireless, but at last, he laid down his pen.

"We'll take this list with us. Let's find the brother. He may know something."

THEY FOUND Lennard von Olsberg at his apartment in a shabby house outside the city walls. The district was home to Vienna's students and those visitors unable to pay higher rents. Klara had pieced together a portrait of him from today's study of intelligence reports: an overlooked boy, cast into shadow by his brother's exploits, who hadn't "taken" to an army career.

The room he lived in had been attractive once. Now, it held discards: a heavy mahogany table, worn leather chairs, a pair of ugly lamps. Lennard von Olsberg, something of a discard himself, slumped in a chair by the window, his thumb tapping against his thigh. He looked sulky, even without the spectacular bruise obliterating his left eye.

Ever polite, Anton masked his surprise and donned a conciliatory face. "Excuse us for calling. I have sad news."

"I've already heard. My sister-in-law told me this morning. You needn't have come."

"Regrettably, we must intrude on your grief," Anton said. "We have some questions for you."

"What kind of questions?"

Klara reached into her portfolio for the list of French names they'd assembled. "Do you know any of these individuals? Did any have business or friendships with your brother?"

Lennard scanned the list, but his answers were brief and unhelpful. Either he was being purposely difficult or he hadn't been admitted to his brother's confidence.

"I'm sorry I can't be of more assistance, gentlemen," Lennard von Olsberg finished, with a pointed look at the door.

Anton coughed. "I'm afraid there's more. You see, the countess implied you had a disagreement with your brother. I see you have a bruise."

Lennard von Olsberg swore under his breath. He left the chair and stalked to the grimy window. "Did she tell you about this too? Sneaking bitch. I didn't kill him, no matter what she says."

“Then your eye—”

He interrupted Anton’s probe. “Oh, this is from Marius, all right, but I didn’t kill him. I can prove it too. Sonia will hate learning that.”

“But you did quarrel the day he died,” Klara put in.

“And again that night, when he gave me this.”

“Perhaps we could sit down?” Anton asked. Receiving a nod, he took a chair. Klara made do with a low ottoman in faded brocade that looked like Lennard had slept on it. Scowling darkly, Lennard von Olsberg resumed his seat.

“We always quarreled. This was nothing new,” he said.

“Perhaps you’ll explain,” Anton said. Klara propped her writing tablet on her knee and took out her pencil. The sight unsettled Lennard, who paused.

“An unfortunate formality, I’m afraid,” Anton said smoothly. “What was the nature of your argument?”

Lennard folded his arms. “I need money.”

“Doesn’t everyone?” Anton smiled, but it failed to mollify Lennard von Olsberg. An angry flush rose in his cheeks, bright against the bruising.

“I asked Marius to recommend me to a better post. He has friends. He could easily get me a place with Hardenburg.”

The hard-working Prussian delegation was churning out a dizzying number of memoranda for the conference already. Posts with the delegation were sought after and not easy to come by. “I’d rather work for the foreign office,” Olsberg went on. “Even Marius admitted I’m poorly suited for the army. It’s mundane and ugly. I have other ambitions.”

“Yet he wouldn’t help you?” Anton asked.

Lennard scowled. “No, but that’s none of your concern.”

“It is if it gave you reason to kill him,” Klara put in.

“Well, I didn’t,” Lennard snapped. “Whether I had a reason or not.”

"We ask only because it's our duty. Is the need for money urgent?" Anton asked.

"It wouldn't be if I had a publisher. I write," Lennard explained. "Poetry. It's good, easily better than half of what you read these days. Of course, Marius had no patience for that either. Not that he ever read anything at all—"

Anton coughed again. "Herr Olsberg, I need you to be frank with us. Your brother is dead, and so far, you're our best suspect. If you did not kill him, we must find the one who did. Time is limited."

After a long stare, Lennard relented. "I need money because of a lady. I met her in Baden this past July while recuperating from a wound. She is—"

"Which action?" Anton asked.

He flushed again. "It was a training accident. Her family...well, they are looking for more than a name. She has a new suitor—older than Adam, but he's wealthy. They want her to accept him and are pressing her to do so. I'll lose her, unless I can afford to marry soon."

"But when you explained to your brother—"

"Marius only laughed. Said it was time I was cured of romantic notions. I should let Anna go and take a mistress instead." A muscle worked in Lennard's jaw.

"And he hit you," Anton supplied.

"In Sonia's sitting room? Even Marius wouldn't do that, no matter how foul his temper. No, this came later, and not, as you think, before I slipped a garrote around his neck."

"How do you know he was garroted?" Anton asked, his brows dropping. They'd told no one that, not even the countess.

"I asked the servants. It's no great secret. Anyone who cares to know will have learned by now."

Anton's mouth tightened. "Why was your brother in such bad temper? He struck you, so your quarrel must have been serious."

"Sheer cussedness? It's not unlike him." Lennard's eyes flicked over Anton, whose face revealed nothing. “I think someone was bleeding him.”

Klara scoffed, ignoring the hairs that prickled along the back of her neck. “That’s an easy accusation to make.”

“No, listen to me.”

“Go on.” Anton leaned forward. Cursing inwardly, Klara pressed her lips together. How much did Lennard know?

“Marius was hopeful when he first came to Vienna. I didn’t understand why. His fields were trampled, his orchards burned for firewood, half his lands stolen by a jumped-up sycophant ennobled by Napoleon. Even his wife, who’s bitter as wormwood over their losses, cautioned him that they couldn’t expect to get everything back.

“I didn’t think much of it until yesterday. When I asked him for help yesterday afternoon, he laughed and put me off. But in the evening, when I spoke to him again at the opera, he was angry.”

“Perhaps he was tired of the subject,” Klara said.

“He said everyone was after his money, and I was asking for preferment. The demand for money must have come from someone else.”

Anton looked skeptical. Encouraged, Klara went on. “You’re guessing. The remark could have sprung from a dispute with the countess. She may have spent too much on a gown, or he could have received an unwelcome bill. It’s expensive to live in Vienna.”

Lennard shook his head. “If Marius and Sonia were arguing over money, it would have been the other way around. She doesn’t like him spending his sons’ inheritance. And there’s more. I knew Marius was expected at the Duchess of Sagan’s party, so I followed him there. He was angry, but I was desperate. I thought if I caught him in a better mood… Except he slipped away from the party almost as soon as he arrived. If I hadn’t been watching, I wouldn’t have seen. I was curious now, and because he was still my best and only chance, I followed again. He was in a hurry. I kept back, thinking over what to say. He walked to St. Stephen's, spoke to a man who was waiting for him, then went into the crypt."

Klara shifted on her seat. It was three steps to the door. If she made it outside, she had a chance of escaping the city, but if Lennard denounced her, she'd have only seconds to run.

"You weren't curious?" Anton asked.

"Yes. That's why I stayed. A short time later—it was too dark to read my watch—another man came. He was let into the crypt too, but he came out an hour or so later—alone. He had to break the lock, and he was running. At first, I thought it was Marius, so I came out of hiding in case he needed help, but this fellow was built more lightly than my brother. He fled, and though I chased him down several streets, I lost him, so I went back to see what had become of Marius. He was out of the crypt by then and in a worse mood than before. When he learned the man had escaped me, he gave me this." His hand hovered over the bruised eye. "Marius was gone by the time I picked myself up from the cobbles."

Klara had stopped writing. Hoping neither her stillness or Lennard's story would convict her, she forced herself back to her notes.

"You think this unknown man killed him?" Anton asked.

"He must have," Lennard said. "How hard would it be to circle back and catch Marius off guard?"

"But why would he?" Klara put in, her pen scratching jerkily on the page. "According to you, he fled."

In spite of Lennard's attempt to throw suspicion on the unknown "man," Klara knew she was innocent and that Lennard was the likelier candidate. Unfortunately, she couldn't tell that to Anton, not directly. "*You* could have followed your brother," Klara said. "You could have hurried to the apartment and waited for him to return home."

"So could the man from the crypt. He must have, because I

didn't. Why would I kill my brother? I still had a better chance of prevailing on him than on his wife. With her holding the purse strings, I won't get anything. I went home, and I can prove I did because the other man, the gravedigger, helped me there."

A tremor rippled down the skin on Klara's back.

"What's his name?" Anton asked.

"Don't remember. I gave him a kreuzer for his help, but he clearly expected more. He spat on it."

"Do you think he knew the other man, the one who outran you?" Anton asked.

Lennard von Olsberg shrugged. "I only care what he'll tell you about me. I left the church and came straight home."

"We'll speak to him and see if he confirms your story. Don't leave Vienna."

Mind in a tangle, Klara put away her scribblings and followed Anton out.

CHAPTER 7

They left the apartment in silence. Klara was too worried to wonder about Anton's thoughts, but when he spoke, his words surprised her.

"Thank you," he said.

"For what?" Klara looked at him.

"You urged me to go immediately to Hagen. You pressed Lennard von Olsberg with hard questions. He might not have told so much if not for you."

"You don't need to thank me." Klara stared at the paving stones.

"I want to be promoted," Anton said. "Unlike my brothers, I can't have the glory of an army career."

"Have they done well for themselves?"

"One died at Austerlitz." He grimaced. "Courageously, of course. Received a slew of medals. The other leads a company of light infantry in the emperor's own regiment. My grandmother thinks he walks on water."

Klara knew little of Anton's family, but it couldn't be easy for him, hindered from birth by his clubfoot. She was so used to his swinging gait she seldom thought of it, but studying him now, she realized he never forgot.

Klara forced a smile. "Don't thank me. I'm just trying to keep my post, same as you." Which wasn't helping Anton, exactly.

"We have some good information."

Unfortunately. "Do you believe him?" Klara asked.

"I'm not sure," Anton admitted. "I want to know if the servants know the count was garroted and if Lennard really found out from them. I won't believe the rest until we hear from the gravedigger." He consulted his watch, then cursed. "He'll have left the church by now. Without a name, we won't find him until tomorrow. We'll have to question him then."

Klara made a disappointed face, concealing the hope flickering in her chest. Her hurried plans went to pieces when Anton spoke again.

"I'd planned to go to the opera this evening. Will you join me?"

Klara shook her head. "I'd better write a report of this interview. One of us should." She needed to rid herself of Anton's company, fast. If he wasn't going to chase down Gunter tonight, there was a chance she could find him first.

"I'll write it. Won't take long," Anton said. "Join me later for supper. We can take in the opera afterward. Tonight's program is—"

"Mozart," Klara finished for him. Her mother was in it. "Thank you. That would be enjoyable." If misguided gratitude was prompting Anton to send her home, leaving him the report, she'd let him have his way. On her own, she could use the hours before supper to find Gunter. The finding would be easy. What she didn't know was what to do with him.

THEY PARTED OUTSIDE THE HOFBURG. Shoving her hands in her greatcoat pockets, Klara hurried away. Gunter was a liability she couldn't afford, and she couldn't buy his silence, not when he'd already proved untrustworthy, selling his allegiance to the highest bidder. She could try to frighten him into silence, but she'd never be as terrifying to him as the secret police.

The safest thing was to kill him.

She licked dry lips, hoping it wouldn't come to that. Plunging into narrow and narrower streets, it was easy to imagine herself in an old-fashioned morality tale, one where the hapless hero makes a mistake, a small sin but one that eventually damns him. Harrowed by the threat of discovery and swiftly diminishing choices, he makes another mistake and another, until Hell reaches up and grabs him.

It was almost the same story as tonight's opera, though Klara felt she had better intentions. Unlike Don Giovanni, she didn't want to do anything wrong. She'd been forced to blackmail Count von Olsberg to help her mother, and if she had to kill Gunter... Her stomach clenched. *Please let me think of some other way.*

Of course, Gunter would have let Olsberg kill *her*, but Klara doubted heaven smiled on that kind of tit for tat. Killing Gunter wasn't taking an eye for an eye—more an eye for a head. She was making herself sick thinking about it.

AS ANTON HAD PREDICTED, Gunter wasn't at the crypt, but Klara recognized some of the workmen still loitering in the square. When she asked them about Gunter, she learned he had packed up and gone home early, complaining of pains in his shoulder, but they told her where to find his lodging. Klara followed their directions to a cramped room in a tumbling-down boarding house and found a surly woman there, who asserted that yes, she was the no-good man's wife.

"Hasn't he come home?" Klara asked.

"Spending his wages on ale again," she fumed, wringing out a mass of gray linen and hanging it on a sagging line in front of the stove. A grubby-faced baby, round as a dumpling, was bound to her back, sleeping between her shoulders.

Klara took inventory of the scanty furnishings. No signs of sudden wealth. What had Gunter done with his money? Surely he hadn't drunk it all. He'd taken a gulden from her, never mind what he'd earned from Olsberg. "Where do you think he's gone?"

The woman jerked her head, a direction that might have meant anywhere. "Tavern at the end of the street." This was a little more helpful.

"If I find him, I'll send him along home," Klara promised, and then remembered she might not.

He wasn't at the tavern, which almost came as a relief. The place was smoky and low-ceilinged with grimy, leaded windows that were temporarily burnished with sunset gold. Klara ate a dish of potatoes and stringy meat and found two men who claimed to know Gunter willing to talk in exchange for ale. The younger man was in good humor, happy to share anything he knew. The second man said less, watching in case they were overheard.

The younger man set down his tankard and wiped his mouth on his sleeve. "Shrewd fellow, Gunter. Thing is, you might have missed him. He's leaving Vienna."

The other man sent him a repressive look.

"Leaving? But what of his family? I just spoke with his wife," Klara said. "She told me to look here."

The younger one chuckled, staring into his mug, while the other snorted. "They ain't married, though she claims the baby is his. Gunter's never been too sure. They've quarreled a few too many times."

"Gunter's come into some money. Said now he's done with her," the younger one added, earning a repressive nudge.

"He can't have left yet," Klara said. "He was at work today."

The younger man shrugged. "Nothing to stop him lighting out of here anytime he chooses. He's got coin. What's to keep him?"

Not the tired woman with the chapped hands, apparently.

"He'll probably have to scuttle off without warning," the younger man said, picking his teeth. "Otherwise, she'll try and stop him. Her brother's a woodcutter. Built like an ox. Last year he broke Gunter's nose."

"He wouldn't have taken her else," interjected the suspicious one. He shook his head. "Plaguey woman."

The other laughed. "You're just jealous of his good fortune."

The man conceded with a shrug. "Would we were all so lucky." He didn't look at Klara, but she felt the invitation and took it.

"You might be yet. Send me word of him, and there will be money in it for you." These men were poor, so it wouldn't take much. She ordered them more ale and told them they could leave any information with the keeper of a kaffeehaus near the river.

"No more ale for you, friend?" the older man asked her, lifting his mug.

"I'll search a while yet." There might be others who knew Gunter on this street.

The fruit seller on the corner recognized him from her description but said he hadn't seen him pass this evening, though Gunter had bought a pocketful of apricots on his way to work. Klara had no success with the beggar on the opposite corner, but farther down the street, she got a nod from a woman selling old clothes from a wheelbarrow.

"Stopped by, he did." She was folding a petticoat, packing her goods to return home.

Klara described him again. "You're certain it was this man?"

The woman smiled, revealing brown teeth. "I've sold on this corner over twenty years. He's only worked at St. Stephen's for five or six. I always see him pass."

"Did he usually stop?"

"No. But today he bought a new coat. Lovely, it was. Thick wool, still had all the buttons. Color of dark wine. I don't often get coats that fine. He must have come by some good fortune." She winked at Klara. "He paid in silver."

Rare indeed, from a gravedigger. "He didn't buy clothes for anyone else?" Klara asked, hoping for the woman's sake.

The seller shook her head. Klara slipped her a coin and walked home, thinking of Gunter leaving Vienna alone in his warm new coat. She was safe from him, or so it seemed. The tightness between her shoulders loosened, except when she thought of the woman and child who'd now have to make their way without Gunter's wage.

Coins were coins no matter where they came from, but she hoped Olsberg's money had paid for the coat.

DINNER THAT EVENING, in the company of Anton's sisters, parents, and grandmother, was a strictly formal affair. Keeping up a tepid conversation with Anton's youngest sister, Klara puzzled over how to tell Anton about Gunter without giving herself away. By the time the servants carried in dessert, she had a satisfactory plan and could devote her attention to the cardamom-flavored ice cream—an extravagant finale to a family meal, but it tasted heavenly. Clearly, Anton's family didn't mind showing they had plenty of money.

Klara told Anton the news at the opera, in low-pitched

murmurs that wouldn't carry over the jostling of the pit or the sinister strains of the opening overture.

Anton scowled. "You're sure the man we want is Gunter Kissling?"

Klara nodded. "The other gravediggers identified him as the foreman. He's the one who keeps the keys."

Anton's *"Verdammt"* was heartfelt and a little too loud, earning a glare from the captain of dragoons standing next to them, who applauded when the curtains opened onto a moonlight garden. As stage scenery went, Klara supposed it was a commendable representation, but she and Anton were concerned with weightier matters.

"This is terrible." Realizing his words could be misunderstood, Anton glanced at the dragoon captain, but the man hadn't heard. "Good thing you started looking for him when you did," Anton added in a lower voice. "I'll question the wife and neighbors again tomorrow and send out a warrant for Kissling's arrest. We might be able to catch him in one of the nearby towns."

For her own sake, Klara hoped not.

"It's suspicious, Kissling leaving so quickly," Anton went on. "Maybe Lennard von Olsberg didn't want us speaking to him."

Klara answered slowly, "He said he did. Seemed to be counting on it. Without Gunter Kissling, there's no way we can prove his story."

"Or prove he's lying. If I was Lennard von Olsberg and I'd murdered my brother, that's just how I'd have arranged it." Anton frowned.

Klara digested this. "You don't like Lennard von Olsberg."

"He's a bad tempered poltroon—did you catch that he was wounded in a *training accident?*"

"And he insulted the countess," Klara added. Anton's mouth tightened, confirming her suspicion. She laughed. "Does the countess know you've taken on the role of knight-errant?"

Anton sent her a dark look. "I feel sorry for her. She lost her husband."

"And is brokenhearted, I'm sure," Klara said dryly.

Anton gave his attention to the stage to save himself from making a reply, but his ears turned pink.

When Baron von Hagen summoned her and Anton to his office the next morning, Klara expected no more than a routine inquiry into their progress. Whispering reassurance to Anton, whose mouth had tightened with anxiety, Klara assembled their files, straightened her coat, and strolled into Baron von Hagen's office behind Anton, who'd insisted, martyr-like, on leading the way.

It was a fortunate chance. Half hidden by Anton's limping frame, she had a second to mask her shock. Next to Herr Hagen stood the man from the countess's bedroom—Josef, fully clothed this time.

"This is Josef von Baeder, my nephew," Hagen said.

Anton bowed. Klara followed a moment behind, still trying to assimilate Hagen's words. Sluggishly, she realized she was wearing the same pair of shoes.

He won't notice, not here. Not while I'm dressed in my own clothes. She stared at a spot on Hagen's desk, hoping petrification would pass for nonchalance.

Hagen grunted. "Apparently, my nephew was with the countess the night of her husband's murder." He spoke like the words tasted bitter.

Josef von Baeder smiled thinly. "Naturally, if I'd known my presence would inconvenience you, I would have stayed away."

"You should have stayed away altogether," Hagen said. "Your self-indulgent affairs—"

"Are a private concern," Josef von Baeder said quietly. "If not for the unusual circumstance I mentioned, I wouldn't have come."

"I'd have found out eventually," Hagen told him.

"Perhaps," Josef said with a shrug.

"Our diplomatic position is precarious," Hagen snapped. "Olsberg was well liked by his countrymen. Once the Prussians learn you were there—"

"I didn't kill him," the nephew said calmly.

"I know that! But no one else will." Hagen folded his arms and scowled from his high-backed leather chair. "Well, Stark? Spaller? What have you found?"

Klara flinched as Baeder's eyes found her. Luckily, Anton managed a response. "Regrettably—"

Hagen turned away and swore.

"The gravedigger that Lennard von Olsberg claims will support his testimony is missing," Klara admitted, pitching her words a half octave lower. The nephew might recognize her voice. Or her nose. She could plead illness and run, except it would make the men suspicious.

"We are expanding the search," Anton promised.

"Sounds like a wild goose chase." Hagen dismissed Anton's efforts with a flick of his hand. "And there's new information. Josef?"

"That night, when I was at the countess's apartment—"

Anton coughed. "Forgive me, Herr Baeder—" He stopped, overcome by his scarlet cheeks. "How long were you with her?"

"All night. I was fortunate."

For Anton's sake, Klara hoped Hagen and Baeder didn't see how much his calm face cost him. Baeder was hiding a smile. "During the interval at the opera that evening, Countess von Olsberg informed me her husband was leaving early to attend a gathering at the Palm Palace," he explained.

Hagen nodded. "The salon of Wilhelmina of Sagan."

"The count left midway through the second act, and neither

Countess von Olsberg nor I felt it necessary to linger. We traveled separately but reached her apartment before midnight."

"And the countess never left?" Anton asked, with a better attempt at indifference.

"Not until morning."

Anton nodded. "Then we know she didn't kill him, at least. Did you hear anything, Herr Baeder?"

The nephew shook his head. "You will be more interested in what I saw."

Klara's stomach clenched. "Forgive me, Herr Hagen." Though reluctant to draw attention, she had to try to stop Baeder—or at least make Hagen and Anton question his story. "Weren't you and Herr Spaller there in the early morning? You did not see Herr Baeder. I do not mean to be a skeptic, but given the relationship he claims with the lady—"

"I'm telling the truth." Baeder gave a tight smile. "I was there. My uncle knows better than to suspect me of chivalry."

"Or murder," Hagen added. "Most of the time."

Klara swallowed, unable to meet Baeder's eyes. "At some point, Herr Baeder, you and the countess must have slept. Either one of you could have left the room."

"We were in a bit of a tangle," he said. "If I'd tried to leave, she would have noticed. I did not relieve her of her husband. I never wished to, lovely though she is."

Klara stared at nothing, hoping Anton or Hagen would second her. No luck.

"Enough, Stark. Diligence is commendable, but you're missing the point. Listen." Hagen motioned for Baeder to go on.

"The countess was summoned from bed early that morning—presumably by my uncle and Herr Spaller," Baeder said. "As I prepared to leave, I discovered a woman searching the rooms."

"You see?" Hagen leaned back in his chair, tucking his thumbs in his waistcoat. "This woman is probably an agent sent to erase any links Olsberg had with the French. But Josef saw her, and she fled before she could recover the ciphered message on that handkerchief."

"She could have been a servant," Klara said. "They often pry."

No one heeded her. Anton's face brightened considerably. "Do you think this woman killed him?" he asked.

Baeder shrugged. "All I know is she was looking for something—and she knew Olsberg was dead."

"You spoke to her?" Anton asked.

"I had her by the arm, but she got away."

Damp seeped onto Klara's palms. "Who do you suppose she is?"

"You're going to find out," Hagen said. "Look over the dossiers of known foreign agents with my nephew. You might find her there. Spaller, I want you to interview Olsberg's banker. See what story his money tells."

Anton bowed with a click of his heels and hurried out before Klara had recovered enough to react.

"Are you coming?" Josef asked, pausing at the door.

"Of course, sir." Klara hurried after him.

"One moment, Josef."

Baeder turned to face his uncle, nearly colliding with Klara. She stepped back, not meeting his eyes.

"This afternoon, you must pay your condolences to the countess," Hagen continued.

Klara was close enough she saw Baeder stiffen and heard his indrawn breath.

"I think that will prove an awkward mistake. She may see our relationship differently now she's lost her husband."

"I need you to find out how much she knows. Her husband may have told her something. You liked her enough before. Just because she's marriageable again—"

"You know my thoughts about unattached ladies," Josef said.

"I can't afford to humor them. You're going to keep up this

affair. Tell her whatever you must, but stay in her good graces. You're my best asset in this muddle."

They exchanged a long look that ended with Josef lowering his chin in a brief nod. "Very well." He straightened and looked at Klara. "Herr Stark? You will show me the files?"

"This way, sir." Pulse thrumming in her throat, Klara led him from the room.

CHAPTER 8

Klara sat down at the table of a small conference room, pretending she didn't feel like she had spiders walking up her spine. Baeder sat across from her, which gave him a view of her face, but at least now she could conceal her feet. He hadn't recognized her or her shoes—unless he was bluffing. But if he knew who she was, why keep silent? He could accuse her right now and save himself time.

He must not know. She'd keep it that way. "These are the foreign agents we know," Klara said, passing him the files she'd collected on their way. It was uncomfortable meeting his eyes, but she forced herself to look at him before glancing back at the sheaf of papers. "Some of them work for us as well."

He grunted, reaching for the dossier on top and scanning the sheet, quickly setting it aside and leafing through the others. "How am I supposed to identify her from these? There's hardly any physical description. I don't know how many languages this woman speaks. I don't know her hair color. We spoke German, and she wore a cap. All I remember is that she was tall—and skittish because I was naked."

"That tells us something," Klara said, pleased it wasn't much.

"This is a waste of time."

Klara said nothing, hoping his statement would prove true. He frowned at the documents in front of him, giving one a closer look, before shaking his head. "You must hate working for my uncle," he muttered.

"I can see you do," Klara countered. "Perhaps calling on the countess will be more to your taste."

He gave her a hard look.

"Were you spying on her?" Klara asked, carefully nonchalant.

"No. But I have to now, obviously."

"How tiresome for you."

Her sarcasm made him arch an eyebrow. "Not so tiresome as this." He pushed away from the table and prowled around the room. "We're stocked with ink and paper, but isn't anyone going to bring us something to drink?"

"You could ask. Secretaries don't drink as they work."

"I'm sorry to hear that."

Klara ignored him, winnowing out dossiers: the wife of an Italian duke, French by birth; a courtesan who'd accompanied a Russian general from Paris; a maid to a Danish princess working for both the French and the Austrians. Josef reached over her shoulder and discarded the Italian lady's file.

"Why are you taking out that one?" Klara asked. "The description says she's tall."

Josef shook his head. "I know Donna Carminati. She has no qualms about intruding in strange bedchambers, but nothing would persuade her to dress as a servant. And she's too pretty. The woman I saw had no breasts."

"You noticed that, but not—"

"I always look. Don't you?"

"Legs for me." Klara had enough practice she could say anything without blushing.

Josef nodded. "Yes, those too, but they are harder to see, even with the current fashion for tissue-thin gowns."

"Would you recognize her if you saw her again?" Klara didn't look up.

"Perhaps. The room was dark. I've never been caught in such a position before. It's proved awkward all around. I'm not sure if it's right yet to call on the countess and offer my condolences."

Klara snorted. "If she is as sincere in her grief as you are in your sympathy, I don't think it will matter."

Josef shook his head. "There's a form to these things, if you didn't know."

Klara pretended to study the dossier in front of her. "Happily, I don't."

He walked around the table back to his chair, sitting down with a smirk. "Too innocent? Or too young? I'd guess the latter. How old are you?"

"Not that young. I'm twenty-five." According to her forged references, at least. She was actually twenty-two.

"You must have experienced uncomfortable moments by now."

He was studying her too closely. Klara reminded herself she had a mustache, cropped hair and a high cravat. For good measure, she leaned back, fully occupying her chair. "If I have, do you think I'd admit to them?"

He smiled. "Probably not."

Klara passed him the descriptions of two more suspects. "What about these?"

"They seem as likely as any of the others."

When they were finished with the dossiers, Klara gathered the likely ones and bundled the impossibles to return to the archives. "Thank you for your help. I'll look into these names."

"You won't be able to recognize her." He reached for the papers, but Klara held them tight.

"Won't you be occupied with the countess?" she asked.

"Not until this afternoon. I'm certain my uncle expects us to work together."

Maybe so, but Klara wasn't about to unless explicitly commanded. The less time she spent with him the better. "You're using me as an excuse to put her off."

"Maybe, but you won't be able to find this woman on your own."

"But I can discover where *these* women were yesterday morning." Or pretend to. Left on her own, she could tackle the real work of finding the killer. Klara handed Baeder half the sheets from her pile. "You take these. I'll look after the rest. Let me know what you find."

He opened his mouth, but Klara talked over him. "This will be faster, especially because I don't care much for our chances. Like you said, this is a waste of time." They'd have better luck finding the murderer by tracking down the French spy who'd given Olsberg the cipher. She would do that.

He stepped closer, dropping his voice. "Don't tell my uncle, but I think you're right."

Klara warned him away with a look and hurried from the conference room, his whisper still tickling her ears. Back at her desk, she scrawled a note to Anton and slipped it under his blotter so only a corner stuck out.

Talk to me before sharing anything with Josef von Baeder. I don't trust him.

Safely alone, Klara settled into work. Once the killer was found and this matter cleared away, she would never have to see or speak with Josef von Baeder again and could stop worrying about being recognized. Unfortunately, there were several people who might have killed Count von Olsberg: his brother, the unknown French spy, perhaps even Olsberg's wife, if she'd enlisted the help and silence of Josef von Baeder. Klara wouldn't dismiss that possibility.

Luckily, she had an advantage. She knew the secret Olsberg had tried to steal from her instead of buy—almost. In her rush from the Hofburg to St. Stephen's, she hadn't actually read the papers she'd tried to sell. Theresa had given them to her sewn shut in a packet, and the note Klara had written was copied from her mother's instructions. Klara hadn't composed the threat herself.

The secret concerned a woman, she knew that much. She'd assumed Olsberg had raped a lady, fathered a bastard, or left a woman dead in suspicious circumstances. All terrible, and she hadn't cared to know exactly what. Last she remembered, the papers had been in the pocket of her coat—the one Levi had thrown into the river. He would have emptied her pockets, but given how angry he was with Theresa and how strongly he opposed the blackmail, he could have easily destroyed the proof. She hoped he hadn't.

Passing Georg Fürst as she hurried from the Hofburg, Klara told him she was searching out the foreign agents on her list in case anyone came looking for her. Then she went home.

The apartment was empty, but Levi had pushed aside the furniture and laid out a sword stick for her, replacing the one she'd lost in the crypt. Hopefully, it was bought and not stolen. The furniture crowded against the walls meant he thought she should practice, but that would have to wait. She needed Olsberg's papers. Klara searched the desk, leafing over news sheets and a few bills. She kept no personal papers, no letters, save the false ones left there to support her pretended identity.

Perhaps Levi had hidden them. That was the wisest course. Klara searched the cache they'd built beneath the floorboards but found nothing. She was taking the pictures off the walls when Levi returned, carrying his luncheon on a tray. The smell of paprika made her realize she was hungry.

Levi didn't allow her time for questions. He took one look at her, then set down the tray. "I'll get another bowl."

"I'm looking for the papers Theresa gave me," Klara said, returning a picture to the wall, the frame containing nothing but a poorly executed mountain landscape. "Did they get thrown out with my coat?"

"I returned them to her. You don't need them." With that, he left for the kitchen.

When he returned bearing another tray, Klara tried again. "I'd like to know what they say."

Levi motioned her to a chair. "Sit down. The food will get cold."

There was no point in wasting their Hungarian landlady's excellent goulash. Klara buttered a slice of rye bread and scooped up a mouthful. The stew was brown, rich, and immeasurably comforting, especially after a morning as taxing as this one had been.

She should tell him about Josef von Baeder and the search he'd started for her. Klara tried to think of an easy way to make the disclosure, realized there wasn't one, and swallowed her mouthful of stew. Before she could speak, Levi coughed. It wasn't the dry rasp she knew. Klara set down her spoon. "Are you ill?" she asked.

"I'm never ill." This was true, but looking closer, Klara saw the shadows under his eyes were darker than usual.

"There's always a first time."

"Should I start expecting you midday?" he asked, avoiding the subject. "You're home two days in a row."

"No trouble this time." None she couldn't handle. "I only came because I wanted the papers. I think they'll be a better lead to Olsberg's killer than anything they've found so far at the Hofburg."

Levi shook his head. "No one knew about this."

"Theresa did."

"Olsberg didn't tell her. She guessed." Levi frowned into his bowl. It was still three quarters full.

Klara pushed the plate of bread closer, waiting for Levi to pick up a slice. "What's so awful about these papers?"

"It's the record of Count von Olsberg's marriage to Elke Fechter."

"Who's she?" Klara set down her bread and passed Levi the butter. He frowned at it, spreading it absently, too preoccupied to eat.

"Does it matter? Olsberg married her."

"He lied to her?" Poor woman. Some mistresses held out for marriage, Klara knew. If this Elke Fechter hadn't known about the countess until it was too late...

Levi coughed again and set down the butter knife. "Not her. He lied to the countess."

Klara's forehead creased as she found her bearings again. If both partners still lived, only the first marriage mattered. Whatever came after was invalid. "You mean he married the Fechter woman first?"

"In 1802. He married the countess five years later."

"And Elke Fechter was still alive?"

"Presumably, because he wanted the papers."

Klara pushed aside her bowl and stood. "Who else knows?"

Levi looked up from his uneaten bread. "He tried to kill you, so I'd guess nobody. He wanted to keep it that way. There's a new sword stick for you," he said, motioning to the corner. "You should practice."

"Later," Klara said. "I must speak to Theresa first."

Josef called on Sonia von Olsberg late in the afternoon, hoping to catch her alone. After quarreling with Uncle Franz and putting up with his secretary, Josef was happier than he had been about the prospect of continuing this cooling affair. Sonia was a beautiful woman; coaxing her into bed with a few well-crafted lies was preferable to shuffling paper in a windowless room of the Hofburg. As Uncle Franz had pointed out, it was unpatriotic to refuse.

Unfortunately, Sonia had company. Hiding his disappointment, Josef strode into the parlor and bowed, not realizing until he straightened that he knew the lady sitting next to Sonia, confidingly close. His smile froze.

"Herr Baeder, have you come to condole this bereaved beauty?" The Princess Bonaccorso stretched out a languid hand, while Sonia used the distraction to dab at her tear-reddened eyes. She didn't look at him.

"I came the moment I heard." Pressing a perfunctory kiss on the princess's pink-tipped paw, he reached for Sonia's but stopped when all she offered was a challenging stare. Feeling like he'd had his wrist slapped, Josef dropped his hand to his side. "Dear countess, I'm terribly sorry."

The only sound was the air stirring from the princess's fan. "Such heavy silence, my darlings. I'll leave you both. I'm sure you have much to discuss." She patted the countess's knee. "I'll call again soon, dear." Rising in a cascade of whispering silk, she waltzed away, murmuring, "So good to see you again, Josef."

"Josef?" Sonia echoed.

The princess turned in mock surprise. "Forgive me. I forget myself. I've used his name for such a long time, you know."

"Since I was in long shirts." Josef's smile failed to lift the downward curl of Sonia's mouth. "Aunt Valeria is a dear friend of my mother's."

"You're related?"

"Only by affection," the princess said with an arch smile. "Dear countess, make sure he entertains you with the good stories. I'm sure he hears the most fascinating things from his uncle." She swept from the room.

Josef went to Sonia before the silence stifled him, taking the empty space beside her on the couch. "Angel, I know you're suffering—"

"You didn't tell me Baron von Hagen is your uncle."

"How could I know it would matter? I suppose he's been here, distressing you with questions. Don't let it trouble you. In other circumstances, he is better behaved."

"Have you been spying on me?"

Josef laughed. "If Uncle Franz had the power to direct my affections, I'd have to sleep with the British ambassador's wife—or the ambassador himself, for that matter."

"You should have mentioned it."

"Would it have changed your mind? Should I have given you a list of all my great-aunts and nephews and godmothers before taking you to bed? At the time, I think you'd have found it an unpleasant distraction."

"I was a fool." She scrubbed the back of her wrist across her eyes. "I won't be anymore." Her chin steadied.

"What are you saying?" Josef asked.

"I trusted you, and you—" Whatever she had intended to say was expelled with an angry breath. "Without Marius, I must think about my boys. I haven't time for you."

"Because you think I'll carry tales to my uncle?" Josef stood. "Don't be ridiculous. You aren't important enough. Your husband—"

"Don't speak of him. I won't allow it."

His temper was getting the better of him. Trying to curb it, Josef brushed at the sleeve of his coat. "Dying doesn't make him a saint. You know he wasn't."

"But he was my husband," she retorted. "And with all the world watching—suffice it to say, I have better things to do than satisfy your vanity. I don't trust you."

"Sonia—"

She interrupted his coaxing with a hard shake of her head. “Leave me alone.”

“But I—”

“I don’t want to see you. Especially alone.”

It took him a second to understand. “You’re afraid? You think I killed him?”

She dropped her eyes, wrapping her arms around her middle. “I don’t know.”

“You ought to.” His tone made her look up, then swiftly away.

“I don’t know, Josef. Please leave.”

Nothing he said would persuade her, and if his suppressed words escaped, they wouldn’t soothe—they’d inflame. Josef bowed, telling himself as he walked from the house she only needed time. She was overstrung from the shock. He’d get her back. And then he’d get even.

CHAPTER 9

Klara stopped twice at Theresa's apartment but failed to find her. Returning home, she let Levi have his way and agreed to some sword practice, but he soon tired, succumbing to a fit of coughing. "Enough," Klara told him, taking away his sword.

Annoyed but unable to argue, Levi let her push him into the armchair and spread a blanket over his knees, though he insisted she continue the practice on her own. He called out parries, grumbling that Klara wasn't fast enough, that she was favoring her injured side. Klara let him drill her until she was sweaty and spent.

"You should be in bed," she told him.

"It's just a wheeze," he said. "I'll be better tomorrow."

When he was safely snoring, Klara patched up her side again. Beneath the plaster, her cut had split open.

HER LUCK WAS no better the next day or the one after that. Although Klara succeeded in avoiding Josef von Baeder, she was too busy at the Hofburg to slip away for a meeting with her mother. Anton's valiant toils unearthed nothing, besides the fact that the servants knew how Marius von Olsberg had died and had told both his wife and his brother. "And heaven knows who else," Anton concluded with a scowl.

Klara worked diligently at her searches, penning precise and pointless reports. Once, Lennard von Olsberg evaded surveillance, which made Anton swear and Baron von Hagen refuse his afternoon cake. The secretaries stepped softly, and the agents responsible for this lapse swore on their hope of salvation that Olsberg wouldn't escape them again.

The countess was proving easier to track, only leaving her apartments to visit Vienna's churches. She had not granted Josef von Baeder a second meeting, and he was, according to Anton, increasingly snarly.

Friday evening, Baron von Hagen informed Klara, Anton, and his tight-lipped nephew that Emperor Francis was displeased at their lack of progress. "I want something by Monday," Hagen ordered. "The emperor expects me to placate the ambassadors by then."

They bowed and left the room in silence, Josef von Baeder turning away from her and Anton as soon as they gained the corridor.

"Sir?" Anton stopped him, wilting under the steely gaze. "Should we confer? Perhaps make a plan?"

"I planned to attend the Palm Palace this evening. Instead, I'll be trying my luck again with the widow. Do you suggest any particular strategy?"

Anton swallowed. "She is a lady, sir. You should treat her so."

Baeder's granite look softened. "You're right. Forgive me."

Anton received the apology with a nod, and Baeder unbent further. "Like you said, we should coordinate our efforts."

"I thought I'd pay an informal visit to Lennard von Olsberg,"

Anton said. "He's always hanging about the house of that lady he met in Baden."

"Anna Stoltenberg," Klara filled in.

"Yes. I'll stop by when they normally receive callers so I can watch him with Fräulein Stoltenberg."

"A sound notion," Baeder said. "Let him feel a little pressure." He looked at Klara. "And you?"

"There are still three agents we haven't eliminated from your list," she said.

Anton looked disappointed at her lack of initiative but was too kind to say anything. Even Josef was unexpectedly forbearing. "There's one more thing we might try," he said. "I was going to look into it myself, but with my time pledged to the countess..."

"What is it?" Anton asked.

"A name dropped in my ear by that priestess of slander, the Princess Bonaccorso."

"Yes?"

"She tells me the late count was an admirer of music, especially of a certain soprano."

Klara licked her lips. She'd expected this and was prepared. "Do you know the name?"

"Theresa."

Anton grunted. "Yes, but which one? Grünbaum or Vogl?"

Klara smiled. She'd forgotten one of her mother's rivals had the same name and was grateful for every bit of dirt muddying these waters.

"You'll have to question both of them," Baeder said.

"I'll speak to Theresa Vogl," Klara said, before Anton claimed her. Earlier in the week, when Klara had gone with him to the opera, he'd been lavish in her mother's praise.

"Why not Fräulein Grünbaum?" he asked.

"Well..." Klara inspected her nails, knowing what both men would think. "It happens I have a slight acquaintance with her."

Baeder chuckled, but Anton shot her a narrow glance. "You do? You never said."

Klara gave Anton an apologetic smile. "There was no reason to mention it before."

Nor was there reason to hurry. Catching Theresa on a Saturday was a gamble, but Sunday morning Klara knew where she would be.

Klara left her apartment at the appointed hour, keeping a hand on her hat until she reached the Graben, where thick crowds shielded her from the plucking hands of the wind. This was the street where all went to see and admire: shop windows, strollers, the princesses and prostitutes nibbling cake beside each other in the konditoreis. Men gathered in kafeehausen on the side streets, lured by steaming coffee, talk, and tobacco. Street vendors sang their wares to the lighter pursed, offering trays of ribbons, combs, almonds, or sugared pastry. Klara bought herself an apricot-filled krapfen and ate as she walked, licking the stickiness from her fingers. It wasn't far to St. Stephen's.

In daylight, there was nothing about the cathedral to frighten her. She entered through the Giant's Door, leaving the sunlit plaza, the hum of gossip, and the smell of September. Inside, it was cool and quiet, earth-made sounds wafting to a roof halfway to heaven. The thousand or more panes of each lofty window were tinted blue and lavender. Only rarely was there a pane of warm-toned gold. Between the windows and spaced along the nave, stone pillars stretched up like summer grass, throwing long shadows across the checkered floor. Theresa Vogl sat in the women's nave, head bent, fresh from the weekly laundering of her soul.

If eyes watched from the corners or from heaven, Klara couldn't say, but the carved stone faces on the walls didn't see.

She sat on the pew beside her mother, waiting for her to finish praying and look up.

At last, her mother straightened, tucking her beads into a sable muff. She was dressed more circumspectly than usual, aside from the furs and the sapphire ring she'd worn as long as Klara could remember.

"Fräulein Vogl," Klara greeted her.

Theresa nodded. "Herr Stark. I didn't expect to see you."

They passed out of the pew into the aisle, their attenuated footsteps making Klara unexpectedly faint, though this place was nothing like the dark warren below. She stopped and took a long breath.

"Have you not been sleeping?" Theresa asked. "You're very pale."

"Stood up too quickly is all."

"Not your wound?"

Klara shook her head, frowning at the floor. "The police know about you and Olsberg. At least, they will by Monday. They chanced on some gossip, but I said I'd question you."

"Don't worry about me." Theresa slipped her hand around Klara's arm and gave her a pat. "You'll come out of this all right. I promise."

Her certainty was irritating. Klara wasn't nearly so sure. "It's a lot to manage." Lost letters, Gunter, Josef von Baeder...

"I lit a candle for you."

Klara resisted the urge to snort. Sometimes her mother was—but there were contradictions she'd never quarrel with, questions she'd never ask. She dropped her voice lower. "Do you have Olsberg's papers?"

Theresa nodded.

"Not in your apartment, I hope."

"No, I keep them with me."

"I'd better take them. Baron von Hagen might order a search

of your apartment, and if that happens, I'm sure Anton Spaller will insist on taking part."

"That friend of yours? The cripple?" She wrinkled her nose, then saw and interpreted Klara's look of surprise. "Levi told me."

"He has a clubfoot. He walks just fine. He's an admirer of yours."

"Then I'll make certain he has to search through my underthings." She fumbled in her muff, surprising Klara by drawing out a bloodstained packet. "Here. You keep it."

Klara stepped forward to shield the paper from view. "That's a terrible idea."

"Teasing Herr Spaller?"

"That too." Klara grimaced. "Don't make him sift through your trifles." Anton was too susceptible. "I'm going to burn this."

Theresa shook her head. "You might need it to blame the killing on someone else—the wife or the brother."

Klara gave her a look. "I want to find the murderer, not frame one."

"Is that wise? Suppose—"

"How did you guess Olsberg's secret? Levi wouldn't tell me."

"Sometimes men get reminiscent. We were speaking of Vienna before the wars. Old loves."

"And from that you guessed he was married? And found proof? He had to have said more than that."

Theresa shook her head. "He said there was a woman he was mad for, yet she'd do nothing but tease him. He said he used to watch her when she went to church, because her father wouldn't let her have anything to do with him. It was only one conversation, and he was halfway drunk."

It was lucky Olsberg was dead. Eventually, he'd have suspected her.

"I was curious, and I knew the church, so I went there and convinced the priest to let me see the register."

No doubt she'd been very charming.

"He left me alone long enough I was able to cut out the page. Then I waited a month. By then, why would Olsberg suspect? All I had was a snatch of conversation, easily forgotten."

"Do you think anyone else knew?"

"Well, the wife does, naturally. The first one," she added, seeing Klara's confusion. "She had to. She was there."

"What if Olsberg thought the blackmail came from her?" Klara asked. "He might have killed her."

Theresa shook her head. "He had no time to make sure. I asked the priest who she was and if she was still living in the parish. Proof of this marriage only damns him if the wife is still alive or was alive when he pretended to marry the countess."

"Is she alive? Could von Olsberg have found her?"

"He didn't. He's dead."

"But—"

"She moved three years ago to Meidling. The priest hasn't heard anything of her since. Why are you so worried?"

Klara pressed her lips together. "Could anyone else have known?"

"Not unless Olsberg told them, and I'm sure he never did that." Hushing Klara with another pat on the arm, Theresa led her past a party of sightseers admiring the pulpit.

"I don't like it." As reasons for killing someone went, Olsberg's marriage gave an excellent excuse to the countess. In a jealous rage, desperate for revenge, what long-suffering wife wouldn't be tempted to murder?

Klara shook her head. This wasn't an opera. If the countess knew of the marriage, she'd either known for some time or discovered it when her husband learned of the blackmail. If she'd known for ages, why kill him now? Olsberg had left the opera soon after receiving the note, so it was unlikely anyone could have discovered he was being threatened and why, then found time and means to kill him. The countess had left the opera soon after her husband and spent the night with her lover—facts that didn't fit with the luck, lightning comprehension, and ruthless speed such a murder required, unless she was complicit with Baeder.

Klara could believe that. All they had to do was pretend surprise the following morning and swear they'd never left each other's arms. With Baeder now part of the investigation, it was easy for him to shift the blame. He'd set them searching for Klara quickly enough, though it was true he'd only accused her of spying. What's more, she'd seen Baeder's surprise that morning. It had seemed genuine. She might want him to be guilty, but wishing didn't make it so.

Lennard, who'd followed his brother from theater to salon to crypt, was a likelier candidate. He could have confronted his brother or overheard him talking and pieced together the truth. It didn't take genius to discern that with his brother gone and his sons declared illegitimate, all Lennard's problems were solved. But if Lennard had learned the truth and killed his brother, why hadn't he revealed what he knew? Even the suspicion that his brother's marriage was invalid could temper his financial problems. Salvation was at hand; why not claim it? Perhaps he'd erred, counting on Gunter for an alibi, and was waiting until he could clear himself of murder before claiming his brother's title. But delay could lose him the woman he loved. Would he allow that when there was a chance he could have her?

Of course, his history wasn't one of daring or competence. He admitted to wounding himself in a training accident, but perhaps he'd finally tired of being the laughingstock brother.

Klara slid the packet inside her glove. She'd find a better hiding place later.

"One of them did it," Theresa insisted. "Don't let them get away with it at your expense. And get some rest." It was permissible, as part of the fiction of a rendezvous, for Theresa Vogl to press a quick kiss onto Kasper Stark's cheek, so Klara didn't pull away when she came close. Theresa smelled of roses.

Hoping the kiss hadn't smeared her pseudo-stubble, Klara watched her mother exit the church. There were too many possibilities, too few ways to be sure. But it seemed truth didn't matter —much.

THERE WERE few things Theresa enjoyed more than a Sunday afternoon ride in the Prater, the royal park and hunting grounds which Josef II had opened to the public sixty years before. Perched on the beautiful chestnut gelding gifted to her by a Russian general—a handsome present, but an expensive one to keep—she walked sedately down the Hauptallee beneath the spreading branches of the horse chestnuts.

Her hair was curled and spilling down one shoulder, her riding habit trimmed with braid and fitted to her waist. Her riding whip had a braided thong and an ivory handle. It was a present too. She knew she looked well, easily controlling a spirited horse, her soft expression denying myriad worries.

She wasn't thinking of her drawer crammed with bills today and whether she'd catch the burr that had lodged in Levi Braun's throat. She wasn't thinking about the luncheon she'd skipped so she could eat cake and drink wine late in the evening or the fat, sweaty, brigade major she must entertain tomorrow. She had a single purpose this afternoon, a difficult one, but she couldn't let it look that way.

Resolutely ignored by a barouche full of ladies, Theresa smiled to herself as she rode past, comfortable in the knowledge that of the three gentlemen escorting them on horseback, she snared two pairs of eyes. Allowing her mount to balk at the whirling red wheels of a passing curricle, she touched the horse's flank with her whip, swiftly proving to man and beast she knew what she was about.

"Well done, madam!" A broad-shouldered Swede drew alongside her, tipped his hat, and attempted to compliment her in faulty German.

"You're too kind, sir," Theresa replied, switching to French. The man smiled with relief at the change and made better progress. He was handsome, displaying all the accoutrements of wealth. Theresa's shrewd eyes detected no faults or camouflaged frugality. He spoke in a velvet baritone, admitting an interest in music and a middling talent at the pianoforte, but was probably being modest. He had the voice and fingers to excel at either. Theresa decided she wouldn't mind singing or sleeping with him. When his friends merged with them at the intersection of one of the allées, he presented her to them with the most sumptuous of compliments.

"If you haven't heard her sing, you've missed the only heaven you'll ever know," he said, laughing with a young lieutenant.

All four of them were handsome, even the one with the missing arm, the result of an injury in the Russian campaign of 1812. She'd happily pair with the Swede—or any of them—but she was hunting particular game today. It was a pity.

There he was. Sitting in a sleek barouche, mustache impeccable, his shoulders admirably set off by epaulettes with fringes of gold braid, he was deep in conversation with an elderly archduchess, decked in fluttering ribbons and a long-fringed shawl. His position made him difficult to flush, let alone catch. Still, he was here, and that was lucky. You didn't capture a king with just one move. It took patience, strategy, and covert traps. She'd be more sure of herself if she had more time.

This wasn't a day for subtlety.

"Oh, look!" Stretching out her whip hand, Theresa pointed past the barouche to a distant carriage. "Is that Princess Marie Louise?"

The Austrian princess, who also happened to be Napoleon's wife, was one of the most gossiped-about figures in Vienna.

"Too far away to tell," said her Swede, narrowing his eyes.

"Do you think she's with Count von Neipperg?" The carriage and the crowd surrounding it was impressive, but it could have held almost anyone. Eye on her quarry, Theresa urged her horse forward. The man she wanted was facing away from her and unaware, his attention devoted to the archduchess, who seemed unable to communicate without gesticulating.

"Wait, pretty one!" The handsome Swede spurred after her, followed by his laughing friends. They closed on the carriage with her quarry, jesting boisterously, swerving close to avoid a high-perch phaeton rolling toward them. Theresa dug in her heel, making her mount sidle. The carriage horses jerked, and the elderly archduchess shrieked with a flutter of ribbons and a flap of her fringed shawl. Theresa's horse whinnied and reared, but she kept her seat, clinging to the reins and the pommel.

"Madam! Are you all right?"

Her horse had four feet on the ground again, and she was breathless and shaken. It was always better not to fake that. Though her Swede was beside her, Theresa patted her horse's neck, focusing on the man in the carriage. She smiled down at him. He'd spun in his seat, the archduchess temporarily forgotten.

"I nearly ended up in your lap, sir."

"Are you all right?" he asked again.

"No harm done." She reached out her whip and straightened the hat that had fallen sideways over his brow. As she did, she let fall the handkerchief tucked into her glove. It landed on his knee, but she only half saw, so intent was she on the man's eyes. Before he spoke, she was away again, straight in the saddle, ignoring the loud imprecations of the archduchess, and trailing a parade of handsome young men.

"Angel, did you mean to do that?"

Theresa looked at the blue-eyed man riding beside her. Her lips parted in a grin. "Old men for comfort, younger for sport." He laughed, keeping pace as she broke into a trot.

Klara had never seen Sonia von Olsberg before, but when she called that afternoon, alone, she discovered the countess was precisely what she'd expected. It was unnatural to have imagined her so particularly, but there she was: graceful slopes of neck and shoulder, skin as iridescent as mother-of-pearl. Her hair was thick, piled about her head in glossy coils accentuating the shapely perfection of her nose, lips, and fingers. Rich blue silk outlined the curves of her bosom and flowed to the floor. She knew her worth and did not invite Klara to sit.

"Forgive me for intruding." Klara bowed. "My name is Kasper Stark. Herr Hagen sent me." Ostensibly, this was a visit to report the pretense of progress, but Klara hoped to resolve her own questions. Somehow, she must gauge how much the countess knew without tipping her hand. It wouldn't be easy. Sonia von Olsberg hadn't killed her husband, according to Josef von Baeder, but had she *known*? Facing her calm, cool stare, Klara could not imagine this woman even suspected she was neither countess, wife, nor widow.

"What news have you for me?"

Klara had thought it might be possible to coax her way into this lady's confidence, skirting close enough to the subject of Olsberg's other wife to learn the truth. It was a stupid plan. One look told her this woman kept her own counsel. "I hope I'm not troubling you," Klara stalled.

Sonia von Olsberg didn't answer.

Klara was seconds from being dismissed. There was no time for finesse. "What do you know of your husband's affairs?"

The countess's eyebrows lifted. "His business or his amours?"

"At present, the leads I'm pursuing concern the latter."

Sonia von Olsberg frowned, but she didn't sweep out or send for a servant to take Klara away. "You're not as gentle with me as the man who came before."

"Herr Spaller, you mean?"

She nodded. "I like him better."

"He's halfway in love with you," Klara said. "You couldn't tell?"

"I might have suspected," she said, hiding a smile by rearranging her skirts.

Klara sensed she was thawing and went to work. "Surely you're used to that reaction by now."

The countess studied Klara, surveying her from top to toe. Klara was still, resisting the urge to fiddle with the hat in her right hand. She never liked being looked at.

"Perhaps I'm waiting to elicit it from you," the countess said.

"Neither of us have that much time." Klara wasn't going to offer adoration, even the false kind. An alliance was better. "I want to help. You and your family deserve justice, though it cannot compensate for your loss."

"No." The countess swallowed. "I'll tell you what I know. It isn't much." She left off plucking at her lace handkerchief and folded her hands in her lap. "I didn't make it a practice to acquaint myself with the details, but Marius always had mistresses."

"And here in Vienna?"

"I expect he had several, but I only know of one: a singer named Theresa. I saw her one day when I returned early from a walk. I'd left the boys at the park with their nurse because I had a headache. I came home to lie down. When I looked out my window, she was leaving by the backstairs. At first, I thought she belonged to that Russian who lives downstairs, but she was wearing a shawl I'd seen in Marius's room. I thought he had bought it for me."

"That must have been uncomfortable."

"Not really. I was in love with someone else."

"Josef von Baeder?"

She closed her eyes. "Yes." Color mounted into her cheeks.

"Did you think we wouldn't know?" Klara asked gently.

"I hoped. He told you, didn't he?" She opened her eyes as she asked, and what Klara saw there made it difficult to reply. That kind of pain was meant to be private.

"I think he did it to protect you from suspicion. He was adamant you had nothing to do with the killing."

The countess's guard came down again, and she turned slightly away, rearranging herself on the sofa. "Then why did you come?"

"He said it, but I wanted to see for myself."

"And?" She drew herself up an inch.

"You're very beautiful."

"You do not trust me."

Klara shook her head. "I don't trust him."

The countess's hands fretted with the lace again. "Neither do I."

"Do you think he killed your husband?" Klara's eyes narrowed. Though she liked the idea of saddling Josef with the murder, she couldn't imagine him going back to bed afterward and pretending so convincingly that nothing was wrong. But the countess knew him better, and it was clear she was both upset and afraid.

"I don't know. I thought he was in love with me, but I'm not sure of anything anymore. He was here that night." She read Klara's expression, her shoulders falling. "He told you that as well."

"Only to clear you of suspicion. It wasn't to help me."

"Or his uncle?"

Klara shook her head. "I'm not sure they like one another. There's distrust there." She shrugged. "These days, it's a common habit."

"A wise one."

Klara acknowledged this and brought them back to the point. "Did you trust your husband?"

"I wasn't asked to. Marriages are words, Herr Stark. I never believed Marius's pledge of fidelity."

"Did you want it?"

She shrugged. "I know how the world works, and I soon learned Marius wasn't the kind who had it in him. I trusted him to guard his name and our interests. He never failed in that, so when we came to Vienna to repair our fortunes, I did not ask many questions." She sighed.

"You only knew of the one mistress? No other women?" Klara asked.

She shook her head. "It doesn't mean he didn't have any."

"Perhaps from a time when he'd been here before?"

"He didn't frequent Vienna much. We spent more time in Berlin."

Klara couldn't get closer to the truth without revealing more, and it was clear the countess didn't know. She was worried about other things—the wrong ones, like Josef von Baeder, who was using her but wouldn't harm her. Sonia von Olsberg had no reason to fear him. Klara did. "Did your husband have enemies?" she asked.

"Clearly, but I don't know them. We did not confide, Herr Stark." Sensing the countess's patience was wearing thin, Klara took a folded paper from her pocket. "I've a list here," Klara said. Anton had gathered the names from Olsberg's servants and known acquaintances. "Would any of these men have reason to harm your husband?"

The countess looked over the list, frowning near the end.

"Perhaps Christopher Magnussen, but I'm prejudiced. I don't like him. When Marius is—" She grimaced. "When Marius was in his company, he gambled too much. Most of these men I don't know, but I've met this one." Her finger tapped the paper. "Alexander Poincaré. He called once or twice, talked about art—the works of Andrea Mantegna."

"Didn't you have one of his paintings?" Klara asked.

"We had three. Marius recovered the smallest just last week. I was—" She broke off. "What is it?"

"Where did he get the painting?"

"He didn't say. I was at the Prater that afternoon with the children." Her lips pressed together. "He was pleased. So was I. We took the boys for ices. He said soon we'd have everything back."

"How?"

"It wasn't my business to know." She studied her hands. "You think that was cowardly of me."

If she did, Klara wasn't going to admit it. "Did you sense he was involved in something wrong?"

The countess shook her head. "No. He wouldn't. But I—" She swallowed. "I think he would do just about anything to get his treasures back."

"May I see the painting?"

The countess rose, pleased to have a distraction. "It's in my room now. I had hung it in here over the fire" —she shook her head— "but I took it down." She walked too quickly to field questions. Klara followed in silence. Behind one of the doors they passed, she heard muffled voices—young boys repeating a lesson. The countess slowed. "I really should—"

"I'll leave once I see the painting," Klara said.

The countess's bed was made today. There were no clothes strewn on the floor, no letters on the desk, no naked man trailing crumpled sheets, but Klara felt him here, her shoulders curling as if he was breathing down her neck. It was nonsense: the windows were open, it was daylight, the bedcovers were crisp and impeccable. Besides the countess, there was only furniture here and a few landscapes on the walls. Klara walked to the largest. "Is this…?" She'd expected more.

"No." The countess laughed. "I don't know where the landlady dug that up. The painting is here, but like I said, I had to take it down." Instead of explaining, she walked to the other side of the armoire and reached for a canvas resting against the wall.

"Let me," Klara said. The canvas wasn't large, though the frame was ornate and unexpectedly heavy. Klara hefted the picture, tilting it into the light.

"Remarkable, isn't it?" The countess stood at Klara's shoulder. "We also had a Mantegna Madonna and child. It was my favorite, but—"

"It's beautiful." Klara had used the word not long ago, applied to the countess. Now she regretted spending the word so freely. Close to, this picture was almost too much to bear. There was not a mark of a brush. The skin looked like it would feel warm, and the shapely hands were elegant and restrained—scarcely noticeable though, below such gentle eyes, the lids half-lowered in pain. Humbled, Klara propped the painting against the dressing table and stepped back for a fuller look.

A naked, beaten Christ filled the frame, but edging around him, tormentors sneered and breathed menace in his ears. They were twisted and grotesque but couldn't dim the glory of the resigned and suffering face in the center.

"After I heard what happened to Marius, I had to take it down. In case the boys… " She swallowed, and Klara freed herself from the picture to turn to her.

"They would damage it?" Only the most outrageous child would deface something like this.

"No. They are excellent boys. It—it was the rope."

Klara looked again. Of course. Captivated by the faces, Klara hadn't noticed the rope on Christ's neck—loose for now, but ready to be tightened at any attempt to escape.

"Marius's brother told me how he died," the countess said. "But I didn't tell the children. Telling them Marius was dead was hard enough."

"I can imagine." Too well. As soon as she pictured a pair of little, wide-eyed boys, she felt her throat going tight.

"You think Marius got the painting from this Frenchman?"

"It's worth finding out," Klara said. "Leave it to the police. You don't want to tangle yourself in anything dangerous."

"No." She licked her lips.

"Don't be afraid," Klara told her. "Herr Hagen has taken steps to ensure your safety."

The countess smiled and looked down. "So I've learned. Must I have these beggars trailing me about?"

The look Klara returned was grave. "Your husband is dead, my lady. Better safe than sorry."

CHAPTER 10

Monday morning came early, and with it came Josef von Baeder. Klara was working at her desk, a quiet, diligent cog, when Baeder strode into the office. Ignoring the other secretaries who, like her, were feverishly copying a stolen bag of diplomatic mail, he pulled up an empty chair and heaved himself into it. "What have you found?" he demanded.

Klara dipped her pen, scribbled another line of English, and watched him out the corner of her eye. If she knew him better, she'd accuse him of indulging in a fit of the sulks. Instead, she frowned at the letter she was copying—was that an *s* or an *f*? Impossible to say. Klara decided the writer loved Colonel Smith, not Frith, and wrote that down, wishing indulgent British husbands wouldn't let their women mingle nonsense with the diplomatic mail. Perhaps it was intentional. They might suspect their letters were regularly intercepted.

"I'm busy," Klara said. "Come back after lunch."

On her left, Anton's scratching pen faltered. "They need to return these letters before nine," he explained.

"Someone else can copy those. I'm busy this afternoon," Baeder said.

"With whom? The countess?" Too late, Klara realized she shouldn't have spoken. Sonia von Olsberg ought to know better than to fall for a blackguard like Baeder, and if she didn't, it was no business of Klara's. Still, Klara felt badly for her and poorly disposed toward the man lounging next to her in a too-small wooden chair.

"Yes, with the countess, if everything goes as planned." Josef crossed his legs. "But I've had a singular run of bad luck, which leaves us with a problem—an urgent one."

Klara kept writing.

"Sonia still won't see me. I don't have any new information to report to my uncle, who I understand is presenting *his* report to the emperor at nine. I expect he will summon us before then?" He checked his watch. "At most, we have about seven minutes. I'm hoping one of you learned something. Anton?"

Anton, pressed by the demands of politeness, set down his pen, though his fidgeting made it clear he was tormented by the looming deadline and his unfinished letter. "The bankers say Olsberg had money but not a lot, and there was nothing suspicious in his account. On Sunday, I engineered a meeting with Lennard von Olsberg at Anna Stoltenberg's—our mothers are acquainted—but it didn't go well."

That was putting it mildly. Anton had given Klara his full confession. Olsberg, already unhappy because Fräulein Stoltenberg had refused to see him in private, reacted to Anton's arrival with angry surprise, accusing Anton of following him. Of course this was true, but Olsberg refused to be placated with polite denials, which led to an unpleasant scene in the Stoltenbergs' drawing room. Swearing his innocence, Lennard von Olsberg railed against Anton and the police, vowing he'd take revenge for such unremitting persecution and the spoiling of his good name. He'd stormed from the house, forbidden to return, leaving the Stoltenbergs angry, Anna in tears, and Anton at the mercy of his grandmother, who of course heard about the whole thing before dinner.

"But there's no need to worry," Anton assured Josef. "Kasper's uncovered a lead." He retrieved his pen and resumed copying with visible relief.

"What is it?"

Feeling Josef's eyes on her, Klara reluctantly looked up. His frown goaded her into a sharper answer than she intended. "When *I* called on Countess von Olsberg, she was alone. We had quite a long tête-à-tête. There's a Frenchman her husband knew. I think he bought information from Olsberg in exchange for plundered art." She folded her arms. "You know, if the countess won't see *you*, your uncle might relieve you of this assignment."

"She'll see me," Baeder countered.

"Kasper's got it all written up and ready," Anton put in, smiling anxiously.

"Good. That gets us through this morning," Baeder said.

"And you'll be busy after lunch," Klara added.

"Can I help you with your letters, Kasper?" Anton asked. He was folding the last of his, waving for the office boy to collect them. They'd be resealed and returned, hopefully before anyone discovered they'd gone missing.

"Nearly done," Klara said.

Josef got up and peered over her shoulder.

"May I have more room, please?" Klara asked. She'd just dropped an ink blot on her sheet.

"*Convey my fondest regards to dear Felicity*," Josef read.

"Thank you." Klara scrawled the last sentence and folded the letter, afraid to look up. He was right behind her, uncomfortably close.

"Gentlemen?" It was Georg Fürst. Klara swiveled in her chair, grateful for the distraction. "Baron von Hagen is waiting for your report," Fürst told them.

"You take it," Klara said, passing her neatly written summary to Anton.

"But you—"

"We're not all needed in Hagen's office. Let me keep working on these letters. Otherwise, we'll never finish on time."

"If that's how you want it." Anton tucked the papers under his arm. He turned to Baeder. "It's good of you to come this morning, especially when you thought you were only here to take a share of the blame."

"Turns out I was luckier than I deserved. Thank you, Stark. You've saved us all a tongue-lashing."

He started off, but Anton hesitated, turning back to Klara. "You're sure—"

"Yes. If I don't keep working, we'll have nothing tomorrow or the next day. Go. I'm expecting a message."

Anton's eyebrows rose, but there was no time to enlighten him.

"Later," she promised.

Alone, Klara copied two more letters. Once the load of mail was carried off, she returned to the notes she'd compiled on Alexander Poincaré. He was thirty-two years old, had brown hair, brown eyes, and side whiskers—a description that could apply to almost anybody, given the right props. He was assigned as secretary to the Duc de Dolancourt, France's expert on German affairs, and his family was from Tours—the father killed in the revolution, the mother still living but sickly. There was mention of a brother, though nothing recent, and a sister married to a prominent royalist. Poincaré had served as aide-de-camp to Marshal Ney, an unfortunate connection now France was back in the hands of the Bourbons. No doubt it helped that Poincaré had left Ney's staff in 1812, after taking a wound at Smolensk.

Poincaré might have left Napoleon's army entirely at that time, but Klara didn't know for certain, though her notes included the information that Poincaré took laudanum, played the violin, and had eaten three capons at a dinner hosted by Countess Zichy. Some agents were too generous with details. Klara hoped for better information from her mother. She'd sent her a message last evening.

There is a Frenchman rumored to be friends with the late Count von Olsberg, a M. Alexander Poincaré. Do you know him? Or a lady who does?

Theresa's reply came just after nine, on scented paper sealed with lavender wax. The message was brief:

I'm told M. Poincaré visits a girl named Clélie in a house on Schottengasse. The woman who keeps the house is called Irmtrude Janke. Used to be a dancer. She might let you in, but don't mention you know me. We took a dislike to one another years ago.

Klara got up from her desk and located Georg Fürst. Though the senior secretary wasn't pleased with the interruption, he answered her questions. Klara left the Hofburg in a rush. If her ploy was to work, she hadn't much time.

When Klara presented herself at the brothel's eminently respectable door, she was admitted by a middle-aged woman with unnaturally dark hair and dramatic cosmetics. Age had whittled her to angular thinness, and she was a suitable match for the giant hound standing beside her, elegant and stretched unnaturally tall. The dog was short-haired and the color of storm water, his head coming well above Frau Janke's waist. He stood silently, obedient beneath his mistress's blue-veined hand. Klara guessed he was not a creature to be taken lightly.

"I'm looking for Clélie," Klara said and brought out her credentials. Letters from Baron von Hagen opened most doors.

Frau Janke frowned through narrowed eyes. Her lips twitched as she motioned for Klara to follow her. Inside, the house was clean and pretty but got shabbier the farther she went upstairs. The dog followed his mistress as closely as a shadow, the sound of his padding paws lost beneath the muffled chattering of girls that coursed through the corridors like burbling water.

The door to Clélie's room was partially open, but when it swung wide, revealing Klara, she jumped to her feet, scowling at Frau Janke. "I told you! Only Alex. He pays you enough. Take this one somewhere else." Her cheeks were mottled with an angry flush.

"I've come from the Hofburg," Klara said, deploying her hands in a soothing gesture. "Merely to talk. We are concerned for M. Poincaré. Your Alex." Guessing from the girl's inflections, Klara spoke to her in French, which didn't please Frau Janke, who must have been hoping to overhear.

The girl's eyes went wide. "What do you mean?"

"May I sit? Or would you rather join me for a walk?"

Clélie stilled her fingers with effort. "Outside is better." She threw the older woman another black look.

Klara waited while the girl donned her tawdry finery. The frills weren't terrible; there were just too many. Swansdown, lace, and ice blue ribbons crowded her face, hiding her hands and making her into a dressmaker's dummy. Klara offered her arm, but the girl kept her hands buried inside a muff too warm for such a bright day. Walking through the ballhausplatz, Klara consulted her watch and bought two paper packets of sugared almonds.

"I'm not hungry," the girl said and pushed hers away.

"I am. Besides, it makes us look natural. You're simply out taking the air."

"With the police," she retorted.

"Yes, but no one knows that. I could be anyone." Guiding Clélie's arm, Klara led her onto the remnants of the city wall, now popular with strollers wanting views of Vienna. A maze of rooftops, spires, and palaces spread in front of them, the streets swarming with people. For a moment, Klara forgot the girl beside her, finding the coffee shops, churches, and street corners she knew. She was fortunate, having gone away with Levi to travel and study, but there was a different feeling in a place you truly knew. Forgetting herself, she let out a sigh.

The wind caught Clélie's hair, teasing it out like the wisps of cloud in the sky. "You belong to Vienna?" The girl had faulty German and phrased it wrong.

"I've lived here for some years." Which was true, if vague, but it fit Kasper's invented history.

"And you love it."

Klara nodded reluctantly. She wasn't here to talk about herself. "Do you love your Alex?" She was counting on it.

The girl nodded. "I don't wish to talk about him with you."

"It's a mistake to keep your lover's secrets." Klara nodded at the view before them. "Look over there."

For a time, there was nothing. The girl shifted with impatience, finally venturing to speak. "I don't—"

"Watch." Klara took hold of her arm again, just as the door to the house opened and a young lady in a yellow bonnet stepped into the street. The man who until now had been leaning against the opposite wall dropped his cigar stub and fell in behind her. An old woman, staggering under a heavy basket, tottered in front of her, blocking her way. The young lady tried to step to the side but wasn't quick enough. She didn't see the man behind her raise his arm to strike. The blow was quick and accurate, sending her tumbling into the open basket. The old woman covered it in a blink, then the pair hoisted the basket between them, jogging to a cart of timber that had stopped at the mouth of the street. They loaded the basket, climbed aboard, and the cart rolled around the corner. Georg Fürst melted out of the shadows, following on foot.

Klara coughed. "When we really want someone, it takes less than a minute."

The girl licked her lips.

"She's a favorite of an Italian prince we think may be passing information to Bonaparte."

"Where are they taking her?"

"Someplace to talk. Would Frau Janke miss you if you disappeared?"

Swearing under her breath, the girl tried to turn away, but Klara kept hold of her arm.

"How much do you love your Alex?" Klara asked. "Will he be this loyal to you?"

"He's done nothing wrong," she said.

"Then it will do no harm if you tell me. Was he buying intelligence from a Prussian?"

"I don't know. If he was, he wouldn't tell me."

"Did he ever mention Count Marius von Olsberg?"

Clélie's breath came out ragged and uneven. Klara waited.

"He had dealings with him. I don't know exactly what."

"But you know who he is," Klara prodded.

"I know what he is—a monster."

Klara raised her eyebrows.

"It's true, no matter how many medals they gave him."

"What's he done?"

She swallowed. "The Prussian army is terrible. Everyone knows."

Klara kept silent. This wasn't a time to remind the girl of the many atrocities committed by the French.

"Listen. At Craonne, a French squadron surrendered to Count von Olsberg's company. They were cut off from their battalion, so it was an honorable surrender. They gave up their muskets and swords, but Olsberg wanted revenge. He ordered his men to shoot them. They were all killed."

"Then how do you know of it?" Klara asked.

"People from the village found the bodies. Alex's half-brother commanded the squadron. He hadn't been shot. Someone cut off his head."

"Olsberg?"

The paper packet of almonds crumpled in Clélie's fingers. "Alex thinks so."

"Olsberg was murdered last week."

She nodded. "I heard. But it wasn't Alex."

"How do you know? Were you with him?" Klara's stern look killed the lie before it left Clélie's lips.

She swallowed. "All right. I wasn't. That will be easy enough for you to discover. But I know he didn't kill him. The count was strangled. Alex wouldn't have done that."

"Why not?"

The girl shivered in a gust of wind. "Because when he came to Vienna, he brought along his brother's sword. Strangling wouldn't be justice."

Klara walked the girl home, not saying what she thought of her logic. If you were set on killing a man, did it really matter how he died? To some men, it might.

On her way back to the Hofburg, Klara walked past the house where Fürst's team had stolen the Italian's mistress. She probably hadn't been missed yet. If Hagen's men brought her back, and Klara had every expectation they would, she'd have a cipher book with her and the invisible ink given to Hagen's agents. Klara couldn't help feeling sad for her and for Clélie. A display of force had defeated them both.

In their place, Klara liked to think she wouldn't have surrendered so easily. Of course, living as Kasper Stark taught her how to use what she could to her advantage. She was lucky, but couldn't help wondering, a shade uneasily, if she lied too fluently.

At least now they had enough reason to question Alex Poincaré.

CHAPTER 11

Anton Spaller was remarkably loyal, Josef decided. He'd declined all Uncle Franz's praise, saying Stark must have the credit. Stark was undeservedly fortunate for a fellow with chronic ill temper, but it was possible he was kindlier disposed to Anton than himself. Inexplicably, Josef seemed to draw more than his share of unpleasantness.

No matter. Once they imparted the good news to Stark, Josef would take himself off for a morning ride, then prepare to storm the barricades thrown up by his wayward Sonia. Except when he and Anton Spaller returned to the office, Stark was gone.

"He does that," Anton explained.

"He could have left word where he went," Josef said, scanning Anton's desk for a message.

"I imagine it's something to do with Poincaré. I'll ask him when he returns."

"Send me word when he does," Josef said, and though Anton looked uncomfortable, he didn't refuse.

That afternoon, Josef set out on horseback, his hair pomaded, his best-fitting uniform neatly brushed, the loops of gold braid falling just as they ought from the epaulette on his right shoulder to the button that tethered them in place on his chest. It was a nice chest, or so he'd been told.

Grateful that Uncle Franz's arrangements made it easy to track Sonia von Olsberg's whereabouts, he rode along Mariahilfestrasse, a busy market street, to the church of the same name. It was white, narrow, and fronted by a pair of towers topped with copper domes that bore an aged green patina. It was a pretty church and, according to the countess's watchers, whom he passed on the way inside, the third on her circuit today.

Her sudden piety surprised him. He hadn't thought she'd be so idiotic, but death affected people differently. If she felt guilty because she'd been in the arms of another man when her husband died, he'd have to convince her such feelings weren't necessary.

The church had been redone, and the white plastered interior was light and pleasing. Ignoring the admirable paintings decorating the ceiling, Josef walked along the nave, looking into the chapels. Here, there was also some fine work, but no Sonia.

In the chapel nearest the main altar, he found her deep in conference with a young priest. Josef hesitated. If she had indeed come for spiritual succor, he couldn't intrude, so he loitered outside, counting cherubs on the ceiling and watching the flickering candles in the opposite chapel. The conversation moved closer. Josef straightened inside his collar.

"...appreciate your interest in our history, but I'm afraid I've rattled on too long."

"Not at all, Father. You've been so kind."

A pause. Josef imagined the priest taking her hands. They were pretty ones.

"I'm sorry for your loss, child."

It would be harder for her to dismiss him in the presence of the priest. Josef rounded the corner. "Oh. Forgive me. I didn't mean to intrude."

The priest dropped her hands.

Josef bowed. "Good afternoon, Father. Countess! What a pleasant surprise."

Perhaps it was all the plasterwork, but she looked pale. "A surprise indeed, Herr Baeder. I did not think you frequented this part of town."

"I don't. That's what makes finding you so delightful."

"And unexpected," she said dryly.

"Indeed." He smiled at her, then looked about as if he was taking the church in for the first time. "How beautiful this is, Father."

"It certainly is. Countess, I hope your visit has brought you comfort." The priest excused himself, pausing to bless them both.

Josef waited until he was out of earshot. "Well, I for one feel much better now," he said.

"Stop it." She hastened away, but before she escaped, Josef grabbed her arm, pulling her back into the chapel.

"I hate that you're taking this so hard," he murmured. There was no chance to say anything else. She turned in his hold, but instead of twisting free, she hurtled close, catching his face in her hands and kissing him.

"Oh, God," she said.

"I imagine he's here too, but my name is Josef." He was unaccountably breathless, unable to speak anymore.

She half sobbed, half laughed, so he hushed her with another kiss and took three steps backward. He wasn't worried about God or His angels, but the priest wasn't far.

"I hate myself for this," Sonia said, "but I can't help it. What are we doing?"

"What we should have done days ago," Josef answered. "It isn't kind to make me chase you all over town." Though this was lovely. She was irresistible when she was hungry. "Take me home?"

She shook her head, shuddering. "I can't. Not there."

"I can sneak you into my house."

"Without being seen?"

"Well, we could stay here."

"Stop. You're making me laugh."

"You need to laugh," Josef told her. "You have your carriage?"

She nodded.

"Send it home. I'll do the same with my horse and get us a fiaker."

Her fingers trembled in his.

AT NINE THAT EVENING, Josef poured himself a glass of his uncle's Madeira. Behind him, Uncle Franz stretched out in his tall armchair. "You've repaired your understanding with the countess?"

Josef nodded. "But I haven't found the right moment for plying her with questions."

"Don't. You're only valuable to me if she trusts you."

"I'm not certain she does."

"Convince her."

Josef sat down again in his chair.

Uncle Franz drew on his cigar. "I feared you were losing your touch."

"So did your secretary. The brusque one. Stark," Josef explained, answering the unspoken question.

"Offended his scruples?"

"He shouldn't have any, working for you." Josef took a sip from his glass. "I called at the Kaunitz Palace an hour ago, but though the Duc de Dolancourt was very cordial, he said his secretary M. Poincaré wasn't in. I think they suspect something."

"We may have to try other means."

Though Josef waited, his uncle didn't elaborate. Well, no doubt if it involved him, he would be informed at a suitable time. Uncle Franz didn't believe in disclosing more than necessary; he was a disciplined man. Josef wasn't, which was why he was the one who dropped in on questionable card parties, finessed his way into foreign embassies, and made love to the countess.

Some people spied for love, others for money. Not Josef. He knew his failing and accepted it, though it put him at his uncle's beck and call. He was obsessed with the game. "Stark seems a clever fellow. Tell me about him." Josef spoke lightly, though they both knew there was no such thing as an offhand question.

"I took him six months ago from Baron von Creuzburg and the tariffs bureau. He's hardworking, efficient."

"Where does he come from?"

"He studied in Heidelberg."

Josef cocked his head. "Not here?" Stark spoke like a long-standing resident of Vienna.

"I gather he's illegitimate. He claims no parents, and his references came from friends of the deceased Cardinal Migazzi."

"I don't think he likes me."

His uncle smiled. "He's conscientious with his work."

"Is that a slight on mine?"

"No. You know I depend upon you."

Josef took another sip, refusing to acknowledge the compliment.

"You were so charming as a child," Uncle Franz went on, exhaling another stream of smoke. He watched it drift up to the ceiling. "I shall never forget how proud you were astride your first pony."

Josef didn't glare at him, though he was tempted.

"I respect you more than you think I do," his uncle said quietly. "But I don't want you keeping secrets."

Josef set his glass atop the leather portfolio resting on the table beside him. "I won't. I've told you everything that matters, unless you care about Countess von Olsberg's beauty mark. It's pink, on the left buttock. Should we add that to the emperor's report?"

Uncle Franz laughed. "That, I don't think he'd want to know." He got up from his chair. "I'm afraid I have to leave you. There's a call I must make."

This was surprising news, but Josef knew better than to ask questions. He stayed in the study and finished his wine.

LATE THAT NIGHT, within a sumptuous room and behind velvet bed curtains, Theresa Vogl breathed softly as she extricated herself from the arms of her newest lover and slid from the high bed. Scattered about the carpet were ribbons and lace, a discarded shirt, her slippers, and diamond-patterned stockings. Their leavings looked dead in the dark.

The candles had guttered long ago, but a glow of moonlight spilled through the windows. It gave Theresa a view of her smooth, white flanks as she passed the looking glass on her way across the room. She could never help looking, but lately she sought more reassurance.

Yes, she'd do, especially in light this flattering.

A faint cough startled her, but it immediately settled into a low drone of a snore. Good. So long as she heard that sound, she was safe. Tiptoeing on fairy feet across the carpet, Theresa slipped through the connecting door and began leafing through the papers in the desk.

CHAPTER 12

Next morning, to her disappointment, Klara learned that Baron von Hagen was against pounding down the embassy door and demanding to question Poincaré. "Josef tried to meet with him and was unsuccessful. I can't afford to antagonize the French," he said. "They are difficult enough already." The peace conference still hadn't officially begun, but already there were signs it was faltering.

"But his mistress claims—"

"She probably claims a lot of things. Why should the powers that be care?"

"You know as well as I do—"

"We don't know. We only suspect. I can't demand him until you find me more."

"They'll never let us get anywhere near him—not unless we take a more forceful approach," Klara argued.

"I can't spend diplomatic favors just to question him. There are more important matters. But if you can find me proof he's guilty, we can use the knowledge to gain concessions from the French," Hagen said. "As it stands, he's only under suspicion. Until we have something truly damning, prudence is our course."

Klara tried not to scowl. She didn't like the idea of giving Poincaré more time to cover his tracks, but she'd never convince Hagen alone. Unfortunately, with Anton nodding and Baeder unwilling to look up from the calm inspection of his hands, there was no help for her. "Sir—" she began.

Hagen didn't let her speak. "Those are my orders."

Klara lowered her chin. "Of course, sir."

"For now, we'll have to try to question him unofficially. Josef?"

Baeder nodded. "I'll see to it."

Hagen grunted approval. "Stark, as you seem afraid Poincaré will outsmart us overnight, you'll help him."

Klara nodded, hiding her dismay. Trying to think of ways to work with Baeder yet still avoid him, she missed the next exchange between Hagen and Anton, but when Anton mentioned Gunter Kissling, Klara's eyes flew up.

"You found the gravedigger?" Her heart stopped as she took in Hagen's satisfied smile. Why hadn't Anton told her?

Anton shook his head. "Just a promising lead I received this morning."

"Pursue it," Hagen ordered. "I want him found."

Anton bowed, clicking his heels remarkably well given his limp. "Right away, sir." He loped from the office.

A lead wasn't the same thing as finding the man, and every other search had failed. She must hope this one failed too. After this many days, she thought he'd slipped the net.

"Coming, Stark?" Baeder paused at the door, frowning impatiently.

"Coming, sir." Collecting herself, Klara bowed to Herr Hagen and followed Baeder from the room, as Hagen, contented for once, reached for his plate of cake. She hurried to catch Baeder in the hall.

"Are you a Jacobin, Herr Stark?" he asked.

Klara nearly missed a step. "No." A radical could never have passed Hagen's screening—except *she* had. Being a woman was less subversive than being a revolutionary, she hoped. "I don't have political opinions," she said.

"Then stop looking like you're plotting to introduce me to Madame Guillotine," Baeder snapped.

"I'm sorry." Klara tried to think of an excuse for her rudeness but couldn't find anything believable. No matter. They didn't need to like one another. In fact, it was better if they didn't.

"So it's me you object to?" Baeder asked.

"I'm not significant enough you should care."

"True." They turned the corner at the end of the hall. "I'd give you a set down but I doubt you'd notice."

"Probably not," Klara answered. "Are you going to tell me where we are going, or shall I just follow silently at your heels?"

Baeder snorted. "If you can."

Klara started humming.

Baeder stopped. Fearing she'd gone too far, Klara swallowed, then saw Baeder's frown wobble. He let out a silent laugh. "Much as it goes against the grain, I'm going to have to thank Uncle Franz for you."

"Why?" Klara's eyes narrowed.

"You're a fit accomplice. Much better for hunting Poincaré than your friend Spaller. How long have you worked for my uncle?" Something in his voice made Klara wary, though the question was bland enough.

"Six months. Before that, I worked in the tariffs bureau, but with the peace conference, Herr Hagen increased his staff."

Baeder made a face. "Tariffs. Must have been dull."

Work in her old department had been less interesting. It had also been safer. "It must seem that way to someone in a military career."

"I just like the fancy coats," he said.

Klara didn't believe him.

"No really, you've no idea how the uniform weakens the resistance of otherwise virtuous women. But speaking of coats—have you a better one?"

"Yes." She tried not to look offended.

"Go home and put it on. And give me your address. I'll collect you at seven."

"Where are we going?"

"To find Poincaré at the opera. Be ready."

"What do we do until then?" It was only midafternoon.

Baeder smiled. "I have an appointment. You'll have to entertain yourself." He strode down the hall.

"Herr Baeder?"

"Yes?" He stopped and looked back.

Klara's eyes narrowed. "Why do you say I'm more fitted for this than Anton Spaller? He's more senior than I am."

"I mean no disrespect to our friend, who is diligent and capable. This gravedigger he thinks he's found, for instance. You'd given up on that."

Klara nodded, glad she needn't explain why.

"I understand him. You, on the other hand, are an upstart of uncertain breeding, murky ambitions, and questionable scruples."

"I have no ambitions. Only to keep my job."

"Then why can't you keep your mouth shut?"

Klara struggled for words. "Anton and I work well together. You and I are a mistake."

"Perhaps." He grinned. "But I still think you'll be more help to me tonight than Spaller. My methods are unorthodox. Be ready."

TRYING NOT to worry about Baeder's parting words, Klara went home to brush her coat, polish her shoes, and fend off questions from Levi. With only half an ear, she listened to his misgivings as he tied her cravat. He was suspicious of social mingling, but then, he suspected everything.

"You just went to the opera with Anton Spaller," he said. "Why go again?"

"I've no choice. Hagen's orders," Klara explained, picking up her other shoe. She might have polished it already but wasn't sure, and Levi wasn't done with her. Interrogation was easier to face when she had something in her hands.

Levi snorted, which turned into a series of coughs. Klara passed him a handkerchief and reminded herself to buy him some lemonade.

"Hagen ordered you to the opera?" Levi rasped, only half recovered.

"To find someone."

"You don't know anyone," Levi countered. "No one important. Keep it that way." Wiping his nose, he set aside the handkerchief and picked up the clothes brush.

"I'm helping his nephew."

"The one having an affair with Olsberg's widow?"

Klara stopped her earnest polishing.

"Theresa told me," Levi explained.

Klara shook her head. No telling how her mother had uncovered that fact, but it shouldn't come as a surprise. Maybe Theresa should work for Hagen. Letting out a sigh, Klara looked for help from the ceiling. Naturally, none came, just another complication. Her only warning was Levi's eyes narrowing.

"Didn't you— Is this the man you discovered in the countess's bed?"

For a second, Klara couldn't speak. "He doesn't know me."

Levi set the clothes brush down with a snap. He glared at her. "That's why you've been taking so long with your shoes. No. You aren't going. He's seen you. He's seen the shoes!"

Klara twitched guiltily. "I didn't mention him because I knew you would worry, and there's absolutely no need." Levi's cough was improving, and she wanted to keep it that way. "I've seen him a half dozen times since then, and he's never recognized me."

"Doesn't mean he can't."

"He won't. Josef von Baeder thinks the girl he saw is a foreign agent. He has no reason to connect her with me. I would have avoided this, but Hagen gave me no choice. There's trouble with the investigation," she admitted.

"How much trouble?"

Plenty. Anton is still looking for Gunter, and he has another lead. Nor am I as easy in my mind about Josef von Baeder as I'm pretending to be. "They know Theresa was his lover," was all she said aloud. "But I think I steered them away from her."

"Let her take care of herself. She won't let anything touch you."

Another time, she'd inquire about the finality in his voice. Tonight, she was simply glad he wasn't throwing her more questions. "I'm hoping we are close to the end of it. I think the man we're trying to sidle up to tonight is the killer." At any rate, he was the likeliest bet, though she had limited faith in Baeder's plan to catch him. Tonight's performance was a premiere, but suppose Poincaré didn't come?

Levi raised his eyebrows.

"I know. I'll be careful," Klara said. Maybe she should write her promise in blood and hang it over the table. Except Levi probably wouldn't think that was funny.

JOSEF VON BAEDER arrived late in a handsome carriage painted dark green with bright yellow wheels. Inside, everything was plush green velvet. Baeder, wearing his dress uniform and a flashing emerald tiepin, looked like the haughty aristocrat he was, until he smiled, motioning Klara into the opposite seat.

"You're sure we can find him?" Klara asked. The late hour had allowed her to cultivate additional worries: Hagen's impatience, the girl Clélie. Suppose she had already told Poincaré they were after him? The fear Klara had planted in her wouldn't last forever.

"I have every expectation of success." Baeder stretched out his legs. Stifling skepticism, Klara slid her legs over half a foot, keeping space between them. Baeder laughed. "I was starting to miss being your prime suspect."

Klara looked out the window. "How is the countess?" He hadn't said anything, but she knew how to interpret the swagger in his step.

"She needs a great deal of comforting."

Klara cocked an eyebrow at him. "I didn't think you were the type."

"Only when I have to be." He sighed. "Do you care for music?"

"Not especially. We'd get there faster walking. Look." Klara pointed outside the window. The clog of carriages along Singerstrasse left no room for them to turn.

"True, but how dreary."

Klara wished she'd said nothing. Her and Baeder's spheres touched, but only barely, and he liked reminding her of it.

It wasn't until they pulled up in front of the Burgtheatre that Klara realized he had no tickets. Of course, Austrian military officers were allowed into the pit free of charge, but she hadn't the advantage of his white and red uniform. Biting back her temper, she was eyeing the crowd outside the ticket office when Baeder stopped her with a hand on her arm. "Wait."

"What for?"

Untroubled by her dismay, he surveyed the crowd. "Ah! Rudi!" Brightening, Baeder hailed a bearded general glittering from the medals competing for space on his chest.

"Josef! How are you?"

"Never better. I was hoping we'd find you. This is my friend, Stark." Baeder indicated Klara with an offhand wave.

"Hoping for an invitation?" The general grinned.

"If you'd be so kind," Baeder murmured.

"Ha! Impudence!"

"I'll make myself useful," Baeder promised, with a sideways glance.

"Come along. Bring that friend of yours." The general swept them inside. The air was too hot and heavily scented to breathe easily and only worsened as they climbed to the general's box. Baeder whispered a dirty aside to him, eliciting another braying laugh. The general was still wheezing when they reached the third-floor balcony, where they were hailed by two more gentlemen and a trio of ladies, two of whom trailed interested eyes over Baeder. The stateliest of these perched herself on the general's arm, but Baeder got the laughing, loveliest one. Klara heard him compliment her necklace of pearls, but it was plain his admiration was more for the flesh beneath. The ladies had their own box but were easily persuaded to join the general for the first act, despite having to squeeze.

There were not enough chairs, so Klara edged her way to the back. She'd avoided the theater since becoming Kasper and had never watched from a vantage point like this. The view of the stage was better from this height. More importantly, she could see into the pit and most of the boxes, but suppose Poincaré was sitting on the same side of the theatre? Or on the balcony beneath them? Baeder was entirely too sure of himself, and now he was drifting into the empty space beside her. She tensed.

"Have you found him?" he asked.

"I don't know what he looks like," Klara said. In this crowd, a written description wasn't enough.

"There." Baeder motioned to a box on the other side of the theater, one tier down. "Rudi knows him. Won some money from him at cards. Here." He passed Klara a pair of opera glasses.

Tall and brown-haired, Clélie's man was also interestingly

pale. His features and tailoring were exceptional. No wonder the girl was in love with him.

"Who's with him?" Klara asked.

"Some Hungarian bankers. Szabo is on the left. Kovacs is behind them."

"Significant?" She handed back the glasses.

"I'm not sure. I'll find out more at the interval." He turned his attention to the lady occupying the chair in front of him, forcing Klara to acknowledge the happenings onstage, where her mother, brilliant in a spangled tunic and harem trousers, lamented man's perfidy with sweet, piercing clarity.

"She's magnificent," Baeder whispered, diverted by the strength of a high E. "I saw her sing Leonora ten years ago, but I think she's even better now, though it should be impossible."

Klara made a noncommittal movement.

"Think she killed Olsberg? She was his lover."

Klara's gaze didn't swerve. "I questioned her. She was occupied that night."

"With whom?"

"It's in my notes."

"I know. I read them at my uncle's."

Klara turned her head. "Does he know that?"

"I'd be very surprised if he hadn't left them out on purpose, expecting me to do so."

"Knows you well, I see."

He didn't react to the gibe. "No one's found the spy I saw in the countess's room yet."

"That was your job," Klara retorted.

"And yours." He said nothing more, but she was uncomfortable, wondering again how much he knew.

At the interval, Baeder found another friend in the hall, who reacquainted him with the Hungarian bankers. Klara never saw him speak to Alex Poincaré, but somehow he secured an invitation to join their party for cards after the opera.

"It will be a better place to corner him," he told Klara as they watched the final act.

The opera ended happily, as shows in Vienna tended to do, to satisfy the royal censors. After the bravas and applause were absorbed by the velvet stage curtains, Klara and Baeder took his carriage to a house near the Am Heumarkt, where they were welcomed into a plush sanctum devoted to high-stakes card games and the consumption of coffee, liqueurs, and cigars. No one questioned Klara's presence, but she kept to the periphery, drank only coffee, and studied the play. She'd been wrong about Baeder. He was skilled, getting them into the general's box, singling Poincaré out of a horde of opera goers, and securing them invitations to this party. He moved effortlessly in the crowd, matching everyone he met with the right words and smile. She'd never met anyone so slippery.

As Klara sipped a Turkish coffee and pretended to watch a game of whist, Baeder insinuated his way into Poincaré's circle with a quip that made them all laugh. A footman passed by, bearing a tray filled with thimble-sized goblets of golden liquid. Baeder took two, offering the second to Poincaré with lazy grace.

Klara's eyes narrowed. She hadn't seen anything definitive, but he'd doctored the drink, she was sure of it. As she sidled closer, Baeder pretended to notice her, motioning for her to join them. "Ah, Stark. Let me introduce you."

Smiling, she recorded the names in her memory: Greystoke, who was English and almost slumbering behind his spectacles; Peter Szabo, a young scion of the banking family and one of their hosts this evening; Poincaré, their target, whose cheeks now held a hectic flush. Klara bowed correctly, carefully, wondering what Levi would think.

The tray came by again. Klara accepted a fingerling glass but only wet her lips on it. Careful experimentation had taught her exactly how much she could drink before her thinking became clumsy, but she couldn't risk unknown potencies on a night like this.

She fielded polite enquiries, admitting only the necessities—that she held a government post, that she'd been a protégé of a cardinal, now deceased. The last was a lie, but a carefully arranged one, supported by impeccable forged letters recommending her to her first employer. The lie was well-aged and felt real enough she did not blink when Greystoke asked if she bore a likeness to the dead priest.

"I'm flattered you think I resemble him in any way," she said mildly. "He was a great man."

No one argued, though the cardinal in question was known more for lechery than anything else.

Poincaré, a little smugly, asked her if the Austrians were working their secretaries very hard—certainly the cooks and musicians were kept busy. "Not sure if I've come to a conference or a fortnight of dress balls," he added.

Klara smiled, ruefully flexing her fingers. "Spare us secretaries a thought, sir! If the conference lasts more than the two weeks they say it will, it's not only going to be the musicians who are worked to death. You won't believe the papers, the memoranda..." She paused, seeing they waited expectantly. "Suffice it to say, I have written a great deal that is best left unsaid."

They laughed, and Baeder turned the conversation to the opera. Here, Klara was in good stead, happier they were no longer talking about her. She knew who'd composed tonight's score and who'd written the libretto, could compare both to other works, and knew how the different performers and productions had been received by the court. She and young Szabo, who proved something of a connoisseur, fell into a friendly argument on the merits of music by Beethoven. Rumor said his newest symphony was to be performed at an upcoming spectacle.

"Well, it will be loud," said Klara, repeating her mother's opinion on the subject.

"Feelings should be," said Szabo.

"I cannot agree," Baeder said. "It's so untidy. Monsieur?" He cocked an eyebrow at Poincaré.

"Some feelings are safer in a quieter, lower key."

Baeder shook his head. "That's when they're most dangerous."

Szabo, tiring of the discussion, glanced again at the tables. "Herr Stark? Can we settle our differences over cards?"

"Not this evening, thank you." She had no money to stake, not in this company.

Szabo bowed and ambled away. The Englishman, Greystoke, had left earlier, not knowing Beethoven. She and Baeder had Poincaré alone.

"Come along, sir," Baeder said. "We'll find a place to sit away from the tables and perhaps something less sweet to drink."

Slightly glassy-eyed, Poincaré did not resist. Flanked by Klara on one side and Baeder on the other, they exited into the hall. Klara wondered if Baeder owned any principles. It seemed more likely he'd gambled them away long ago. Of course, she was no lily-white soul herself. Her heart thumped.

Down the corridor, they passed another salon where men were drinking and singing. Poincaré veered toward it, but Baeder nudged him away. "I'm not in the mood for loud company," he said. With admiring remarks for the paintings decorating the walls, he led them along until they reached an octagonal room, pocket-sized and built for secrets. Rosewood flowers climbed the dark paneling.

"No one will mind if we make ourselves comfortable here," Baeder said, sinking into one of the chairs and reaching to the nearby table to pour out three glasses. "He has another ten minutes or so," he whispered as he passed Klara her glass.

If that was all, they had best start questioning. There wasn't much time. "M. Poincaré, you said you're from Paris?" Klara asked.

"I don't recall that I did, but I am," he said, sinking into the damask embrace of a chair.

Klara didn't want to sit, fearing Poincaré would bolt when the questions got harder, so she moved to the fire, setting her glass on the mantelpiece. "What brings you to Vienna?"

"I'm attached to the French delegation," he said, his hand dipping precipitously as he lowered his glass.

Baeder sipped and smiled. "But what did you come here to do?"

"So far no one has done anything but talk and dance and attend parties." Poincaré laughed, not noticing the brandy that splashed onto his coat. His eyes were watering, his face flushed. Klara threw Baeder a worried glance.

"You're wrong," she said. "Someone murdered Count von Olsberg."

Poincaré's reaction was slow. Carefully he set down his drink. "Not sure I know him."

"You do. Clélie told me." Klara pressed on, watching the color drain from his cheeks. "What was it like, drinking and gambling and buying information from the man who struck off the head of your brother?"

"You're with the police." His eyes darted from her to Baeder.

Two long steps put Klara in front of him, blocking his path to the door. "Don't try to leave. You won't get far." Behind her, she heard Baeder rising from his chair.

"I'm surprised your superiors asked such a thing of you," Baeder said. "But perhaps they did not know. I do not think you are a forgiving man, but—"

"What he offered was important. He was too valuable to kill, but I was willing to wait."

"Except he's already dead," Baeder said. "Can you explain it?"

"I'm not his only enemy."

"But you brought along your brother's sword. Why? To strengthen your resolve?" Klara asked.

"It's strong enough. I never had the opportunity."

"Why should we believe—" Klara had no time to finish. Muscles bunching, Poincaré lunged from his chair, shoving her back. Struggling to keep her feet, Klara snapped her elbow up, catching Poincaré on the chin. He staggered into the table, toppling it, crashing with the decanter and the half-empty glasses to the floor. Panting, he fixed his eyes on the wine soaking into the carpet. "Drugged." He laughed. "Doesn't matter. You won't get a confession from me."

Klara knelt beside him. "We know your secret."

Poincaré grinned. "You know nothing." Slowly, like falling sails, his eyes closed.

Baeder swore.

"We can rouse him." Klara slapped his cheeks and shook his shoulders.

"Too late. He can't hear."

Scowling, Klara sat back on her heels.

"You didn't have to hit him so hard," Baeder said.

"He moved slower than I'm used to." Breathing heavily, Klara straightened her cuffs. "You could have helped me."

Baeder flicked invisible lint from his coat. "I try to avoid wrinkles. Come on." He righted the table. "Best if we leave him facedown."

"He'll vomit?"

"Likely."

"Then we should wait. He might—"

"He'll be in no state to speak for a while. We'll get nothing else. We should go."

Klara shook her head. "We've gained nothing."

Baeder shrugged. "We tried."

"How long will he be like this?"

"Hours."

Hours they didn't have.

"You shouldn't have poured him another glass."

"By then, it hardly mattered. I didn't expect you to bludgeon him."

"That wasn't exactly planned."

"No." Baeder grimaced. "Effective, though."

"What do you think Olsberg was selling if Poincaré says he was too valuable to kill?"

"Prussian troop movements. Government memos. The Prussian ambassador's love letters." Baeder shrugged. "Plenty of possibilities."

Klara braced her hands on her knees. "Think he still has any of them?" She jerked her head at Poincaré.

"The ambassador's love letters?"

"No. The other things."

Baeder frowned. "He might."

"It's worth the chance. Come on." Klara seized Poincaré's deadweight arm and slung it over her shoulder.

"He'll sleep it off," Baeder assured her. "No need to—"

Klara shook her head. "We're salvaging this, but I need your help. The French delegation isn't far. We'll take him inside, then search his room and any other places we can before they stop us."

Baeder pursed his lips. "I'm not sure my uncle will approve."

"There's nothing wrong with two drunks helping a friend home."

Baeder nodded, his mouth slowly widening into a smile. "I suppose not."

Klara smiled back. "Plenty of ways to get a man's secrets."

CHAPTER 13

Anton Spaller shrugged within his coat, but it merely improved the set of his shoulders, failing to put the world right. The street ahead of him was grim and seedy as ever. His destination—a brothel at the end of the alley—would be even worse. Stepping aside for a roughly dressed laborer in heavy boots, Anton avoided brushing both the man and the moldy wall of the house beside him. The smell, alas, was not something he could dodge. Yet again, Anton wished he'd planned more carefully instead of leaving the palace in a rush; he could have brought a guardsman with him or at least changed into plainer clothes. He'd expected to find the gravedigger long before dark, instead of tailing him for hours.

Following a lead from an unemployed wagon driver, Anton had trailed his quarry from a lumber mill to a cook shop to a cockfight, each place grimmer than the last. There was worse to come. His feet ached, he had dusty smears on his coat, and the mere idea of venturing inside Squint-Eye Tina's brothel made him uneasy. It was the kind of place where men could easily disappear.

In which case, he shouldn't waste any time, or Gunter Kissling might elude him again.

The brothel slouched at the end of the passage, looking like one good shove would send it over. Its timbers and plaster were stained a patchy gray-brown. Even the windows were the same dull color. The only jarring thing about the place was the shine on the door handle. Anton wrapped his hand in his handkerchief and knocked.

The girl who opened the door was cleaner and kindlier looking than he'd expected. "Sir?"

Anton held out his credentials, not wishing to be mistaken for a customer, not in a place like this. "I'm looking for a man named Gunter Kissling. He came here half an hour ago wearing a red coat."

The girl licked her lips.

"Where is he?" Anton asked.

She was saved from answering by the arrival of a giant through an inside door. He came in sideways, too wide to fit. "Trouble?"

Anton reminded himself the man couldn't really be as large as he seemed. This was simply an effect of the low ceiling. Congratulating himself on his cool tone, Anton repeated his question, though his hand tightened around his sword stick.

The girl turned to her colossus, whispering. All Anton caught was, "We don't owe him."

Clinging to courage, Anton was about to explain to her the duties owed him as a representative of the crown, but the giant forestalled him with a shrug.

"Bring him along." He looked square at Anton. "Kissling's here, all right."

Anton held back a sigh of relief, which was premature, as there was still the unsettling business of following the giant up the stairs. "After you." He made the girl go ahead, not wanting to be caught between the two of them. Most assuredly, he shouldn't have come alone. A sword stick would only irritate the monster in front of him.

"We don't want any trouble," the girl murmured humbly.

Anton nodded with a loftiness he didn't quite feel. "My superiors will be pleased to hear of your cooperation."

The giant turned. He shook his head. "They aren't going to hear anything about us."

Anton swallowed. "If you prefer it."

He wished they weren't so stingy here with lights. It would be easy to stumble on these uneven steps. There weren't doors in the upstairs hall, only tattered curtains. The giant tugged one back, curtain rings clattering. The girl sprawling on the faded velvet cushions sat up and swore, clutching her arms to her naked chest, but the man beside her snored on. He was harder to distinguish in the gloom than the girl, who stood out because she was pale.

"Gunter Kissling!" Anton's impressive shout was not as good as a nudge from the giant's boot. The gravedigger started up, grumbling and rubbing his eyes. The giant hauled him to his feet, lifting him into the air until they were nose to nose.

"We don't want trouble brought to this house."

Mewling for mercy, Gunter wiped his stringy hair out of his eyes. His scrawny legs were bare, but he still wore his shirt and coat. The red wool was only slightly diminished by dirt and wrinkles. "I'm no trouble! I swear!"

"That's better." The giant dropped him to the floor.

"You have to the count of ten to dress yourself," Anton explained. "Your assistance is required by the state police."

Eyes wide with horror, the man fumbled for his trousers. The whore threw them at his head, hissing insults. Anton closed his eyes, assuring himself these were words he'd eventually forget.

Still, he was pleased. He'd found the man at last.

"God, he's heavy," Klara muttered.

Baeder tightened his grip on her arm, steadying her as they dragged Poincaré between them down the street. "We may have trouble getting into the French embassy. The servants—"

"If you can't hoax your way past one butler…" Klara swallowed a grimace and kept walking. The week-old cut on her side burned. "Just try to be faster this time. All that chattering back there, I thought my arms would fall off." She mustn't look like she was struggling. Even a slightly built man was strong enough for this.

Peter Szabo had seen them lugging Poincaré out of the house. It had taken some minutes before Baeder, pretending drunken assurance, had persuaded their host it was unnecessary to send M. Poincaré home by carriage. They hadn't far to go—Baeder's house was just around the corner. M. Poincaré could sleep off his wine there.

Szabo had been convinced, though it had taken so long Klara's arms had begun trembling. Just a little further. Once they were out of sight of the Szabo house, she could rest for a moment. Unfortunately, the Kaunitz Palace, home to the French delegation, was a ways off yet.

Baeder grunted, taking more of Poincaré's weight. "Keep singing. Szabo might be watching from the house."

Counting steps in her head—another thirty would carry them around the corner and out of sight—Klara sang breathlessly.

"Without friends, what is the hero? What are the lords of the land?"

Her breath failed in the next line, but Baeder took over in a loud baritone.

"Without friends, without wine…"

He stumbled artfully, and Klara's legs almost gave under her. "Stop it!" she hissed. "Do you want to pitch me right over?"

Baeder stopped singing, looking at her over Poincaré's slumped head.

"It's like dragging an elephant!" Klara snapped before he could speak. In spite of Levi's training, she wasn't strong enough for this. Not for this long. The French delegation was at least another two streets away.

"We'll set him down for a minute." He steered them to the closest wall. "No one will see us here."

Releasing Poincaré, Klara bent forward, bracing her hands on her knees. A sticky warmth crept along her throbbing side.

"Are you all right?"

Klara glared at him. "Fine."

"Take as long as you need."

She'd like to, but the way he was studying her made her nervous. "I think he has lead in his boots." It certainly felt that way, dragging him over the cobbles.

"I suppose you don't carry unconscious men often."

"Do you?"

"Sometimes. During the war."

Klara swallowed her barbed reply. "Of course." It surprised her to learn he'd fought in battles. She'd assumed he'd been the ornamental kind of officer—a liaison to the emperor or the general staff. "I hardly recognized you tonight. You're a different man in a crowd."

Joseph snorted. "Everyone is. Even you."

Fair enough. It had been an idiotic thing to say. She'd choose a safer topic. "How much will he remember in the morning?" she asked, nodding at Poincaré's slumped form.

"Some. We'll find some garters and stockings. Drape them around. Leave a good scene."

Klara grinned. "All right. I'm ready."

Hoisting Poincaré upright, they stumbled down the street. A hundred yards to the next corner... Seventy...After lugging Poincaré this far, they had better find something worthwhile.

At forty yards, pain seared across her side. Klara bit on her lip and stopped breathing.

Baeder halted. "Something's wrong. Aren't you well?"

"I'm fine. We'd better keep moving."

"We have time." Baeder propped their burden against another wall. "Don't hurt yourself."

"Nothing's wrong. Let's go."

She could tell he didn't believe her, but at least he didn't challenge the lie. "If you wish."

Turning right again, they lumbered north, Poincaré's feet still trailing, his head lolling from side to side. Baeder was breathing heavily now too. Klara watched for uneven cobbles and counted her steps, fighting the urge to stop and examine her side. They turned into Johannesgasse. Fifty steps done, again. She could do fifty more. The embassy wasn't much farther.

She counted to eighty-seven before they reached the door. "I need to put him down for a minute," Klara said. They laid him on the steps while Klara bent to catch her breath. When Baeder looked away, she probed at her ribs. Her coat was damp and her shirt clung; she must have split open her wound again. She prayed the blood wouldn't show against the black wool.

"Ready?" Baeder asked.

Whether she was or not, there was no time. She couldn't stand here bleeding in the light of the flambeaux that flanked the door. They muscled Poincaré to his feet again.

"Leave the talking to me," Baeder whispered.

Together, they staggered up the palace steps. Baeder knocked, a sharp *tak-tak* defying anyone to shut him out.

Moments later, a candle-bearing servant cracked open the door. Reviving in the bright light, Poincaré lifted his head, swore with surprising eloquence, then went limp. Klara closed her eyes, murmuring silent thanks.

"What do you want?" the servant asked.

"Our friend Alex needs to be put into bed." Baeder's words were slurred. "Let us in so we don't drop him." He leaned against the doorframe, stumbling past the servant and dragging Poincaré along.

"If my lord would leave him in that chair—"

"Don't trouble yourself, Your Excellency," Baeder said, waving his free hand grandly, weaving under Poincaré's weight as Klara tried to catch up with him. "Brought him this far. Might as well finish." He shuffled to the stairs. "Where do we take him?"

"M. Poincaré's chamber is on the second floor," the servant warned. Deep in shadow, Klara grimaced. "Down the east corridor, third door on the left."

"Stark, you up to the challenge?"

Klara sighed. *"En avant."*

Baeder grinned at her and grabbed the servant's candle. "Thank you, Your Excellency."

"If I might—forgive me, sir, but there are ladies sleeping." Anxious now, the servant trailed after them.

"We'll be quiet as ghosts," Baeder said and hiccuped. "Go away."

The man hesitated.

"Go away!"

The servant ran.

"Come on," Baeder said.

The steps were broad and shallow, stopping twice on wide landings where sculptures in alcoves loomed over them, casting threatening shadows. Hurrying past, they escaped down a second-floor corridor that looked endless. "There's his door," Klara gasped.

They jostled their way into the room. Klara elbowed the door shut.

"Drop him," Baeder said. "This is good enough."

Poincaré toppled to the floor, making Klara wince and not for her own sake. "Hurry. We haven't long," she said. The servant would soon fetch someone capable of clearing them out. "Is there another candle?" She didn't want Baeder seeing her pained face or her bloodstained side, but searching in the dark was impossible.

“Found one.” Another light blossomed in Baeder’s hand. He passed it to her, and she went to the bed, running a quick hand under the mattress. Nothing. She went to the desk, combing through papers: letters from a man named Denon about paintings and long missives from Poincaré’s sister. Klara siphoned away the Denon correspondence while Baeder searched the desk drawers.

“No false bottoms,” he said.

“Try the bookshelf,” Klara said.

“Certainly. You tackle the clothespress.”

Klara ransacked the top drawer, but found only gloves and trifles.

“Too many novels,” Baeder said, flipping books open and shelving them again with remarkable speed.

“What about this?” Klara picked up a leather box from the second drawer and tried the lid. “Locked.”

“Give it here,” Baeder said, before she set it aside.

“I’m not sure we should break it.”

“Don’t need to.” He held a pick in his hand and sat down with the box on the bed. The lock gave easily, and he opened the lid. What he saw made him sigh reverently.

“Well?” Klara peered over his shoulder. Baeder was lifting out a knife. It was a beautiful weapon, sweetly lethal. He drew it partway from the sheath. “A blade this thick would leave a hole wider than my thumb,” he whispered. “Didn’t Olsberg have a wound in his thigh? Maybe this is the blade that belonged to Poincaré’s brother.”

Klara said nothing. She lifted her candle, sweeping the light around the room. “The girl said it was a sword.”

There it was. “Look.” She nudged Baeder’s arm, nodding at a battered saber propped against the far wall. “That must be his brother’s.”

Baeder turned. He stared for a long time. “That’s a Titian.”

Klara frowned.

"Above the sword, you idiot. Look at the pictures."

Klara raised her candle higher. Three paintings hung closely together.

One was a Madonna and child. "Is that a Mantegna?" she asked.

"I think so. Olsberg is missing one. And a Titian. And a Lippi." As he spoke, his candle moved, illuminating each canvas.

"Spaller has a complete list. Olsberg itemized everything in his petition," Klara said. "We can check these against it."

Baeder chuckled, his attention on the Madonna. "This one is special. Wouldn't you have wanted her back?"

"They're too big to take with us," Klara reminded him.

"But we know they're here. This proves the French were dealing with him."

"Admire them later." Klara turned back to the box. All that remained inside was a book sized to fit in the palm of a hand. Klara picked it up and turned over the well-worn cover.

"An appointment diary? Why lock that away?" Baeder took it from her. She hadn't noticed him move so close. Klara shifted, putting more inches between them. She didn't like the feel of his breath floating over her shoulder.

"We're running out of time," she said. "Just take it."

"I don't think it's his," Baeder said, ignoring her. He went to the bookshelf, flipping open a volume to the title page where Poincaré had scribbled his name in the top right-hand corner. "See? The handwriting doesn't match."

Ignoring her discomfort with his method, Klara asked, "Do you think the diary is Olsberg's?"

"I'll have to ask his wife." He slid the book into his pocket. "Quick, put the box back. Keep the knife."

There was no time to argue. She heard footsteps. She shut the box and shoved it back into the drawer.

"Hurry—"

"We're out of time. Someone's coming. Put out the light."

They'd be less likely to notice anything amiss in the dark. Klara blew out the candle beside her. Baeder snuffed his in almost the same moment, suspending them in velvety dark.

"Laugh," he whispered, gripping her arm and towing her to the door, humming a rude army song.

She let out a snigger that sounded more like a cough, but the second attempt was better. The door moved before Baeder touched it, letting in a blinding shaft of light.

"Here they are, sir." The dour servant surveyed them with his candle.

"Why, hello!" Baeder dropped Klara's arm, blinking and bowing unsteadily. "Good evening, gentlemen."

"*Bonsoir*." This time it wasn't the servant who spoke. The voice was quiet, sliding from the netherworld outside the candle's glow. This did not sound like a butler.

Baeder switched to French. "M. Poincaré is well. He's sleeping."

"On the floor?"

"He's very heavy," Klara put in.

"But you've lost your light. I'd hate for you to wander astray on your way out. Jean, if you will attend to M. Poincaré, I will see his friends to the door. Just get me another candle."

It was too dark to see the speaker's face, but Klara sensed his eyes following Jean as he circled the room, looking for the recently snuffed lights. Instinct told her he noticed everything: Poincaré's lax mouth, the hastily tidied papers on the desk, a drawer left open half an inch, the rumpled bed linen.

Jean passed their new adversary a candle. Klara's eyes widened. The man was black.

He smiled. "I'm afraid we haven't met."

"Mikhail Yaroslavovich." Baeder gave a beautiful bow. "Your servant, sir."

Klara followed, using the exaggerated care of the very drunk.

"I'm Vasily Georgi," she said, trying to sound as if she had more than a few words of Russian.

"And you, sir?" Baeder prompted.

"Call me Durachit. I believe it's the word for fool, but if we are being Russians for the evening... This way."

No choice but to follow him. He walked quickly, too quickly for a confused drunk to follow, but persisting in the charade was useless. Klara glanced at Baeder. "Who is he?" she whispered.

Baeder's shoulder twitched—a covert shrug.

No mention of a black man had been included in the reports she'd seen of French embassy personnel, detailing everyone from Prince Talleyrand to Antonin Carême, his talented chef. This man spoke with authority and was clearly important. Of course, it was foolish to suppose Hagen didn't keep some files to himself. Whoever this man was, he would be known to him.

The dark enigma stopped by the front door, which was open, footmen stationed on either side. "Good night, gentlemen."

Baeder cursed softly as the door closed behind them, stranding them in the moonlit street. The bolts slid shut.

"That was a real cock-up." Klara said. She felt as sick as if she'd been caught by Prince Talleyrand with dispatches in her hands.

"I'll say."

"I wish you hadn't chosen Russian," Klara said.

"I had no time to decide. How was I to know? You've never told me what languages you speak."

"You never asked."

"Would you have told me the truth?" He watched her closely.

She made herself meet his eyes. "Of course. Honesty is critical in our assignment."

"Hmm." He shoved his hands into his coat pockets, striding ahead of her.

"Herr Baeder?" Worried now, Klara hurried after him,

ignoring her aching side. She caught up with him at the end of the street.

"There are permissible lies, I suppose," he said, his gaze on the night sky. "Like giving those false Russian names. Not that we fooled anyone."

"That man worries me," Klara said.

"But as you said, there are times when honesty is critical." Baeder's hand closed on her arm. "This is one."

For the second time this evening, Klara threw up her arm to slam it into a man's face, but Baeder was quicker than Poincaré had been. He blocked the blow, catching her other arm and forcing her back.

"What are you—" Klara struggled and tugged, but now a wall was right behind her. Baeder pinned her with his shoulder, freeing his other arm. Klara closed her eyes, flinching from the expected blow, but instead his hand closed hard between her legs. "Get off!" She bucked, but it was too late. His fingers had pushed past the padding and found her shape.

"Shall we talk about this?" he asked in a frightening, friendly whisper. "Or would you rather start with the blood seeping into your jacket?"

CHAPTER 14

All she could do was breathe. Somewhere in the silence, a dog barked.

"Take your hands off me."

Unexpectedly, he listened, pulling a few inches away, but she still couldn't say who the breath in her ears belonged to. She had space now, but he was threateningly close. It wasn't like her to be trapped with no idea what to do or say. She felt tired and pinched and worn to blankness.

"Don't look at me like that. You—" He stopped, and Klara saw his face change. He drew a long breath. "You're *her*. No wonder—"

Klara stopped the reflexive shake of her head. It was too late. His eyes were on hers, completely certain, and the weight of his arm and the brick at her back made it impossible to run. "Was it the shoes?"

"Shoes?" He looked baffled.

"Then how do you know?" She had Poincaré's blade as well as her own, but neither was any good to her. She couldn't kill him. She couldn't even make her fingers twitch.

"You couldn't carry Poincaré. And when we picked him up

after resting in the street, some of your stubble rubbed off on my cuff. I realized you were a woman, but not—" Breaking off, he shook his head. "I thought— Christ! I thought my uncle knew, but he doesn't, does he?"

Klara shook her head.

"Then that morning at Sonia's—what were you doing?"

"I had a reason." Klara licked her lips. "Same as you. And I didn't kill him."

Baeder scrubbed a hand through his hair. "But why—"

"I didn't kill him," Klara repeated. "Though I doubt your Uncle Franz will take my word as readily as yours. Olsberg—" Her voice failed. She tried again. "He had something that could hurt me."

"He knew? No wonder you were so frightened." He shook his head again, then peered at her. "My uncle truly doesn't know?"

"No one does." Her breath shook, and she feared she might cry. Part of her wanted to. It would be such a relief.

"Shh." He was close again, close enough she could almost feel the cloth of his coat on her face. Cautiously, his fingers spread over her stinging side. "Why are you bleeding?"

Klara stiffened. "It's nothing."

"I don't believe that. You're hurt."

Klara shrugged. "I can't see a doctor."

"Let me look at it. My house is close by," he added before she had time to refuse. "Didn't you hear me say so at Szabo's house?"

She hadn't thought it was true, something he read from her face before she could stop him.

"*I* don't always lie. Come on."

Her head spun and her feet felt dead, but she couldn't refuse. She followed, wishing she could be sick.

House, he'd said, not apartment, Klara thought numbly, as

Baeder let them into a slim townhouse. He was richer than she'd thought, but she should have guessed—she'd seen the way he spoke, his infallible confidence. The house matched him perfectly: elegant and artful as his sideways glance or the pin poised in the folds of his tie. Klara balked in the hall.

He looked back at her. "I'm too tired to run. Don't make me give chase."

Where would she go? If she was lucky, she might escape the city, but on her own, with little money in her pockets, she wouldn't remain free long. And how would she warn Levi? She was caught, and the only thing she could do was persuade Baeder not to tell—a task that was surely impossible.

"I've stopped bleeding," she said, not wanting to go farther inside. "Once you tell him, Hagen will have someone tend to me." In more ways than one, she was sure.

"I'm not letting you out of my sight. You have no idea how awful you look. Come on." He crossed the hall to the table and picked up a branch of candles.

"Please, Baeder. You needn't—"

"Call me Josef. Who says I'm going to tell?"

Klara was too stunned to reply.

"I want to know who you're afraid of."

"Your servants—" Klara began.

"Only my valet is awake."

This proved true. The house was still, save for the stout man sleeping in a chair at the end of the hall. He woke at the sound of their approach, rising and greeting Baeder with a bow. He didn't blink at Klara or at his master's request to provide them with wash water, merely relieving both her and his master of hat and gloves and leaving them in the library with a brandy decanter.

"I'll pour," Klara said.

Baeder stepped away from the tray. "How do you know I didn't doctor it before leaving the house?"

"I'm not going to swallow anything," Klara countered. "But I can make it look like I am, if that satisfies you."

"Then there's no reason you can't allow me to pour." Returning to the tray, he splashed generously into two glasses. Klara accepted hers but set it straight back onto the table.

"I've done nothing wrong," she told him. Not terribly wrong, anyway. "Please let me go. I'll leave. I'll never—" She sounded too abject, but what else could she do?

"When did you start living as a man?" he asked.

The question surprised her. "I was twelve."

He settled onto the sofa with only the smallest of pauses. "How old are you now?" He sipped, motioning with his eyes for her to take a seat.

Klara perched on the edge of an upholstered chair like it was a cliff. "Two and twenty."

"Your records say twenty-five."

He'd read her file. "My records say a good deal," she admitted.

"Is any of it true?"

"I did study in Heidelberg."

"So how did this happen?"

Unsure what he meant, Klara glanced at her side. A dark patch spread from her ribs to the flap of her pocket, but it wasn't easy to see against the black wool.

Baeder shook his head. "Not the wound, though I'll hear that later. I meant *this*." His hand swept over her.

"My—my family thought it the best thing. I'm not pretty."

"So? There are plenty of ugly girls."

"Ugly men fare better."

"Sometimes."

The valet coughed outside the door. "Everything is ready."

Klara stood nervously, not looking at Baeder, who'd also risen. In silence, they followed the valet up a flight of stairs and down a corridor, farther into the house. When the servant motioned Klara to a room on the right, she couldn't find anything to say and was unaccountably relieved when Baeder spoke behind her.

"Herr Stark prefers to look after himself."

The servant left them, but Baeder stayed, following her into the bedchamber. Tensing, Klara shot him a glance.

"Don't look at me like that. I could never ravish anyone wearing a mustache, not even at this hour."

"I'm not afraid of that," Klara retorted, but his brows tilted skeptically.

All right, maybe a little, she conceded. Which was foolish. When a man could have a woman like Sonia von Olsberg, what would he want with her?

"Much as you might wish it, I can't see your wound through your coat," Baeder reminded her. "You need to lose some of your clothes."

"The hurt's not serious. I can manage on my own."

"Do you? Every day?"

Klara colored. "I have a servant who knows. He helps me."

"Is he your lover?" Seeing her recoil, he gave a silent laugh. "Clearly not. Am I going to have to help you from your coat?"

Not wanting him anywhere near, Klara doffed it and her waistcoat. Without them, the outlines of her corset were visible through her shirt. Shoulders hunched, she set aside Poincaré's stolen letters and knife.

Josef nodded. "You don't need the knife. I won't hurt you."

"I don't need that knife. I have my own," Klara told him.

His eyes narrowed, but she wasn't going to say where it was.

Twisting in front of the mirror, Klara inspected her blood-stained shirt. Moving was painful, but there wasn't a lot of blood now. Straining for a better look, she flinched when Baeder thrust a wet cloth in front of her.

"How did it happen?" When she said nothing, he reached for the tail of her shirt. Klara sidled away.

"It was Olsberg," she said, too off-balance to parry well.

Baeder frowned.

"He would have killed me if I hadn't escaped."

"When? How did you manage it?"

Klara swallowed. "I was the man he met at the crypt. He was bigger, but I surprised him—"

"How?"

"With my knife."

"Is that how he got the wound on his leg?"

Klara nodded. "But he gave me this."

"Let me see."

Throat tight, Klara gathered up her shirttail, waiting for questions that didn't come. Surely he expected her to tell him more. It was hard to see the gash on her side beneath the loose plaster, but she wasn't taking off the corset, not willingly. She stretched, lifting the bottom edge and probing beneath with her fingers.

Baeder sighed. "Let me." Forestalling argument, he put his hands on her waist and pulled her closer.

"Don't—"

"You can keep your clothes on."

He bent, prodded, then frowned. "Pass me the cloth. It's not bad, just wants washing." He dabbed at her side, peeled away the old plaster, then folded up a clean handkerchief and pressed it against her skin. "This harness of yours should keep it in place. You can get your servant to patch you up again later. I'm guessing you don't trust me with a needle."

Klara swallowed with an almost audible clunk. "No."

"Did you follow Olsberg from the church?"

Klara shook her head.

"Did his brother?"

"I didn't see him. All I could do was run. I didn't know Olsberg was dead until morning, when I saw the guardsmen bringing his body into the palace. When I learned Herr Hagen was making a search of the house, I had to look first, in case—"

She stopped, hoping Baeder's nod meant she'd be spared from saying more. Not so.

"How did he come by your secret in the first place? Did you know him?" Baeder asked.

That was easy to disprove. Klara shook her head, hoping he couldn't tell she was sweating. The truth was in her mouth, but it was like sugar, dissolving in an instant and leaving only the taste behind. "Olsberg and I had never met until that night, but he knew my mother. Theresa Vogl."

"The singer?"

Klara nodded.

"So you really do know her, just not the way Spaller thinks."

"She never would have told, but Olsberg discovered the truth about me by accident." A careless, flighty courtesan could let anything slip, and this lie was close enough to the truth he might believe it. If he knew the whole, she'd never convince him to spare her.

"And he threatened you? Why not your mother? He could have made her—"

It was a chance. Klara took it. It wasn't hard to make her voice emerge as a croak. "He did. We hoped he'd only want money, but—"

Josef turned away. "You were valuable to him as a source of information, especially because he was already selling to the French. What did you tell him?"

"Nothing. I refused."

Josef's look was flat and disbelieving. She had to make him buy her tale. "All right. I gave him some papers, but I forged them, made everything up. I would never betray—"

He covered his eyes with his hands, silently chuckling. "Schätzen, slow down. I can't keep up with you."

Klara eyed him warily. Schätzen, he'd called her. Little treasure.

He studied her, running a hand along his chin. "So you retrieved the false papers before my uncle could find them."

This she didn't have to fake. Her throat was dry again. "Your uncle would have recognized my handwriting, but I couldn't find the papers."

"Olsberg didn't have them?"

"I persuaded Anton to let me search the body before I went to the apartment."

"Then he must have already given them away," Josef said grimly. "Almost certainly to our Frenchman. Weren't you afraid I'd find them in his room?"

"I hoped I'd find them first. Ever since Olsberg died, I've been searching, trying to keep myself out of trouble, but I could barely keep ahead of you and Anton and Hagen. I swear I didn't kill him."

"You had good reason."

"Not as good as some, but that doesn't matter. It wasn't enough." Her voice dropped to a whisper. "You know my secret, and I haven't killed you."

Baeder lifted an eyebrow. "Could you?"

Bloodstained, white-faced, half-dressed—no doubt she looked pitiful. Holding his eyes, Klara's fingers stole to the place above her wound where a sheath was stitched into the boning of her corset. She drew out her knife, making it dance between her fingers. "There's another up my sleeve. I could have silenced you, if I were the kind that didn't mind killing."

His breath hitched, but only once. He didn't retreat a hair—he came closer, nose to nose, except his was higher. Klara wanted to squirm away, but he was in front, the washstand behind her. She went utterly still, her hand with the knife landing on the table behind her.

He leaned in and kissed her forehead. "I'm not going to tell, schätzen."

CHAPTER 15

Klara didn't know a potent enough curse in any of her languages, so she blinked, which was wholly unsatisfactory and made Baeder laugh.

"Frightened? Did you forget what I told you about the mustache?"

She decided it was best not to point out it could come off, settling instead for: "I don't like you standing so close to me."

"I know. That's what makes it enjoyable."

"Why aren't you going to tell?" She believed he meant it, but not that he wasn't perfectly capable of changing his mind tomorrow or any day after that.

"It may surprise you—hell, it surprises me—but I don't want to see you in that much trouble. I don't think you killed him."

Which begged another why, but she was too afraid to ask. "I don't understand. But I'm grateful." Doubting was her habit, but in this case, it was better not to question such unexpected luck. Baeder wasn't leering at her or asking *how* grateful she was, like the villain in a French novel. He wasn't coercing her or asking for anything in exchange for his silence, so he probably wasn't a villain at all, just mercurial and self-indulgent—understandable faults in a man of his position. All he did was smile, pick up her coat, and hold it out for her. Tentatively, Klara found her way into the sleeves.

"If you and I are careful, we should be able to keep your feet from the fire," he said, and it sounded like a promise. Still, the image was too close to the truth for Klara to smile at it. Hagen's officers were not above torture.

"Go home and sleep," Baeder said. "If we didn't find your forged papers tonight, I doubt my uncle will pry them from the French. They'll have sent them on to the powers in Paris by now, so let's hope you wrote something good and misleading."

"I can spin a good yarn," Klara told him.

"I'm sure." He yawned.

Klara finished fumbling with her coat buttons. "Thank you." It was a difficult word. "Good night."

"I hope so." He rubbed his eyes tiredly. "I still have a call to make."

Klara frowned. At this hour?

"Not my uncle. Stop worrying." He laughed. "You've forgotten the countess."

Tonight? "You said— I thought she— Weren't you just with her this afternoon?"

"Yes, but visiting her now will be more interesting." The slant of his smile brought a flush to her face. "Besides, I want to ask her about that appointment diary. If you're headed in the same direction, you could drive with me and keep me company."

The thought was enough to make her recoil. "I'd spoil the mood," she retorted. "I can find my own way home."

"Then I'll see you tomorrow, hopefully with some more color in your face. Get some rest." He leaned past her and inspected his hair in the mirror.

Retreating, Klara bowed, though it felt ridiculous now he

knew her true sex, then spun around and walked out the door. Listening to her heels clicking on the tiles, she wondered how many secrets Baeder kept from his uncle. He was trouble, as she'd known from the start, but she needed him now—or his silence, at least.

Her position was more precarious than ever. Josef might only be waiting to use her, frame her, or give her up to his uncle. Still, she walked home unafraid. Josef had a string tied to her, it was true, but she was good with knots.

RISING AT AN UNHOLY HOUR, Josef murmured the required inanities and left Sonia von Olsberg. She smiled sleepily at him, watching from her pile of pillows. Forgetting her, he hurried home to change, wondering all the while how, in six months, Uncle Franz had failed to discover the truth about Kasper Stark.

Josef was back at the Hofburg before eight. There was much to report to his uncle, though he didn't intend to share all his discoveries. He smiled as he laid Marius von Olsberg's appointment diary on his uncle's desk. "It's Olsberg's. His wife confirmed it."

"And you think the paintings are his as well?"

"I haven't checked the list, but I'd be surprised if they weren't."

Uncle Franz nodded. "You did well. We're making progress. Spaller's brought in the gravedigger."

Josef kept his face smooth, only lifting his eyebrows. "Excellent." Inside, he cursed.

"Spaller is questioning him now, and I've sent for Lennard von Olsberg," his uncle said as he gathered papers into a leather portfolio. "After I give today's report to the emperor, I'd like you and Stark to go with me to call on the French."

"Sadly, I'm promised to the countess," Josef said.

His uncle made an inquiring grunt.

Josef sighed. "I don't think she'll keep on with this absurd tour of churches." He hoped not. Last night's loving had been good, but there had been entirely too much weeping afterward.

Uncle Franz snorted. Josef supposed he would think it funny too, if Sonia's companion were anyone else. "I deserve a medal," he said.

"Pah." Uncle Franz waved aside his claim. "It will have to be me and Stark then. Where is he?"

"I'll find him," Josef said, speaking smoothly, lest he betray anxiety. He bowed and went out.

Where was she? Not in this corridor, nor in the mostly empty secretaries' office. Her desk was clear, the papers all in locked drawers. Josef drummed his fingers on the desk. Stark ought to be here by now, especially if Spaller was already busy with the thumbscrews—though not literally, not yet, Josef hoped. If that gravedigger spotted Stark—

Josef hurried to the dungeon, where Spaller was diligently writing down a grubby man's repeated denials.

"Have you seen Kasper?" Josef asked.

Spaller shook his head without lifting his pen. "Has Herr Olsberg arrived yet?"

"I'll send him if I see him," Josef promised, hoping he wouldn't have to make good. This gravedigger could botch everything. He hurried upstairs and into the courtyard.

Stark was striding through the mill of palace servants, a half-eaten pastry in her hand.

Relief washed over him. "You're late," he called.

She pushed the last bite into her mouth, dusting sugar from her fingers. The sun glanced off her hair, and she scowled, speaking as she chewed. "I didn't sleep. Did you?"

Josef couldn't help a smile. She got so tetchy over the countess, almost as if she were jealous. "You're in trouble," he told her, serious now.

"Can't be. Haven't done anything yet. I've only just gotten out of bed." But as she watched him, her insouciance faded. "What is it?"

Josef shook his head, studying the shine of his boots. "You may want to adjust your face a little."

Her hand flew to her mustache.

"I meant your expression." Josef sighed. "You're looking that way again. People will notice if you insist on looking at me like a child whose dog has died."

Klara settled her shoulders. "Has it?" Her voice was tight.

"Anton Spaller found the gravedigger."

She took a moment straightening her cuffs. "What does he say?"

Did she never panic? "The usual. He wasn't there, we've got the wrong man...but if he sees you, he'll know you."

Klara nodded. "He'll recognize me. But I never gave my real name."

"Kasper Stark? You think of yourself that way?"

"Most of the time."

Josef grunted. "Careful when you go inside. You don't want him getting a glimpse of you from the cells. You might want to hide. They've sent for Lennard von Olsberg."

"I'll check on the cryptographers. They're on the second floor."

Josef nodded. "I'll find you later, once it's safe."

Klara stopped him with a hand on his arm. "Thank you. I don't—" She shook her head. "What did Herr Hagen say about Poincaré?"

"You're to go with him to the French embassy once the emperor is finished hearing his report. Wait for him in his office around the time he usually comes back. That should keep you out of trouble. And until you hear from me, stay out of the dungeons."

She nodded. Josef walked the opposite direction, resisting the temptation to watch her go. Since last night, his mind itched with questions. How had she learned to hit so hard? Did those little, tightly hidden breasts hurt? But if he acted differently around her, someone would notice, and for now, this was a secret he wanted to keep for himself.

KLARA PASSED a half hour irritating Herr Krampitz, the chief cryptographer, with what he termed meaningless questions.

"If I solve the French code, I will tell Herr Hagen. Until then, have the goodness to leave me alone," he said, his heavily emphasized words scattering the fragments of burned paper laid out in front of him. "Verdammt! Get out of here!"

Klara fled, avoiding her own desk and loitering instead in Hagen's office, wondering if she dared shave off a slice of the gugelhupf waiting for him. She'd overslept, and her single pastry wasn't proving sufficient for the morning's anxieties.

Better not. Hagen was particular about his cake, and food wouldn't solve her worries. She should stop thinking about Gunter, unless it was to indulge the cheering hope that he was even now proving to everyone's satisfaction that Lennard von Olsberg had killed his brother—negating all the work she and Josef had done last night.

No, Poincaré had killed him, but Olsberg's murder was no longer her most pressing problem. Josef was. Klara stopped chewing her lip and stared again at Hagen's cake. Her stomach rumbled.

"Herr Stark?"

Klara turned around and found herself facing Lennard von Olsberg. She didn't jump, but her eyes went wider than they should have. "Good morning, sir."

"Herr Hagen summoned me?" He sounded impatient.

"Yes, I believe Herr Spaller has finally found the man you told us about."

"Then why am I needed?"

"I imagine they want you to identify each other."

"Oh. Of course."

"Your eye is looking much better." He might have powdered over the last traces, but from this distance, the bruise was gone. She wondered if he was glad, knowing his brother would never mark him again.

"Have you been able to settle matters with your fiancée's family?" Klara asked. Surely, if he knew he was his brother's lawful heir, he'd have intimated that to his fiancée. They might have to wait until the dust settled to marry, but that wouldn't matter against the knowledge that their future was secure.

The lines around Olsberg's eyes drew tighter. "Not yet." Which must mean he still wasn't allowed back inside the Stoltenbergs' house.

"I'm sorry."

"At least now I can prove my innocence. Where is he?"

Klara was about to tell him where Spaller could be found when Baron von Hagen returned, striding into the room.

"Stark, are you ready?"

Klara nodded.

"Excellent. Hello, Olsberg."

Lennard von Olsberg nodded. "Herr Stark was just explaining why I'm needed. I don't imagine it will take long?"

"Not long at all." Hagen was in unusually good spirits. "Stark, show Herr Olsberg to where he needs to be."

Klara coughed to conceal her dismay. "The cells, sir?"

"Yes, I've a few things to tidy away before we venture out."

"You're taking me to the cells?" Olsberg echoed, indignant.

"It's where we're keeping the gravedigger," Hagen explained with a smile. "No need to worry, unless this fellow's got a different story than you do." He chuckled. "Stark?"

"At once, sir." She shouldn't need a second prompt. "Herr Olsberg? This way."

Olsberg's disgruntled frown grew, and Klara's heart sank with every downward stair. Her palms were sweating by the time they reached the basement corridor.

"They should be farther on. Just that way." She could hear shouts and the tones Anton used when he was keeping a firm grip on his temper.

"Awfully grim down here," Olsberg said.

"Hmm? Well, it's not where the emperor lodges his welcome guests. They'll be in one of the rooms just ahead of you."

As he walked, Klara tried to fall behind, but when she slowed, Olsberg did too, reluctant to move if she wasn't with him. Klara gritted her teeth. She could get close to the doorway, she supposed, so long as she wasn't seen. Gunter, in all probability, would be bound, sitting against the wall.

"I have some matters I should attend to," Klara began.

Something crashed. This time, Klara jumped. She heard Josef now, angrily ordering silence. If they moved Gunter or brought him out into the hall…

Lennard hesitated outside the door, glancing at Klara, who hung back little more than a yard behind him.

"In there," she said, nodding at the door. No matter what Olsberg thought, she wasn't stepping any closer.

"It's Lennard von Olsberg," he said, rapping on the door.

A chair screeched against the floor. Klara turned around, hurrying away so anyone who looked out wouldn't see her face.

Behind her, she heard a harassed-sounding Anton answer the door. "Ah, Herr Olsberg. Thank you for coming. Perhaps you can set matters straight for us. This is the man who helped you home from St. Stephens? I'm afraid he's having some trouble remembering."

"Then he's a damned liar," Lennard von Olsberg said. "I tell you—"

"Never been to those crypts in my life," a man yelled. "I told you. This isn't my coat. I found it on a body—"

Klara stopped breathing.

"What's the matter, Olsberg?" It was Josef's voice.

When Olsberg spoke, his voice cracked. "This isn't him. I've never seen this man before."

CHAPTER 16

They dismissed an irate Lennard von Olsberg, who clearly wasn't finished complaining about the inadequacies of police who wasted his time and failed to protect important witnesses. "That gravedigger helped me home. I went to bed. I don't know anything more than that," he insisted.

The coat thief, who claimed his name was Jan, was prouder than ever of the garment that had gotten him into trouble, preening even during close questioning. They forced him to admit he'd found money inside the coat pockets, but nothing more than that. They released him with a warning, telling him not to leave Vienna, but Klara knew he'd disappear. Flighty transients who lived off pickings from the streets always had places to hide.

It was possible Jan had murdered Gunter for the coat—robbery was not uncommon—but they had no way to prove it, no more than they could prove Anton's theory that both Count von Olsberg and the gravedigger had been done in by Lennard. Anton was especially frustrated his efforts had come to nothing and limped from the room, his lips pressed tightly together.

She and Baeder exchanged a glance, then followed him

upstairs to Hagen's office to tell him the news. Klara was quiet. It was a relief, knowing for the moment she was safe, but when she thought about what had happened to Gunter... "Do you think we could find the gravedigger's body?" she asked.

"I'm sure the anatomists have him by now," Josef said. "He won't be any help to us in bits and pieces."

Anton grimaced. "I still say the brother killed him."

"He was just as surprised as we were," Josef reminded him. "Besides, without that unfortunate gravedigger to prove his innocence—"

"Or testify to his guilt," Anton put in. "Without him, we can prove nothing. It leaves us in a perfect quandary. You wouldn't believe the places I went to find that fellow. All for nothing."

"No. We're close. You're forgetting Alex Poincaré," Klara said.

Anton's frown didn't lighten. "Let's hope."

Minutes later, Klara left the Hofburg again, this time in an imperial carriage. Indifferent to the luxurious fittings, Hagen sat across from her, reading notes. He barely looked at her, which seemed to prove that so far Josef had kept his word—and that Hagen was irritated by this morning's mistake.

Studying her hands, Klara tensed as the coach swung around another corner. The driver, who'd recognized the significance of his chief passenger, barreled along at an intimidating pace.

They lurched to a stop. Klara climbed from the carriage, clutching the portfolio holding her report of the interview with Poincaré's mistress along with their evidence: the diary that Josef had confirmed as Olsberg's and descriptions of the paintings in Poincaré's room, which matched three listed in Olsberg's petition.

Following Hagen was like being borne aloft by a strong wind. The palace doors swung open as they approached. With low bows, a pair of footmen swept them into a magnificent room. All the furnishings were the best of their kind, save the hastily made portrait of Louis XVIII, who'd retaken the throne only months before. Dull and flat amid such splendor, the royal presence dwindled even further when the room's lone occupant rose from his chair.

It was the black man she'd seen last night, but today, he looked even more intimidating. He was tall—taller even than Baeder—and his forehead was high, his cheekbones proud, his jaw commanding.

Hagen stopped midstride. "Where is Prince Talleyrand?" he demanded.

"Baron von Hagen." The black gentleman bowed. "Forgive me. The prince was expected yesterday but has not yet arrived in Vienna. Unforeseen delays. My latest information says to expect him in two days' time." Just a day before the arrival of Emperor Frederick and the tsar. "I'm authorized to tend to all matters in his absence."

Hagen raised disbelieving brows. The look on his face told Klara he had no inkling who this man was or what place he held on the diplomatic chessboard. Concealing her surprise, Klara studied the man more closely, wondering who he could be. Hagen knew everyone of importance in Vienna, knew who had authority and who didn't. He knew secrets Klara wouldn't even guess at, schemes that would frighten, amaze, and bewilder. He didn't like being confronted with an unknown.

Smiling thinly, the gentleman enlightened them. "I'm Jules LeMaître. Our good king has entrusted me with matters of intelligence. How may I assist you?"

Smiling diplomatically, Hagen effected a swift recovery. "My apologies. You understand, when I was expecting to be received by the prince—"

"Perfectly." The black man bowed again, and this time, Hagen answered the courtesy. Rising, he indicated Klara with a casual hand. "My secretary, Kasper Stark."

"How may I assist you, Herr Hagen?"

"I've come about a man attached to your embassy. Alex Poincaré."

LeMaître smiled. "I thought as much. Let us sit down."

Growing portly around the middle and hampered by his bad leg, Hagen took the offered chair, clearly unhappy at displaying his physical disadvantages. It showed in the way he irritably motioned Klara to take the adjacent chair.

Sensing Hagen's impatience, the Frenchman made a show of building up the fire and pouring out drinks. This once, with the tension in the room thick as blood, Klara would have liked to gulp down a glass, but Hagen hadn't touched his, so she set hers aside. When she looked up, she met LeMaître's cold glance. His eyes didn't linger—she was unimportant—but he recognized her.

He sipped his drink and leaned back in his chair. "What is your interest in M. Poincaré?"

"A most serious one. We believe he may have committed murder."

"How troubling," LeMaître said, still as evening water in a deep pond.

"No doubt you've heard of the death of Count Marius von Olsberg."

"The Prussian colonel. Yes."

"Did you know he—"

"Slaughtered Frenchmen who'd given up their arms in honorable surrender? No, I only recently became aware. M. Poincaré told me a week ago."

"Did you also realize he'd—"

"I expect you know M. Poincaré had been entrusted with some delicate negotiations about the return of misplaced art."

"Misplaced?" Hagen's brows drew together. "Much has gone astray in the wars of the last twenty years. With so many claims, I'm curious why Count von Olsberg's were attended to. Many are not so fortunate."

"I'm no connoisseur." LeMaître sipped again. "If you have

questions about the merits of the property in question, you will have to write M. Denon."

"I'm not interested in art," Hagen said. "Only what you were buying with it and why you allowed it to be the business of a man who could only have been interested in personal revenge."

"That was a mistake," LeMaître admitted. "But not a fatal one."

Hagen snorted.

"Let me explain," LeMaître said.

Hagen folded his hands together.

"Matters of intelligence leave me little time, so I do not make it a practice to scramble hither and yon. Happily, Prince Talleyrand has assembled a numerous staff here. Many are willing to complete errands for me. In this case, M. Poincaré had helped me before, so I unfortunately allowed him to develop a friendship with this Prussian. By all accounts, it seemed genuine. I doubt Olsberg ever suspected their true connection. Luckily, I uncovered it myself."

"How convenient," Hagen scoffed.

"It is amazing how many things swing on chance. You doubt me, but I assure you my story is genuine. I sensed something wrong in M. Poincaré—a restlessness I couldn't quite explain—so I tested him. The details are not important, but he was most distressed when I ordered him to accompany the Duc de Dolancourt on an evening visit to Lord Castlereagh instead of his planned card party. This was the evening of September tenth, you understand. If Poincaré had killed this Prussian, it would have happened then."

"So he waited another three days."

"My assistants are not often foolish enough to disobey me. I would be greatly surprised if—"

"He'd already kept one scheme from you."

"But by then he'd admitted it. M. Poincaré knew perfectly well that if I suspected him of harming this Prussian, I would have no compunction turning him over to you or punishing him myself. I told him so, explicitly. I expect, given the choice, he would prefer to have been punished by you. He was quite frightened when he learned of Olsberg's death, until he learned the killing was done the night of September thirteenth. He was lucky."

"Very," Hagen said.

"I'm afraid it's quite true. You see, fortunately for M. Poincaré, he passed that evening with me."

"I don't believe you." Hagen leaned forward, bracing his elbows on his knees and weaving his fingers together. "Listen, LeMaître. I have his mistress's statement that he hated Olsberg, that he came to Vienna for revenge. My agents have seen his knife and his brother's sword."

"But not a garrote." LeMaître smiled.

"Olsberg's appointment diary was found in Poincaré's possession, and I also know, from his mistress and from an officer in Olsberg's regiment, that he ordered Poincaré's brother's men shot and killed the brother himself."

"I do wish I had known of the tragedy," LeMaître murmured. "I fear my oversight has caused you a good deal of trouble."

"Trouble isn't the half of it!" Hagen slammed his hand against the arm of his chair. "I was willing to let you keep Poincaré for sufficient consideration, but now—"

"My dear sir, you must allow me to finish. I said I do not care to run about, but I have hobbies that interest me. On the night of September thirteenth, Alex never left my company from nine o'clock onward. We didn't return to the palace until nearly dawn."

"Anyone can conjure witnesses," Hagen scoffed.

"Mine is Andreas von Ettingshausen." LeMaître smiled. "I think his word will be beyond question. I understand he has an acquaintance with you. We passed the evening together—I had some questions about his latest treatise, you see. Alex was bored with our discussion, not being of a mathematical mind, but because he was in disgrace, he had to pass the time in a chair on the far side of the room, getting drunk and playing patience."

Hagen had gone deathly still. "I did not realize you were acquainted with Herr Ettingshausen," he said at last. "Still, I'd like to speak to Poincaré. Hear him confirm your story."

"I'm afraid that's impossible. He's been called away from Vienna."

Hagen squared his shoulders. "Emperor Francis will appreciate the courtesy if I'm allowed a few words with him before he goes away."

"I wish that were possible," LeMaître said softly. "He's already gone."

"How?" Hagen demanded. The back of Klara's neck prickled. Without a false passport, Poincaré couldn't have gotten far, especially in the state they'd left him.

"He left in Duchess Varen's traveling trunks at half past four this morning. It was an unorthodox departure. After being sobered so roughly, he was displeased with the arrangement, but I didn't wish him to be detained. I thought he'd endured enough Austrian questions."

Hagen's eyebrows rose in mock innocence. "My dear M. LeMaître—"

"My dear Herr Hagen, a perfectly understandable mistake. Until now, you could not know how well I understood the matter. Or even who I am. I trust your secretaries will conduct themselves more discreetly in future. I shouldn't like more embassy personnel to be drugged and questioned."

"I do not interfere with my secretaries' private time," Hagen informed him. "But I'm happy to pass on your request to those persons in question, if I'm able to find them."

"You're very good," LeMaître said softly.

"You have been to Vienna before? No? Well, do make sure to enjoy your time in our city. You'll find our people are perfectly hospitable."

The two men smiled at each other, like dogs baring teeth. Klara didn't speak until she and Herr Hagen were alone in the hall. Warily, for Hagen's brow promised thunder, she asked the question that was burning inside her.

"Sir? Who is Andreas von Ettingshausen?"

"One of *my* agents. He teaches mathematics at the university here in Vienna. If LeMaître reads his scholarly papers, I'd bet my life he's the French cryptographer. He's playing with me."

He stormed into the waiting carriage, and Klara just escaped being caught in the door. Quietly, Klara wondered if, after being bested himself by LeMaître, Hagen might be a little gentler with Herr Krampitz. Judging from his face, she thought not.

CHAPTER 17

Josef understood the day's mishaps were disappointing: first, the discovery that Lennard von Olsberg's gravedigger wasn't a gravedigger at all, and second, that Poincaré wasn't their man, and they'd been hoodwinked by the French. Uncle Franz was nearly sick he was so bad tempered and would probably be just as angry tomorrow, which gave Stark and Spaller ample reason to wear long faces. Josef could have left them to tidy away their files and maunder dispiritedly on home, but abandoning them felt like bad form. Besides, he liked watching Stark, studying how expertly she behaved.

"I need a drink," Josef announced, setting his hand down on the papers that Anton was putting away. "You should join me."

Anton looked up in surprise.

"What place do you suggest?" Josef asked.

Stark, predictably, resisted, but Anton brought her around. A short time later, the three of them were in a nearby tavern, drowning defeat with dark brown ale. Spaller sat glumly on Josef's right, Stark on the opposite side of the table. She was dejected enough to actually drink today, though she spaced her swallows, progressing slowly to the bottom of her tankard. A dice game jostled along farther down the table, but this they ignored.

"To brothers in arms." Josef raised his mug.

Anton smiled as he raised his, but Stark repeated the toast half-heartedly, avoiding Josef's eyes. She knew he was teasing and didn't like it.

"We'll never know who killed him," Anton said, setting his ale down with a sigh.

"Will it matter?" Josef asked. He'd reached the fatalistic stage. "I like to win as much as any man, but—"

Stark drew her finger through a puddle of ale on the table. "It might." Matter to her. As he knew quite well.

"It's been nine days since the murder," Josef reminded them. "Most of Vienna has already forgotten. Even my uncle is more concerned now with the discovery of this French code master than the murder itself."

"Because finding the killer doesn't win our government any leverage," Stark muttered.

Josef considered this, then nodded, conceding the truth. He was not an idealist. Was Stark? He'd have thought her too well acquainted with life's practicalities for indulgences like that. Probably she just wanted it settled so she could feel safe in her own skin.

Lately, most rumors he heard were threats of war: cities demanding the end of Prussian occupation, squabbles over the kingdom of Saxony, and dark muttering about Russian plots to annex Poland. To men with power, a single death didn't weigh much against these bigger concerns, especially when they couldn't squeeze the culprit's government for favors.

"Be glad it doesn't matter. In a few more days, this will all be forgotten." He meant to reassure Stark, but it was Anton who answered.

"But I fear Hagen will not trust me or Stark with such an assignment again."

Josef spread his hands. "What more could you have done?"

Stark frowned. "There's still Lennard von Olsberg. And the countess."

"I was with her," Josef reminded her. "She—"

"Hagen's not going to keep watchers on them forever. He'll need them elsewhere." Anton sighed. "Even if they had something to do with it, we'll never find any proof. If we... But there's nowhere else to look."

Jules LeMaître had seen to that.

"I think it was the Prussians," Stark said. "If they found out Olsberg was selling information to the French, they'd make sure to silence him."

"Why not order him home?" Josef said. "Besides, there's nothing to indicate Olsberg's treachery had been found out."

Anton only shook his head. "Hardly matters now."

"This won't be your only opportunity," Josef told him. "You've chased all over the city after the faintest traces—"

"And found nothing." Anton took another long swallow.

"And Stark—" Josef broke off as she stopped him with an infinitesimal shake of her head. Anton might appreciate praise, but she didn't want him drawing attention to her and what she'd been doing. "—is a capital fellow," Josef finished, hiding a smile in his cup, waiting for her glare. It came, making her look more masculine than ever, the mustache bristling, the thickened brows drawing low. Wearing this face, he could see why he was the only one to have tumbled onto her secret. Everything about her—the bluntness of her hands, the low voice she used to curse, her square shoulders and long stride—was copied perfectly. Everything except that look she had when caught by surprise. It made him think of Antigone, accepting her punishment of being buried alive.

He supposed that was one reason he wasn't tempted to tell.

His stomach had twisted into knots this morning when he thought she might be exposed by the gravedigger, but with attention shifting to other intrigues, this problem would soon be buried and forgotten. Stark would be safe, or as safe as she ever was.

"The conference will be over in a couple of weeks," Anton grumbled. "When that happens, Hagen won't need half of us. I'll be transferred back to the exchequer, if I'm lucky, and Stark—"

"Will land on his feet, I'm sure," Josef put in. "Enough of this." No one liked failure, but they'd lost a trick, not the hand. The world was here in Vienna, watching, scheming, deep in his favorite game. "Everyone else is celebrating the peace. Shouldn't we?"

He watched Stark from the corner of his eye. They had a whole night ahead of them. He suspected he'd enjoy it very much.

ANTON LEFT them outside the tavern, promising Josef he would hurry home to change. Klara turned to Josef. Time to tell him she wouldn't be joining them.

Josef was watching her. "Why won't you come?"

"I just want to go home."

"Brooding alone isn't going to help." He waited for her to deny it. She didn't. "Are you not coming because there's blood on your evening clothes?"

She shook her head.

"If you're adequately supplied with coats and satin breeches, why closet yourself at home?"

It was impossible to explain that she couldn't come because of Levi. "I can't."

"Schätzen, you're missing the point. Your life, as you've designed it, would give you extraordinary freedom if you ever let yourself enjoy it." He gestured at the crowd of carriages in the street, the first crush of partygoers making the rounds. "The parades and fireworks and waltzes won't last forever. Anton will be mortified if you don't come."

"It won't kill him."

She began walking away, but he fell in beside her. "I'm not letting you refuse."

"The only place I'm going is my rooms."

"Well, I wouldn't mind seeing those."

Klara shot him a look. "Why?"

"I wouldn't mind a glimpse of this servant of yours. I suspect he's the one who makes all these rules. Does he breathe fire? Or have very sharp teeth?"

In spite of herself, Klara laughed. "He isn't frightening. It's just that he cares."

"Terrifying in its own way."

She could forbid him from following her, but she doubted he'd listen. And it was wrong of her, but if she brought Baeder home, she could change and go out again. Levi would say nothing. In Baeder's presence, he'd have to act like a valet, not an overcautious parent. He'd be furious, of course, but time would show him his worries were groundless. At least for now, Klara felt safe with Baeder.

They were allies, of a sort. Perhaps even friends. Since last night, it felt harder not to be. Why should she resist? Like Baeder said, she should take advantage of the freedoms she had. If she did, she might feel differently—not so trapped and dissatisfied.

Buoyed by the prospect, she sailed into her rooms, Josef in her wake. Levi immediately swallowed what he'd been going to say. "Welcome home, sir."

"I must change." There was nothing wrong in her decision. She shouldn't feel like a truant youth.

"You'll be out this evening."

"Yes." She tried not to say it like a challenge and walked into her dressing room. Levi followed. When Klara glanced back, Josef winked at her from the armchair.

Levi shut the door. "Are you going to explain?" he whispered.

"No. This is not for Hagen, but there's no reason why I can't. I'm Kasper Stark, not a hermit."

Levi must have seen something in her face. He looked disapproving but didn't argue. "Very well."

Immediately, Klara felt guilty. He did so much for her. She took the clothes brush from him as soon as he was done with her shoulders, not wanting him to stoop to reach her breeches or the sides of her coat. He never admitted it, but she knew he had pains in his back. "You've taught me perfectly. I'm ready."

This provoked only a half smile. "Perhaps you are."

"I'll be careful."

In the sitting room, Josef was reading one of their books by Sheridan. She wouldn't have expected him to choose an English comedy.

"Are you enjoying it? You're welcome to borrow the volume," Klara said.

"I've read this one before. I was just passing the time." Josef set the book aside. "Now, if you'll come with me, I'll have time to freshen my own feathers before Spaller arrives."

It felt strange to leave without bidding good night to Levi.

At Baeder's house, he left her to change, leaving her in the drawing room where she looked over his collection of musical instruments. Most of the sheet music was written for the cello, so she guessed that was his instrument, not the pianoforte or the neglected harp in the corner. She didn't know enough about art to judge the quality of his pictures, but she knew enough about Baeder to guess they were distinguished.

Anton arrived, looking handsome in his evening clothes, but

he didn't look as well next to Baeder, once he rejoined them. If Baeder were painted in the glory of his uniform, the only way an artist could possibly flatter him was to soften the cunning lines around his eyes. They enjoyed a light supper and talked about books, without a single sentence about murders, ciphers, or diplomacy. Flattered by Josef's attention and mellowed by good wine, Anton became more generous with his opinions. They all did, and the meal passed in carefree debate.

When they left in Josef's carriage, Klara expected they were bound for a card party or the theater like the night before. Tonight would be easier because she wouldn't be drugging anyone or trespassing in diplomatic strongholds. Then the carriage halted, and Klara's mind-cogs stopped with it.

She knew this place. Without her noticing, they'd driven through the grand gate she recognized but never used. Outside the carriage, a red carpet led the way up the steps. They'd come back to the Hofburg, to an imperial ball.

Anton cleared his throat. "I'm not sure I—"

Klara was more decisive. "You can't bring us here," she hissed.

"Why ever not?" Climbing from the carriage, Josef smoothed the sleeve of his coat.

"Anton and I have no invitation."

"Why should that stop us?" He grinned. "Spaller, stop looking like you've swallowed a wasp."

Anton composed himself, straightening his jacket. Klara followed them out of the carriage, trying not to think of the state of her coat. Her best-cut black wool and crispest linen felt insufficient for an event with this much sparkle. "I'm not dressed for this."

"Here." Josef slipped something into her hand. Klara winced. It was his tiepin, and the end was sharp. She stuck her finger in her mouth.

"I want it back afterward," Josef told her.

"I've no use for emeralds."

He watched her place it at her throat, which made her feel clumsy, as if she hadn't carefully learned everything Levi could teach about this particular gentleman's art. "You'll do, Stark. Stop fussing."

"Well, if you think it's all right, I suppose we can give it a go," Anton said. He might be nervous too, but he would be all right. His family moved comfortably among Vienna's bourgeois and boasted a nebulous court connection. It was how he'd come by his post. She was the one who was impossible—daughter of a courtesan, disguised as a man. Hiding in a bureaucratic phalanx of secretaries was one thing, attending an imperial ball quite another.

Klara glared at them. "I—"

Josef leaned over her to murmur in her ear. "Don't expect me to resist the temptation of seeing you dance." Prodding her arm, he walked her up the steps. Klara drew a long breath, trying to look calm and disinterested as he spoke with the liveried doorman, even when he murmured something that made the servant stifle a smile. A coin flashed in Josef's hand and disappeared between the doorman's fingers. "Three?" the servant whispered.

"Two. I have my own."

Behind the screen of their bodies, the doorman slipped two used invitation cards to Josef, who made it look like he'd drawn them out with the one from his coat pocket. Flourishing the three gilded cards for the benefit of the party approaching behind them, Josef returned the cards to the doorman, who bowed impressively and ushered them inside.

"How many times will he resell those invitations?" Klara asked.

"Half a dozen, at a guess," Josef replied.

It seemed likely from the crowd choking the entrance hall. Klara couldn't say which was more dazzling—the guests or the thousands of lights in the massive chandeliers. Anton swallowed nervously, opened his mouth, then shut it again, unable to speak.

Klara kept her lips in a straight line and edged past a lady in gauzy muslin, trying not to stare at the diamonds stitched onto the plunging bodice of her gown. This horde was so over-trimmed with jewels, medals, and gold braid, it was a miracle no one became tangled, she thought—and nearly stepped on Josef's heels when he halted suddenly, the buttons of his cuff caught in a lady's lace overdress.

"Hold a moment." He slid his free arm around the lady's waist. She started to draw away but was stopped by the pressure of his hand and the sound of tearing stitches. "Keep still. I'll set you free."

The lady's cheeks went as pink as her hair feathers. She licked her lips. "Am I badly torn?"

"No irreparable damage." His head was bent so close, Klara half expected him to kiss the lady, but Josef retreated, putting a scant two inches between them.

"Thank you, sir." The lady spoke breathlessly, peering back over her shoulder.

"It was a pleasure. Good evening." He nodded, as there was no room to bow, and let her be absorbed into the crowd. Klara counted one more backward glance.

Anton nudged Josef's elbow. "Was that a happy accident or—"

"There's no such thing," Klara muttered.

"It's the only reason I endure this kind of press," Josef explained. "You're a fool, Spaller, if you don't seize the opportunity."

Anton looked skeptical.

"There's nothing impertinent in an accident," Josef assured him.

Anton looked around, unconvinced. His eyes traveled over the crowd, then stopped, widening with surprise. "I know that gentleman," Anton said, indicating a vague direction with a tilt of his head. "He's my grandmother's physician. Just there."

Klara looked, but it was impossible to tell who he meant among so many.

"Hundreds will be here on reused invitations." Josef smiled. "You'll recognize quite a number of the guests."

"But what about the real guests? Don't they mind? I would think infiltrations by the hoi polloi—"

"They make agreeable company. The daughters are surprisingly willing to be lured into corners. This way." Josef motioned them on.

As they walked, Klara edged closer. "I hope you aren't playing with Anton."

"Not at all. I'm playing with you."

Klara compressed her disapproval into a one-word reply: "Splendid."

"Isn't it? If you find one willing to go with you, you must promise to let me watch."

She made a face, deciding it was better to ignore him and study the colonnaded walkway instead. It was a sight to behold. Heaps of flowers and fragrant orange trees flanking the arches made it seem as if they walked through the gardens of paradise—or Eden. Clearly, temptations abounded here.

There were too many guests to be accommodated in the ballrooms of the palace, even without extras like Anton and herself, so a parquet floor had been laid down over the indoor performance grounds of the Spanish Riding School. Pinked out and pomaded, ladies and gentlemen danced instead of the famous Lipizzaners for the crowds watching from the galleries. Klara, who'd seen the horses and riders perform, decided that elegant as the dancers were, they couldn't compare to the horses' disciplined art.

Josef stopped. "Spaller? I see someone you should meet."

He led them to a pale, pretty girl, under the loose supervision of a gawping chaperone who was more interested in memorizing the details of the ball than safeguarding her charge. Within seconds, Anton and the girl were galloping across the floor.

Josef winced. "His paces are off, but given his deformity—"

"He's not a horse."

"I have the utmost respect for our friend. I just wonder why you think he needs protecting."

"I do not."

Josef raised his eyebrows, but before he could speak, a uniformed Englishman claimed his attention. Two ladies were with him, and it was impossible for Klara to escape the formality of an introduction.

"This is my friend Kasper Stark," Josef said. "An invaluable member of my uncle's staff but also a sublime dancer. Miss Standish, could I persuade you to take my friend's arm?"

She twittered something Klara assumed was affirmative. It was impossible to show Josef what she thought, but if there was any justice in the world—something she doubted—she'd give him the rough side of her tongue before this night was over. For now, the only thing to do was bow and take the lady's hand, wearing a masklike smile.

"You honor me, Miss Standish."

The laughter in Josef's eyes was unmistakable.

Klara knew how to waltz, if not as well as Josef had promised, but the lady was light on her feet, hiding Klara's deficiencies as a partner. After their first circuit, Klara took her eyes off the bouncing curls in front of her and looked at the girl's face instead. She was pretty, with a slim straight nose. Her best feature was her eyes—peat brown, with a twinkle.

"Herr Baeder never mentioned you were so solemn," she said.

"Forgive me. You see, I'm humbled to have such a beautiful partner."

The girl trilled a laugh that almost made Klara flinch. "Herr Stark, you underrate yourself. Don't go on, or you may convince me."

"If I could make you believe otherwise—" This conversation was as florid as something from Levi's satirical plays, an exchange as artificial as this whirligig parade. "You're a sublime dancer," Klara finished.

"That's what they all say." She looked at Klara from beneath her eyelashes. "But I like hearing you say it."

"I'm happy to please you." Klara spun into a faster turn, hoping to dislodge that steady gaze.

"Don't overset us, please."

"Never," Klara promised. She knew this tune. If there was no extra reprise, she had at least one minute left. *Damn Josef and his games,* she thought, watching him waltz by with a bright-eyed blonde. "Are you enjoying your time in Vienna?"

"I love Vienna," she admitted. "Never have I met so many intriguing ladies or such well-mannered gentlemen."

"Miss Standish, I suspect that wherever you travel, you'll find gentlemen eager to please."

She laughed at the compliment, but Klara suspected she was waiting for this kind of reply, like a songbird performing for caresses and treats. In Klara's mind, it was a baffling existence for a person and a troubling one. Miss Standish was not so much younger than she—vapid but happy, a pretty ornament and pleased to be one. Klara wasn't made to subsist on a diet of sugar, yet she envied the girl, who knew how it felt to be admired, perhaps even adored.

"You're frowning. Am I too giddy for you, Herr Stark?"

"Not at all. There's a couple behind us veering off course. I don't want to get in their way." Josef and his partner were slipping away from the crowd. Miss Standish spotted them, just before they vanished into an alcove.

"It is a little shocking," Miss Standish confessed. "Manners are not so free in England." But she didn't seem the least dismayed by continental customs, not like, so rumor went, the British ambassador's wife. When the dance ended, Klara returned Miss Standish to her brother with as much expediency as she could manage. Josef found her again, smirking and asking if she'd enjoyed her partner.

"She's a pretty idiot. Like you," Klara retorted. "How was yours?"

"Tempting, but the wrong sort. Unmarried ladies are dangerous."

"You only meddle with wives and widows?"

He answered her needling with perfect sincerity. "Widows are dangerous too. If it weren't for my sense of duty—"

Klara snorted but was unable to reply because they were greeted by another party. Once more, Klara found herself matched with a young lady, traversing the floor. This time, she planned better. When the dance finished, Klara thanked her partner and escaped upstairs to the first gallery. She walked around sipping a glass of champagne, watching Anton escorting a bored young lady off the floor.

She'd lost Josef. Not wishing to interrupt Anton, whose next partner looked more interested, she tried to think of ways to occupy herself without drawing attention. It was awkward to stand too long in one place, so she started walking again, making slow progress through the crowd, eventually climbing to the second gallery, right below the white plastered roof. Flushed and overwarm, she envied the ladies in their light gowns. Klara drank another glass of icy champagne and rested her hands on the wide railing of cool stone, letting the chill at her fingers and in her throat calm her. The great chandeliers hung well below, level with the first gallery, floating like frigates over the sea of dancers.

She'd read of these fabulous balls in newspapers and police reports, extracting facts and impressions from descriptions that seemed to belong to fairy tales. Tonight, the heat, the music, and the crowd were all too real, while she was entirely false. This whirling multitude made her realize, more than ever, that she could never belong. She must always be alone. The friendships she'd imagined were only tinsel.

There was no point brooding on it.

Looking down, Klara saw Miss Standish charming a tall hussar. Behind her—yes, that man was Lennard von Olsberg. Klara became sure of it, watching as he was dismissed by a young lady in pale blue, whose vehemence drew more than just Klara's eyes. All around them, heads turned and mouths dipped behind fans, whispering.

Even from this distance, Klara saw Lennard von Olsberg turn scarlet. He stalked away, and his place beside the young lady was immediately filled by an old gentleman with a gray mustache. He touched the girl's arm, inclining his head solicitously and was rewarded with a surprisingly warm smile, given his age and growing paunch.

Olsberg had reason for his fears, it seemed. If this young lady was Anna Stoltenberg, she was clearly too lovely to last.

The orchestra finished their lively ecossaise with a pronounced flourish and set aside their bows. The order of the dance disintegrated, filling the room with chatter, as people made their way out of the hall in search of the buffet. Anna Stoltenberg and her elderly suitor were lost to view. Klara decided she'd had enough. It was time to leave. She was halfway down the stairs when Anton found her.

"I've been looking everywhere for you," he said. "Come and meet Fräulein Rohmer. She—"

"I was planning to slip out while the orchestra rests."

Anton stared at her. "You can't! It's not even midnight."

Klara smiled tiredly. "If I don't leave now, I'll fall asleep against one of the pillars. I'm exhausted."

"Don't go yet," Anton pleaded. "In half an hour, there's to be a promenade with twelve ladies dressed as the elements. Can you imagine how they'll clothe the ones who are meant to be air?"

It wasn't hard to guess. She'd seen plenty of filmy gowns

already. Klara shook her head. "I'm tired. Will you tell Josef I've gone?"

"Gone where?" asked a voice behind her. Klara spun around and saw Josef, coming down the steps behind her. He must have climbed to the gallery without her seeing him.

"I'm tired. I'm ready to go home," she told him. "But there's no need for either of you to—"

"I've had enough myself. Spaller, stay and enjoy yourself. I'll send back the carriage for you."

"I'd rather go alone," Klara said. Josef couldn't insist on escorting her.

"Let me walk you to the doors, then." Josef lowered his voice, smiling at her. "I've learned something you'll find amusing."

"What is it?" Anton asked.

"Gossip about a lady Kasper danced with."

"Oh?" Anton's eyebrows rose. "Then I'll come along too. At least to the doors."

It wasn't the secret exit she'd planned, but she could endure one more of Josef's asides if it got her out of here. Klara followed Anton down the stairs, moving out of the way for a pair of plumed ladies climbing up to the gallery. As soon as they were past, Josef fell in beside her.

"Is your wound troubling you?" he whispered.

Klara shot him a repressive look and shook her head. They descended the next flight in silence and had just reached the landing when a gentleman barreled through the door, colliding with Anton. "Have a care, sir," Klara snapped, grabbing the fellow's arm so Anton would have time to steady himself. The man looked ready to plow right through him, and Anton could easily stumble.

The man rounded on her with a curse. Klara drew back. It was Lennard von Olsberg. "Forgive me," she said. "I thought you didn't see my friend."

"What are you doing here?" Olsberg demanded.

"Trying not to be knocked down," Klara said. She didn't like the way he was looking at her.

"I don't take scolds. Not from you." Olsberg said.

Blood rushed to her face. "I'm sorry for any offense."

His eyes narrowed. "I'm not interested in apologies." There was liquor on his breath.

Anton moved forward, trying to edge between them, but Olsberg wouldn't cede any ground. "This is a small matter, gentlemen. Not worth getting angry about," Anton said.

Olsberg sniffed. "You might have small care for your dignity. I value mine."

"So I see," Klara said dryly.

"Do you?" Flushing, he stepped closer.

"I don't make a habit of quarreling with drunks," Klara said and found herself shoved against the wall, his hand frighteningly close to her throat.

"Do you often lose your temper?" Klara asked quietly. "Did you lose it with your brother?"

The words worked. His grip slackened, and she shook him off. Klara went to smooth her coat and suddenly found herself stumbling back, lights dancing in her eyes. Only as they cleared did she feel pain and realize Olsberg had struck her in the face.

There was a terrible silence. Anton stared at Klara, stricken.

"We do not brawl in the palace, Herr Olsberg," Josef said. "You're attracting a crowd."

There was only one thing to do. Olsberg had struck her in public. Ignoring her throbbing cheek, Klara found her tongue. "Herr Olsberg, my friends will call on you in the morning." This time, she succeeded in smoothing her coat. "Perhaps by then you'll have reconsidered your actions."

"There's nothing to reconsider," Lennard said. "Meet me or prove yourself a coward."

Pain pulsed in her head, making it difficult to speak. "I will. Consider what you are proving about yourself."

"Enough. Come away," Josef whispered. He took her arm as Anton closed in on her other side. "Good night, sir." Josef nodded to Olsberg, glacially cold.

Klara kept her eyes straight ahead, unable to hear the whispers that must have followed them outside above the pounding in her ears. It was cool outside the palace and comfortingly dark. The air felt good on her face.

Josef stalked ahead, then spun around and glared at her.

"It doesn't matter," Klara said, sensing a storm of profanity coming. Duels were not disasters.

"I suppose not," Josef said, startling her with the venom in his voice. His eyes glittered. "When word of what you said to Olsberg travels around, everyone will think he killed his brother. Uncle Franz will love it. He'd rather score over the French, of course, but he'll happily accept a reason to reproach the Prussians."

Klara would have protested that wasn't why she'd done it, but her head was swimming. She shut her eyes. Didn't he see she had no choice?

"The Prussians will order Olsberg home, perhaps discharge him from his regiment," Josef said. "Especially if he kills you in a duel."

Klara smiled. "Especially that."

Anton's voice was hollow. "You shouldn't have interfered, Kasper. I don't mind a slip on the stairs."

"Yes, you do." Klara wasn't going to let him lie.

"Olsberg wouldn't have challenged a cripple," Anton said.

Probably not. "It's done. Don't worry about it," Klara said. "His fiancée is going to marry that elderly brewer. Olsberg would have picked a quarrel with anyone." It was just bad luck it happened to be her. "He struck me. No man endures that."

Anton nodded reluctantly, but Josef just glared at her.

CHAPTER 18

Josef and Anton flatly refused to let Klara leave on her own, insisting they take Josef's carriage together. Somehow, Josef arranged that Anton was returned first, though his home wasn't the closest.

"I'm taking you to my house," Josef informed Klara once they were alone.

Klara shook her head without lifting it from the padded carriage seat. It was hard to think, but she was clearheaded enough for that.

Josef ignored her protest. "You need someone to look at your face. You may have something broken."

"Nothing's broken." It hurt, but not that much.

"How would you know?"

"Stop trying to play doctor," she told him. "He struck my face, so you won't get to take off any of my clothes."

The look he gave her made her regret what she'd said. "You told me you can't see a real doctor," he said.

"I have Levi." Once she said it, she realized another difficulty and bit her lip.

"Then I'll take you home. He can help you."

Klara shook her head again, more slowly. "Not yet. I don't want him to know about this."

"Fine. You're coming to my house. Don't argue. If you're not going to confide in Levi, we have things to discuss."

"I shouldn't have grabbed Olsberg's arm."

"It wasn't your fault. He was drinking heavily all evening, mooning over that bird-witted girl," Josef said. Somewhere between the palace and wherever they were now, he had lost his scowl. Klara hadn't noticed until now.

"You saw?"

"It wasn't difficult. If that fool wants a bullet in him so badly, it would be more courteous to put it there himself. Can you shoot?"

Klara turned her head to see him better. They were sitting on the same side of the carriage. She hadn't thought to move when Anton left them. "Yes."

"I thought so. Well, it should be a simple matter, then, so long as you don't kill him."

Klara wasn't going to think of the alternative.

Josef drummed his fingers on his knee. "I still don't like it."

The carriage stopped, and he climbed out. Klara hesitated. If she walked for an hour or so, letting the swelling fade from her face, she could go home once she was sure Levi was asleep. "I'm feeling quite a bit better. I'd rather not go inside. I need some air."

"There will be a surgeon at the duel," Josef said, not listening. "In case either of you is shot. If you're injured and he examines you—"

"Let's hope Olsberg misses then. Or shoots true," Klara said, climbing out of the carriage.

"Come inside. We've got to think this through."

He might not notice if she argued but probably would if she walked off, so she followed him up the steps.

"Have you fought before?" he asked, unlocking the door.

Klara shook her head. "But I know the theory." Duels were

governed by a strict code of rules. Tomorrow morning, Josef would meet with Lennard von Olsberg's seconds and try to resolve the dispute. Hopefully, Olsberg would have more sense once he was sober, but because he'd struck her, she'd lose face if she didn't demand satisfaction, even if he could be persuaded to apologize. Klara didn't care a rap about honor for her own sake, but if she didn't see this through, she'd be branded a coward. Kasper Stark wouldn't live that down.

"Come on," Josef said. "Let's get something on your face."

She followed him into the drawing room, where Josef's servant built up the fire.

"Herr Stark needs something for this." Josef motioned at Klara's face.

"Yes, sir."

Klara waited for the door to close behind the servant. "When will the duel be?"

Josef rubbed his jaw. "Probably the day after tomorrow. Early morning, in the Prater with pistols."

Klara nodded. "Is he a good shot?"

"I have no idea."

The servant returned with towels and a dish of crushed ice. "I'll see to it," Josef said, waving the servant away.

"This isn't necessary." But she'd never procure ice on her own at this hour. Even by day, it was far too expensive.

"I don't want my valet to notice your stubble washing off. Sit down. Lean back." He motioned Klara onto the sofa. She sank onto the cushions, tensing when Josef leaned over her.

"You're very skittish," he said, wrapping a handful of ice in the towel and gently applying it to her face. "This will lessen the bruise."

With one eye, she watched him walk to a table and pour out two drinks.

"Toss it down," he told her. "You'll feel better."

Her fingers closed round the glass. "Until I wake next morning, not sure where I am, and remember that you and Anton are scheduling an appointment for that idiot to shoot me. How do men stand still and let that happen? I've never understood it."

"Ladies aren't meant to," Josef retorted. He considered her through his glass. "Of course, you aren't exactly a lady, are you?"

It would be petty to take offense. Klara drank, letting the liquor scour the impolitic words from her throat. Josef sat down at the other end of the sofa. From her one eye, it was easier to look at the room instead of him. There was the cello, with different music on the stand today. He must have played since the other evening. Next to the brandy, a bronze sculpture of a long-dead hero wrestled a lion, his bare muscles straining. There was another bronze on a matching table across the room beneath a painting of Venice. She thought it was Venice, at least. The bronze wrestler was easier to guess: Hercules. Next to her, on a low table, a lacquered box held fresh packs of cards.

"Will you have another?" Josef asked, gesturing with his empty glass, and Klara realized she'd finished hers.

"Are you trying to get me drunk?"

"I expect it takes more than a couple glasses."

Not much more, not with spirits this strong. Still, she let him fill her glass and return it to her hand. She might be dead or discovered the day after tomorrow. Josef knew her secret, so she was in as safe a place as any, and she had no one to talk with but him.

"I didn't tamper with it," he said, smiling.

"Tonight, I might not mind if you had." Her cheek was numb, but an icy trickle ran down her jaw, making a mess of her stubble. Her shirt collar was damp.

"Are you afraid?"

She shook her head, suspecting he wasn't convinced. "It's been long enough." She lifted the towel.

"Give it another quarter hour," Josef said. "You'll need to look halfway decent tomorrow."

True enough. "It does help," Klara conceded. "But if I drink too much, I might end up saying too much to Levi, and he can't know. Back when I was at university, there was another boy—and I mean, a *boy*—who tried to quarrel with me. Everyone was fighting duels then, and like tonight, I couldn't escape the challenge. I was frightened, though I wasn't bad with a sword. I thought I could match him. I was taller than he was and practiced much more than anyone knew."

"What happened?"

"The morning we were to fight, they found him beaten senseless. Levi never admitted to it, and I knew better than to ask. If he knew what I'm going to do, I think he'd try to injure Olsberg, maybe even kill him."

"Would that be so terrible? Why not let him spare you?"

"He's past sixty. Killing a man is different than beating a boy."

"You consider him a great deal for a servant."

"He only pretends to be one. He's more to me than a valet. I couldn't manage this without him. He taught me all I know."

Josef stretched his feet out in front of him. "So what is he like when he's not playing a part?"

Klara hesitated, but they had to talk about something. Levi was as good a subject as any. The warmth of the fire was comfortable, as was the glow of brandy in her belly. "Levi doesn't talk much about himself. He comes from a Jewish family in Prague, but I don't know anything more about them. They quarreled when he was young, I guess about the time he came to Vienna. I don't think he even knows if his parents are still alive. Anyway, he came here to write for the theater. Occasionally, he still does under a false name."

"You're not related."

She shook her head.

"So why did he take charge of you? When you were twelve, you said?"

"I knew him long before that. I was only a child when he began teaching me Greek. He was a friend of my mother's."

He lifted an eyebrow.

"No, it's not what you think. They were never lovers. I'm reasonably certain of that."

"Or maybe you just want to be." Seeing she was prepared to argue, Josef shrugged. "I don't suppose it matters what they were to each other, only how they matter to you." He sighed, staring into the fire and fiddling absently with a coat button. "I wish you hadn't let yourself be drawn into this."

The duel? Or her double life? The duel was easier to talk about. Klara scooped more ice into the towel and put it back on her face, pretending an assurance she didn't feel. "You don't need to worry. I wish you wouldn't."

He got up and went to the fire, nudging a log into the coals with the point of his shoe.

"What does Sonia von Olsberg tell you?" Klara asked.

"Not much. I must be slipping. But the diary was Olsberg's, like I said."

"Her brother-in-law doesn't like her."

"Well, if we find her garroted in an alley, we know who to blame."

Klara shivered. "Don't."

"I'm sorry."

She shouldn't look at him so long, even though he appeared almost perfect with one arm resting on the mantelpiece and one foot propped on the fender. If he wasn't so wrapped in thought, she'd accuse him of posing.

Stop watching. If it weren't for the melting ice dripping from her face and hands, she could get up and admire the bronzes. "It can't have been easy, having Count von Olsberg for a husband," Klara said.

"I'm sure it wasn't. Luckily for me."

Klara frowned at him, but all he did was smile wearily. "Should we take a look at your eye?"

She shivered and inched back into the cushions. "I'm all wet."

"I don't mind." He picked up another towel. "I'm sorry you're cold, but it will help with the swelling." He sat beside her, swabbing her cheek with the dry cloth.

"It feels much better," Klara assured him. "Am I a terrible mess?"

"You'll do." He dabbed gently around her eye, along her cheek, and at the edge of her mustache.

"Wait. I can do it."

"No, let me. Sorry, does that pull?" He smiled, and her pulse quickened.

"The gum sticks sometimes," she told him, hoping it would explain her nerviness.

He dipped the cloth in the dish of dwindling ice and glacially cold water.

Klara shook her head. "No, let it stay. I'll just have to put it back on again before I leave."

Josef shook his head. "Let me have a look. I can't see if your lip is swelling with this on."

She shut her eyes, but that made her edginess worse, not better. She opened them again and caught him looking her square in the eye. Her breath caught, her nerves screamed that here was danger and—

"You don't need to take so long about it," she grumbled, sliding away. She only gained a couple inches, stopped by the arm of the sofa. "I don't know why you want it off. I can stand a dirty face for an hour or two."

"I can't kiss you with your mustache on," Josef told her. "It's a little daunting."

"You did before." She felt like she'd been running.

"On the forehead. I'm aiming nearer the mark this time." He

swept the cloth over her mouth again, and the mustache peeled away.

Her lips, traitors that they were, fell open, but she had other, smarter instincts. "Why tease me tonight? At the ball," she added, seeing he didn't understand that her mind was running to safer places. "Why make me dance?"

"It was amusing. Also, I was genuinely curious. I wanted to know if you liked women."

"I don't understand them," Klara said, but it wasn't true. Just now, she understood what made them want him well enough.

"I'm glad you'd rather kiss me."

It was too late to bring another lie to her lips. His were already there.

Klara drew back. "What did you put in my glass?"

"Only brandy. You must lose the idea that I have to drug women to get them into my bed."

"But you want me there." Klara bit her lip, fearing he'd laugh.

"Assuredly." His eyes gleamed. "How could I not? You're nothing like anyone I've known before."

"Is that why you haven't told?"

"Shh." The sound came with his lips onto hers, making her weightless again. Her thoughts were scattered beyond recall.

"Is that how the countess likes it?" Her breath was coming much too fast, though her eyelids were heavy.

"Don't be a cat." He eyed her closely. "You've never kissed before."

"I've been a boy since I was twelve," she reminded him.

"Then this is long overdue." He moved closer, pushing her down. His mouth moved with hers, like their lips were dancing.

"You taste like brandy," Klara murmured.

"And you've had too much." One side of his mouth hitched up, and he pulled away. "I keep forgetting."

Klara sat up. "I can't stay here." She should leave. At once, before she lost her head completely.

"You're bosky. You can't go home." He kissed her on the forehead. "Sleep here. No one will find you. I'll leave you be."

She wasn't brave enough to tell him that might not be what she wanted.

WHEN KLARA WOKE, she only vaguely remembered how she came to be in this blue brocade bedroom. Then the details returned. Bolting upright, she threw off the covers. She was clad in a shirt, and a quick pat of her chest, hips, and stomach told that her apparatus beneath was intact. Her heart slowed down again. Climbing from the bed and crossing the carpet, she twitched aside the window curtain. The street outside was bathed in sunlight.

Levi was going to kill her.

She reached for her trousers and discovered they were brushed. Someone had laid out a fresh shirt and cravat and left a note resting beside them. Klara unfolded the paper.

I helped you into bed, nobody else, so your secret is safe. Unfortunately, as I've ordered you be left undisturbed, you won't get any breakfast. I shouldn't have, since you were asleep, but after I undressed you, I kissed you again—couldn't help it. On the eyebrows, so don't be in a panic. You have such beautiful bones.

Sorry I had to go out, but if you recall, I'm obliged to make an appointment for you and Lennard von Olsberg to shoot holes in each other. It's a damnable business, schätzen. Don't go too far.

Her apartment was close enough, Klara decided. Hurrying into her clothes, she combed her hands through her hair and reaffixed her mustache, which was wrinkled from being in her coat pocket. More servants were about Josef's house this time of day, but none said anything to her as she made a hasty departure.

There was a slight shadow on her one cheek, but she wouldn't draw notice in the street.

Levi was another matter.

"Have you anything to say?" he demanded when she rushed inside.

"I can't stay. I'm late. I know you've been worried," Klara said.

"That's a reasonable conclusion," Levi said.

"I was with Baeder and Anton. There was drinking and cards. I ended up falling asleep on the sofa." That last part was nearly true.

"Tell me the truth, Kasper." Everything about Levi was angry, from his bristling brows to his quivering chin.

"I'm a grown man," Klara told him. "At least, we make it out that way. I don't need to account for everywhere I go. I can't do this, on and on, day after day." She bit down on her lip and drew in a steadying breath. "I'm late for the office, but I don't need you to help me. I can do it myself."

She slammed the bedroom door behind her, then, as she dug a fresh pair of stockings from the bureau, she started to cry.

CHAPTER 19

When Klara's sobs subsided, she looked up into the mirror and realized the door was open. Levi stood with a glass of water in his hand.

"Would you rather have something stronger?"

Klara shook her head. Drink had given her enough trouble.

"It will be all right." Levi came up behind her chair and set the glass of water on the dressing table. He laid his hand on her shoulder.

Klara scrubbed at her eyes. "I haven't time for this." Kindness was the one thing she wouldn't be able to resist.

His hand stayed. "What's the trouble? Is it serious?"

She nodded. "I got into a quarrel. It was forced on me. People were watching, and there was no way to back out." She hadn't intended telling him, but once begun, the relief overwhelmed her.

"Will there be a duel?"

"I have to." Seeing his face harden, Klara turned in the chair and took hold of his hand, smoothing her thumb over his knuckles, grown knobby with age. "No. I won't let you. This isn't Heidelberg or a match between boys. You've only just got well again."

"Klara—"

She ignored the whispered name. "I won't tell you who he is. You can't fight for me." Straightening, she added, "That was why I didn't come home last night. I was afraid to tell you."

"You shouldn't be afraid for me."

"Caring doesn't only go one way," Klara told him. "I don't want to talk about it. I tried to avoid it, but—" Levi had caught her in a moment of weakness, and it didn't do to dwell on why.

"We always knew this could happen." He squeezed her fingers and let them go, then ran a hand over her wild hair. "Are you afraid?"

"A little."

"There are more dangerous things. You do them every day."

Klara looked at him, her lips unsteady. "You ought to read me a lecture—"

Levi shook his head. "You're grown. I know that, not simply because you keep telling me."

Klara nodded and went to wash her face. She was expected at the Hofburg. As she toweled dry and powdered over her faint bruise, she watched Levi through the mirror, wondering what it would be like if things were different. They could go to a small town and live cheaply—an elderly man and his daughter. She would take care of him for a change.

"Why do you love me so much?" Klara asked.

"I never had a child until you became my own. Haven't I told you?"

"Not for a while."

"I'm sorry." Levi held out a clean handkerchief for her to put in her pocket. "This duel is with the man who put that mark on your cheek?"

Klara nodded.

"What about this one on your neck?"

Klara frowned.

"The love bite. It's hard to spot, but I see it."

There it was, just beneath the edge of her shirt collar. Her hand flew to it at once. "Please don't ask."

"I want you to be safe."

"I'll never be. Can we wait a few days and see if I'm still alive? We can talk then."

He waited a long time before nodding. "When do you fight?"

Klara shrugged. "Spaller's friend is arranging it."

"They will second you?"

She nodded.

"I'll come with you. We can say I'm a doctor. If you take a wound that's not serious, I'll take care of it and keep you from the hands of a real one."

"All right."

"We'll need to practice your shooting. And remember, a good many men miss."

He brushed her coat, though it didn't need it. As he finished, his fingers swept the place on her neck she'd carefully powdered over. "Is it Spaller? Or the other friend?"

Klara swallowed. "I wasn't forced to it."

She waited for the next question, but Levi said nothing.

AT THE HOFBURG, it swiftly became clear the entire department knew of her upcoming duel. Even without the pointed disapproval of Georg Fürst, she felt the scrutiny of the other secretaries, and Anton was unusually solemn.

"Do we have an appointment?" Klara asked with studied unconcern.

"Baeder told me to leave that to him. I'm to arrange for the surgeon."

Klara told herself it didn't matter if she and Olsberg shot at each other tomorrow or the next day and tried to concentrate on her work. It wasn't easy.

In the afternoon, Hagen himself paused by her desk to congratulate her on her unorthodox but excellent solution. "This settles the matter in everyone's minds. Lennard looks guilty. It will serve very well, but you must try not to kill him. I can pry more from the Prussians if he's guilty and alive." He leaned in to whisper. "Unless he's tremendously lucky, you'll come out all right. I made inquiries. He's a dreadful shot."

In spite of the circumstances, Klara's spirits lifted. She took her afternoon coffee with the other secretaries and didn't let herself wonder why she was more welcome among them now than she'd been before.

There was a message waiting for her when she returned to the office. It said almost nothing, but as she read it, she blushed.

I'm calling for you at five to go riding.

It was from Josef.

WATCHING FROM HER APARTMENT WINDOW, Klara saw him arrive on horseback. A second horse, ridden by a groom, trailed behind. Acknowledging Levi's pained and knowing look with a guilty flickering of her eyes, Klara hurried downstairs.

"Excellent. You're ready." Josef signed to the groom, who handed Klara the reins to a well-mannered black.

Klara took time to admire the horse—not too tall or showy, but fine-looking nonetheless. "Should I have asked my groom to wait?" Josef asked. While she'd been looking over her mount, he must have dismissed him.

Klara shook her head and pulled herself up into the saddle. It had taken hours of painful practice, but she'd learned to mount unaided.

Josef looked pleased. "He's the right height for you."

"Do you have news for me?" Klara asked, smoothing one glove as the horse sidled, adjusting to her weight.

"Later."

Klara tilted her head, inquiring. She didn't like that single, uninformative word.

Josef sighed. "Olsberg is an ill-mannered buffoon. After dealing with him, my patience is too thin for a genteel parade around the Prater. Let's ride in the woods. We can dine at a tavern, then lose ourselves in the forest." He gave a smile that made her stomach flip.

They rode from Vienna. Josef was a born horseman and knew it, but with taut nerves and a racing heart, Klara kept pace. When Josef surpassed her, soaring over a moss-covered log or a ditch of black water, the warmth in his eyes as he waited for her made it worth coming second place.

"Slow down or I'll lose you." Klara laughed, trotting up beside him beneath a canopy of lush green. As yet, there were only hints of the coming autumn gold.

"You aren't a bad rider," he said.

"I'm a better shot. And illustrious among the secretaries now. Your uncle was pleased."

"I said he would be."

"He tells me Olsberg's bad with pistols."

"He is." Josef nodded, but there was grimness around his mouth.

"Where were you all day?" Klara asked.

He shrugged, urging his horse forward, picking a path around the trees. "An assortment of drawing rooms. Most tedious, I assure you."

"I was waiting to hear from you. Even after your uncle told me there was little need to worry, I was unsettled by the delay." His horse was a pace or two ahead. Klara nudged her mount to walk on the other side of the next tree, so she could draw even.

"I'm sorry. I'd have come earlier, but it couldn't be helped."

She believed the tone but not the offhand, obscuring words. Klara watched his face, firmly set amid the leaves' moving shadows. Suddenly, she knew. "You were with the countess."

He shrugged.

"You went to her? Today?" She kept control of her heels and didn't spur off into the trees, but her voice rose, angry and strident.

Josef spun around, pulling on his reins, making his horse balk. "Do you think I wanted to?"

Maybe. It wasn't something she could say. "You could have put her off."

"She was expecting me. I hadn't planned on kissing you last night."

"No?" Looking back, it felt calculated.

His eyes dropped. "Maybe I hoped for it, but I didn't know it would make me—"

"Make you what?" Klara demanded.

"Miserable without you." He scowled. "Isn't that enough? What more do you want me to say?"

Klara swallowed. Her horse, impatient with the delay, stamped a hind foot.

Josef's shoulders twitched. "Show a little mercy, schätzen. I can't have this conversation until I've had something to eat."

She was almost dizzy after this turnabout. Food would help. "All right."

Relieved, he smiled as he turned his horse and led them on through the woods. Before long, they came to a road, then a white-walled tavern on the outskirts of a village. "Supper will be good here," he promised as he brought her inside. It was—a skillful selection of wines taken with thinly sliced venison and buttery dumplings topped with mushrooms. Josef swore he hadn't tasted better since his childhood.

"We had wonderful dumplings back then." He sighed. "Until the cook quarreled with my mother. She's a difficult lady to please." He quirked an eyebrow at Klara and smiled. "I suppose all ladies are—at least the ones worth having."

Klara poured more wine into her glass, pretending a calm she didn't quite feel. "Think she's worth it? This new one of yours?"

"I don't know yet. She's asking a lot from me."

Klara snorted. "That must be new."

"It is." He grimaced. "There's something I have to tell you. I've been putting it off."

"Yes?"

"Let's go for a walk."

Klara collected her hat and gloves and followed him outside. They walked past their tethered horses and along the quiet lane.

"I told you this was a damnable business," Josef said. "Olsberg is a devil. He and his seconds insist he never offered the challenge."

"He struck me in the face," Klara protested.

"After you rough handled and insulted him—or so they claim. Strictly speaking, they are right. You did offer to send your seconds to wait on him."

"After he told me he wasn't interested in apologies," Klara retorted. "If that's not issuing a challenge—"

"I know. It's cagey, but they insist." He hesitated. "He's also insisting on swords."

Klara digested that. "I can fence."

"Unfortunately, Lennard von Olsberg's much better with a blade than a pistol," Josef said quietly. "Seems it's about the only thing he's good at. Nearly always wins his regimental cup. He's broader than you and at least a couple inches longer in the arms. He'll tire you out, then finish you." His lips pressed together, and he stared straight ahead.

Klara found her voice. "A wound won't satisfy him?" She didn't want another, but it was better than dying.

"Not since you brought his brother's murder into it. He equates killing you with proving his innocence."

Her chest felt tight.

"I tried to dissuade him. I told him you already carry a wound, but the craven still insists on swords. I was only able to convince him to put the fight off for a week. It gives you a little time to make ready." He studied the ground at his feet. "Or disappear. You could, you know."

"Is that what you think I should do?"

They turned onto a path through the woods. Josef looked at her. "Do you want to continue as Kasper Stark?" he asked.

Did she have any other choice? "I'd rather fight than leave." He might soon forget how he felt about her beautiful bones, but until he did, she wanted to stay. "I know how to be Kasper Stark. I'm not sure how to be anyone else."

"Don't look like that."

"Like what?"

"Like you're about to be buried alive." He hesitated. "It pains me."

Her laugh was bitter. "I'm more likely to be buried dead. Soon."

Josef shook his head. "It won't come to that. I'll let the rumor spread that he knows of your wound and that's why he's pressing for swords. Once everyone he knows starts cutting him, he'll reconsider."

"So I should practice shooting after all?"

"I'm hoping in a week I can persuade you both to apologize."

"I'll say anything necessary," Klara said. "So long as Kasper can keep his pride."

Josef smiled. "Isn't it the same as yours?"

It wasn't, Klara realized. The thought made her uncomfortable. "I'm not sure you're right about this. If, as you say, Olsberg thinks dueling me will absolve him of the murder, why should a few turned shoulders and sidelong glances make him give it up? For that matter, why does killing me make him innocent?" None of it made any sense.

"These are old ways and old rules."

"It's not the twelfth century anymore." It was ridiculous being governed by a centuries-old knightly code.

"Let me take care of it. It's what seconds are supposed to do."

She studied him for a while before nodding. He didn't know it yet, but she'd reached more than one decision. Maybe Josef was right, maybe he wasn't. The only certain thing was that she had a week left.

"Schätzen." Josef stepped closer, dropping his voice to a whisper. "You're giving me that face again. Trust me. It will come out right."

CHAPTER 20

Levi Braun was not used to taking his supper alone. He didn't like it. Klara ought to be here, telling him about her day, arguing over obscure lines of poetry that were two thousand or so years old. She didn't come back until after dark.

"I was riding in the woods with Josef von Baeder," she said. Seeing that he was looking, she took off her coat and stretched out her neck. "No more damage."

"None that I can see."

She smiled. "I'm practicing swords with him tomorrow. He has a garden behind his house. We won't be seen."

"Why swords?"

"My opponent dislikes pistols. The duel is set for next week. My wound should be better by then."

"Better enough?"

"It will be," she said, unwilling to consider anything else.

He wouldn't either. He had a whole week. More than enough time to learn the name of her challenger and solve this problem. The fist around his heart loosened. "I saved you some Rehrücken," he said, uncovering a piece of cake. She'd always had a weakness for apricot filling.

Smiling her thanks, Klara sat down and picked up her fork. "Thank you. Not just for the cake."

"This is good news," Levi said. "There's always less danger with swords."

She nodded, but with her mouth full of cake, she said nothing.

JOSEF DECIDED that evening parties were less enjoyable with his head full of his schätzen. Normally, he had a good ear for music, but tonight he'd scarcely heard a note. Nor had he arranged a quiet meeting with the Tyrollean countess who was the latest bedmate of the Duc de Dolancourt. He must see to it now so he could go home.

One way or another, they would find a way into the French camp.

He leaned over to the lady next to him. "I wish it weren't so warm in here. It's a pity gentlemen no longer carry fans."

"Do you want mine?" Her blue eyes sparked up at him.

"Maybe you could ply it a little closer."

They were friends by the time the concerto ended, and she brought him along when she rose to speak to her cousin, the fair-haired Tyrollean countess he was seeking.

"It's very kind of you to introduce us, Maria," the lady said. "But Herr Baeder and I are already acquainted."

Josef bowed. "Let me fetch you both some lemonade."

"I'll go with you." They walked off together, arm in arm, leaving the young girl alone with her fan.

"Don't abandon her for too long," Josef whispered. "Who knows what kind of man will next give her trouble?"

His companion laughed. "We need only go a little ways along

the corridor. You, I daresay, will discover an urgent reason to leave, and I will remember how cold I am without my shawl."

"Quite right." Josef bowed over her hand, and a folded paper slipped from her fingers into his. "You must excuse me. I have business elsewhere."

The lady smiled. "Find me again next week, but don't use my cousin. She's had her heart broken twice already since coming to Vienna."

The door beside them opened, and Josef started in spite of himself. Jules LeMaître stood there, bowing and apologizing for the interruption.

"There's no interruption," Josef said. "I'm just on my way out. Sir. Countess." Bowing to each in turn, he hurried away, relieved to escape the house. He'd have to report LeMaître's presence to his uncle and feared within a day or two they'd learn Dolancourt had found a new mistress.

Josef swore under his breath. Although this countess looked nothing like Sonia, she put him in mind of her, and she was another person he'd rather not think about.

An hour of swordplay against Josef early the next morning was depressingly difficult. Pained and sweating, Klara was blocked again and again, and she was forced to retreat, taking his blunted foil on her leg, arm, and twice on the heart.

"It's no good," she said, bracing her hands on her knees to catch her breath.

"The trouble is your wound. It's crippling your lunges. You'll be in better form by next week. Let's try again. Keep the attack close. You're better there."

Klara tried, but she was already exhausted. "That's enough for today," she said and went to the garden bench to pick up her coat. "Your uncle won't like it if I fall asleep at my desk."

Josef spoke in a low voice at her shoulder. "You must only look as if you're prepared. It won't come to a fight."

Klara wanted to believe him, but she couldn't escape her foremost thought: six days left. She licked her lips, wondering if they were watched from the windows of the neighboring houses. Probably. "Will I see you later?"

"I've calls to make. Tonight, I'm expected at the British ambassador's." He made a face. "I'd bring you with me, but I wouldn't inflict one of his dinner parties on anyone I like."

Liking. It wasn't the same as being miserable without her. Did his affections melt away as quickly as that? Klara realized he was still speaking, looking at her sideways as he stripped off his gloves.

"You could come by later. I'll be home by eleven." He met her gaze. "We could play cards."

Her tongue was too clumsy for words, so she nodded.

"Are you any good?" Josef asked.

"Wait and find out." She knew how to play, of course. And how to cheat.

THE DAY PASSED SLOWLY, Klara's stomach working itself into tighter and tighter knots. Anton noticed and spoke to her with bracing cheerfulness, telling her she'd feel better next week, after the duel. Klara only half listened. Back at home, she choked down a quarter of her supper, then pretended to read alongside Levi, listening to the bells of the nearby church count out the hours. Blind to the words before her, she watched as Levi turned pages and emptied his glass of wine. He retired at half past ten. Klara waited another half hour, quietly washed and dressed, then set out.

There was hardly a house without lights in the windows, and the streets were filled with muted strains of Mozart and Haydn.

Klara's tongue was dry, her palms were damp, and she'd forgotten to put on her gloves.

There were lights in Josef's house, but only on the ground-floor windows. Klara pulled her hat low and rapped softly on the knocker, fighting the urge to run. Josef answered the door. "I sent the servants to bed before I went out," he explained.

"I can't play for large stakes," Klara told him as she passed inside.

"We don't need to play for money," he said.

Klara walked into the drawing room, to the box where she remembered he kept his cards. She lifted out a fresh pack, unable to look at him. "You don't have any counters."

The door closed and locked. "We could play for our clothes." His mouth twisted in a smile that looked a little pained. When she said nothing, he shrugged. "Too childish? I can find us some counters—"

Klara laughed, her chilly determination vanishing. She felt safe with rules. "I'm not a bad player," she said. "Build up the fire. You're going to get cold."

From that moment, it was easier, for they were talking and joking again, smiling at each other as Josef built the fire to a bright blaze. It warmed his face and gleamed on his ring as he dealt out the cards. Klara lost the first hand, grumbling as she began to struggle out of her coat.

Josef shook his head. "I want the mustache first."

"I'll need water." Without, it would pull and stick.

"I think we can manage." He blotted his handkerchief with brandy and walked around the table to press it to her lip. Klara gripped her knees to keep her hands steady as the mustache peeled off.

"That's better," Josef said. He didn't kiss her, just dabbed away the extra brandy and reclaimed his chair.

You'll win this time, Klara told herself, but she didn't. Josef smirked as she surrendered her coat and then her cravat. "You're a complete degenerate," Klara told him.

"Unrepentant too," he said, his eyes trailing down her neck.

"I'm not losing again."

This time, she was right. She claimed Josef's shoes, stockings, his ring and tiepin, his waistcoat and watch. By now, she was jumpy again, intent on the cards, for all he had left was his shirt and trousers. She won the shirt, watching him stand and shrug it off in the firelight.

He sat down and poured himself another brandy, hiding a smile.

At once, she understood. "You're losing on purpose." She dropped her eyes to the cards lying faceup on the table.

He reached for her hand, picking it up and slowly uncurling her fingers. "I thought it the easiest way. Now I'm not so sure."

Klara swallowed. "Unless you blindfold me, I'm going to start losing." As he knew very well.

"Let's call it a game, then. Will you come upstairs?"

"Yes." It was what she wanted and why she had come.

CHAPTER 21

Klara lay awake, smiling into the dark. With a sigh, she rolled onto her side, deeper into the sea of pillows. As she moved away, Josef hummed a weak protest and stretched out a hand, fumbling for her fingers. Hooked together, his breathing slackened, sinking into the song of easy sleep.

The even sounds reminded her of a night she had spent on Lake Mondsee, lying on the shore and listening to the lap of the water. She'd been happy then, though in an entirely different way than she was now. She'd been only twelve on that first journey with Levi, after Theresa had decided what her life should be. She'd been too uncertain and excited then, lying under the night sky, to make any use of Levi's astronomy lessons.

Now there were bed curtains above her, not a canopy of stars, but it was impossible to read her future in either. Even if she could, it was probably better not to know. Her hand twitched beneath the covers, prompting a reassuring sweep of Josef's thumb. Perhaps not asleep, then. Klara turned her head, studying his careless, beautiful features. His eyes did not open, and, after a time, the sight of his face turned painful. Doubt, unwelcome companion of the small hours, had found her.

Moving like a shadow, Klara climbed from the bed and went to the window.

It was dark and chilly outside the covers. The strip of jeweled night visible above the opposite row of houses didn't give any answers, but looking at it was reassuring, until she began shivering. Wiggling cold toes, Klara looked around for her clothes. Her shirt was draped over a chair on the other side of the room. She tiptoed there and pulled it on.

"Schätzen, are you sad?" Josef whispered.

She hadn't realized he was awake. "No. But I want to think."

His head lifted. "I don't know if I should let you be so serious. You look cold." He stretched out a hand to coax her back into bed. "Don't go yet."

"I have to think about what's coming."

"The duel?" He sighed and sat up, drawing her in and under his arm. "I suppose you can't help it." He pressed a kiss on her forehead. "Don't think too hard, schätzen. Promise." He waited for her nod, then lay back, tucking his hand around her waist.

When she woke again, it was still dark. The other side of the bed was empty. Klara sat up, clutching the sheet.

"Do you want me to help you dress?"

Klara twisted around. Josef was coming from the adjoining dressing room, fully clothed save for his hat.

She scrambled from the bed. "Yes. I must go. Aren't you—?" Clearly, he was dressed to go somewhere.

"I'm going riding," he said. "I go most mornings."

"Except for nights when you sleep with the countess." She had tried to sound lighthearted, but her voice was sharper than a joke should be. "When I found you there, it was after nine."

"So it was. I'd keep you if I could, but we must stick to our usual habits if we want to maintain your secret."

"All our habits?" She was still thinking of the countess.

"Most." He smiled and leaned in to kiss her. "There are differences between duty and pleasure."

"Which one am I?"

"I think you know. Haven't I given sufficient proof?"

Perhaps he had. Klara blushed. In any case, there was no time to argue. She must hurry home. She had five days before fighting Olsberg, unless she wanted to pack up and run.

"Here's a fresh shirt."

She stripped off her old one, and Josef helped her into the corset. "I hate to hide you, but there is a certain thrill in being the only man who knows what you are—and appreciates it." He pressed a kiss on her shoulder. "When will you let me see you again?"

"I don't know. You might have calls to make."

"I'll put them off." He grinned at her in the looking glass.

"I need to rest. To prepare for my duel."

"You can sleep here, afterward. Come every night."

"And claim we're playing cards?"

"I'm about to become an inveterate gambler."

His persuasiveness was flattering, but she couldn't agree too readily. "I'm not sure it's wise. With this duel— "

"Making love is the only thing to do the night before a duel." He finished with her laces and planted a kiss on her other shoulder.

Maybe it was, but Klara didn't want to think about it now. She ducked into the clean shirt. A minute later, she was in her coat and breeches too, finishing her cravat. Smoothing on her mustache was all that remained. The gum that held it in place wasn't all that sticky anymore, but it would last long enough for her to get home. Her apartment wasn't far.

"It's strange to see you turn back," Josef said. "I hate that mustache."

"What would people think if I started to shave?"

"I'm more worried your Levi won't let you out again," Josef grumbled. "Will he be awake when you arrive home?"

Klara glanced at the clock, dimly lit by the candle left burning in the dressing room. "Not if I hurry."

"Be quick, then. And remember you've promised me not to worry. Olsberg will change his mind."

JOSEF WATCHED until she turned the corner, then walked out the front door. Seconds later, he climbed into his carriage. He hadn't wanted her to see it, for he'd told her he planned to go riding. The lie didn't trouble him, though he wasn't entirely easy with his conscience. She wouldn't have made love to him if not for this duel. Of course, without the duel, he wouldn't have realized how much he wanted her and how important it was to keep her alive.

The knowledge had struck him that instant in the palace stairwell, watching her issue her challenge. She'd been hit hard across the face, good reason for any woman to cry or cower, but she hadn't that day or since. He'd been furious with her for giving Olsberg a chance to kill her. The man was a blackguard who ought to be shot, but he wouldn't be, unfortunately.

The carriage rolled past Vienna's old, broken walls, heading north. Josef consulted his watch. He'd arrive in good time, before sunrise, and for now, he had time to think.

His schätzen was sweeter than he'd imagined, but then, she'd always surprised him, right from the first. Beneath the bravery, false assurance, and hardheaded distrust, he'd discovered a girl who was breakable. It made him feel unexpectedly tender, though he did not doubt that if she tried, she might very well kill him. Perhaps that was what made her so fascinating.

She was also unduly jealous of Sonia, which amused him. He was flattered she was so jealous. Well, if things this morning fell out as he hoped, he'd be free of his unwanted connection, and

Sonia would still have reason to be pleased with him. He'd engineer their parting today, one way or another.

Josef had never seen Olsberg fence, but the man was reputed to move as agilely as a lizard. Certainly, he'd been quick to strike that night on the stairs. Josef thought his schätzen could kill Olsberg quite handily if she caught him by surprise in a tight corner. It was her wound and the formality of dueling that would make her lose, and she knew it.

Perhaps he should have told her his plans. No, this way was best. He'd manipulated her into bed, but she'd come willingly, not because she was afraid of him, or worse, grateful. He looked forward to seeing her expression when she learned she could trust his promises—assuming he lived until luncheon.

Across from him on the seat was a selection of three swords, though Josef knew perfectly well which one he'd use. He had a favorite, but it was a nice effect to practice a few thrusts with each one before settling on his choice and giving his most formal bow to his opponent. Humming to himself, Josef leaned back into the carriage cushions. A church bell tolled the quarter hour. It was not yet seven. In another five minutes or so, he'd reach the Prater.

CHAPTER 22

Levi was too silent and suspicious this morning to be pleasant company. Klara wondered if he knew she'd gone out last night and if he suspected where. If he did, he wasn't saying anything, and for that she was grateful. Klara gave him a shyer smile than usual as she went out and promised to be home for supper.

Anton was not at the Hofburg, so Klara worked without interruption until ten, when she went out for a cup of coffee and to read the newspapers. She was halfway finished with her mélange, a mix of milk and strong coffee, when Anton walked in.

"Good. You're here," he said as he spotted her.

Klara moved over to make room on the wooden settle. Anton sat heavily beside her, waving away the offered newspaper. "Josef asked me to find you. He wasn't sure where you would be, but he wanted you to know as soon as possible. It's over."

Klara set down her cup. "What do you mean?"

"Olsberg's dead. Josef fought him this morning on your behalf."

"Why would he do that?" Her voice sounded thready. "The duel's not until next week." Fighting her light-headedness, she watched Anton stick his hands in his pockets, wondering how he could look so pleased.

"Josef said you wouldn't suspect. I thought you'd catch on, but he was right. When Olsberg wouldn't relent because of your wound, Josef insisted on taking your place but didn't wish you to know. Said you'd be too proud to agree to it."

In certain circumstances, it was permissible for a second to step in for his principal, but—Klara pressed her lips together. She knew the response expected of a gentleman. "I'm not the coward Josef thinks me. Perhaps I should challenge him."

"You can't. Besides, no one will think you a coward—not with your wound. You knew nothing about the plan, as Josef and I will make plain to anyone who asks." Anton's brows tilted with concern. "Why didn't you tell me?"

"About my wound? It's a small thing. Josef worries too much."

Anton shook his head. "It wasn't fair for Olsberg to insist on swords with you at a marked disadvantage. Everyone recognizes that. It's better this way. Josef can stand the rough from Hagen better than you."

Klara remembered Hagen hadn't wanted Olsberg dead, merely injured and dismissed in disgrace. "You said I can't challenge Josef. Why? Was he harmed?"

"Took a wound in the thigh."

Klara pushed to her feet. "I must see him."

"No need to panic." Anton stood, laying a hand on her arm. "He'll limp for a few weeks, but he says it won't trouble him because it puts him in such good company."

Klara stared.

"He meant me and Herr Hagen," Anton said.

Of course. "This is my fault," Klara said.

"You don't look well. Sit down." Anton pulled her back into the wide seat. He looked around, making sure they were private. "No one blames you, least of all Josef. He chose to step forward. He's quite a swordsman. Not as skilled as Olsberg, but he had the stamina to fend him off and finally outlast him. If he hadn't been so tired, he might not have made it a killing thrust, but—"

"Tell me everything that happened," Klara said. "And take me to Josef at once."

SHE EXTRACTED the details as they rode to Josef's house in a rattling fiaker.

They had met shortly after dawn, Anton told her. The air was chilly, and there was dew on the grass. "He had to practice while he waited to keep warm. I counseled against it, fearing he'd tire early or give Olsberg too much knowledge of his skills, but he said he'd rather risk that than begin with cold arms and numb fingers. He hates to be cold."

"He does," Klara said, thinking how Josef slept buried beneath a pile of eiderdown.

"Don't look so tragic. You know he won," Anton scolded and went back to his story.

They had sparred politely at first, getting each other's measure. Olsberg nicked Josef on the wrist only a few minutes in.

"You spoke only of a wound in his thigh."

"This was only a scratch," Anton told her. Though it had bled into Josef's cuffs and down the length of his hand. "Worried me, that. Didn't like to think what it might do to his grip."

Anton claimed never to have seen a fight like it, not that he'd witnessed many, but even the doctor and the other seconds had been impressed at the flashing bladework and quick stepping of the combatants back and forth across the grass. Olsberg had pressed the advantage, making the most of his strength and technique. Josef worked harder, blocking the killing thrusts again and again, for Olsberg offered no quarter. Sweat soaked their shirts and ran into their eyes, though the watchers stood shivering.

Anton feared the worst. It was plain Olsberg was tiring,

diminishing the number if not the speed and strength of his blows, but Josef was exhausted, barely holding up under the relentless assault. Then, on a riposte, Josef stumbled and took Olsberg's blade deep in his thigh, but he parried and broke free before Olsberg stabbed him again. They'd circled, feinting and drawing back, unwilling to spend strength on unnecessary strikes. On a lunge, Josef faltered on his wounded leg, scrambling away from Olsberg's sword point with a torn coat and a gash on his chest. Sensing victory, Olsberg quickened, drawing back for a hard, swift strike. In that instant's reprieve, Josef twisted, throwing up his blade. It rammed through Olsberg's stomach and out the back of his chest.

"He just crumpled," Anton said. "Like a puppet with the strings cut."

"Did it take him long to die?" Klara asked.

"There was a lot of blood."

She could imagine it, bright, hot, seeping into his clothes, dripping to the ground, bubbling into his lungs. Josef was safe, and so was she. For that, she must be thankful.

"You lied to me," Klara said, charging through the door of Josef's bedchamber. He was on the bed, nearly naked, with a surgeon wrapping a linen bandage around his thigh. At the sight of her, his grimace turned into a grin.

"I had reasons."

Saving her was one, luring her into bed another, but she couldn't accuse him of that, not in front of the surgeon, the valet, and Anton.

"Don't be angry with me," he said.

Klara brushed at her coat. "If you had died, Herr Hagen would blame me."

Josef laughed. "Luckily, it didn't come to that." He motioned her closer to the bed and spoke in a softer voice. "I knew if you fought him, your death was a certainty. He showed no mercy."

"I can't be glad you fought, but I'm grateful."

"Keep the gratitude. I don't want it. There's nothing worse than a friend who feels obliged to you. It was my choice, Stark. You owe me nothing." He turned his eyes to the surgeon. "Are you finished, sir? Though I appreciate your efforts immensely—" He winced again.

"It's done, my lord. Be gentle with it, and I'll look in again tomorrow."

"I'm afire with anticipation."

The surgeon smiled. "So long as you aren't burning with fever. That was a pretty bit of swordplay, my lord, even if the end was rather ugly. I've seen a good many contests in my time, but never one to surpass yours."

Josef nodded at the compliment, and the man withdrew, accompanied by the valet. Sighing, Josef reached for the shirt that lay at the foot of the bed and shrugged into it. "Don't look so stricken, Stark."

"Grant me some time to recover from the shock," Klara said. She blinked the sting in her eyes away and settled her gaze on Anton, who was safer to look at. "You're both far too good to me."

Any answers they might have given were silenced by a commotion in the hall.

"No, I won't wait. I'll see him now."

Anton stilled. "It's Herr Hagen," he mouthed. No time for anything more. Baron von Hagen swept into the room and glared coldly at his nephew.

"They tell me you'll live."

"It's good of you to call," Josef said.

"How badly are you hurt?"

"I shan't be dancing this week. Give it a month, and I'll be recovered. I've suffered sword wounds before."

Hagen grunted.

Josef steepled his fingers together. "You're displeased I fought in place of Stark."

"You're more valuable to me than he is." Hagen frowned at Klara and rubbed his jaw. "At present."

Klara wasn't sure if she should laugh or take offense and decided it was best to do neither. "I'm sorry, sir. I'd have stopped him if I'd known."

"That would have been a damn fool thing to do. I didn't say I didn't need you, just not as much. What's this about a wound?"

"Truly, it's nothing serious. Herr Baeder worries unnecessarily."

Josef opened his mouth to protest but fell silent under his uncle's gaze. Within a moment, he recovered. "I did the only thing I could do."

"You should have told me what you intended."

"I'm not one of your secretaries."

"No, but as two of them are here"—Hagen glanced at Klara and Anton—"we might as well finish this. Josef, if you're in pain, you've no one to blame but yourself. You'll have to endure. Stark, write this down."

When Hagen was seated and Klara equipped with paper and pen, he began dictating.

Count Marius von Olsberg, identified in police investigations as an informant of the French, was murdered eleven days ago on the thirteenth of September by Lennard von Olsberg, his brother.

"We think he did it. I'm not sure," Josef interrupted.

His uncle shrugged. "In a balance of probabilities, I think it's most likely. Olsberg tried to establish his innocence and failed. Besides, it will embarrass Hardenberg." He cleared his throat and Klara lifted her pen.

This was in response to a quarrel where Count von Olsberg refused to assist his brother in furthering his career. It is supposed that Lennard von Olsberg, fearing discovery by the Imperial Police, subsequently killed one Gunter Kissling, a gravedigger, who'd witnessed this quarrel.

Oppressed by his conscience, Lennard von Olsberg provoked a man into a duel over insults regarding police suspicion. He was killed in this action, leaving me, as head of the Imperial Police, no alternative but to close this inquiry.

"We've done what we can," Hagen said and stretched out his hand, impatient for Klara to finish the statement and hand over the pen so he could sign it. Affixing his name with a flourish, he handed the papers back.

"Write out a copy to deliver to his widow, the countess."

Klara nodded and set to work.

"I can deliver them, sir," Anton said.

"No, let my nephew—" He broke off, frowning at Josef, who was shaking his head.

"You must see that I can no longer carry on with her."

Josef was taking care not to look at her, so Klara bent her head and went back to copying the report. She dropped a blot on the last word and had to cross it out.

Hagen grunted. "I don't suppose you can, after killing her brother-in-law. I wish you had considered that."

"Without her husband, she has little influence."

"But there is the question of who will claim her and her son's allegiance. His inheritance, if it's returned to him, is of interest to many parties."

Anton shifted in his place on the carpet. "I don't believe the child is of age."

Hagen nodded. "Makes him easy to trade, if his mother is amenable."

Klara misspelled another word. Pretending disinterest was impossible. She let herself look up. Anton was nearly squirming under the weight of the objections he felt but would not say. Klara's conscience pricked, but her lips stayed still. She wanted Josef to be free of Sonia von Olsberg.

Pale and pained, Josef sat in his bed, exchanging looks with his uncle. "I'm finished there. Find someone else for her."

Hagen shrugged. "I'll have to."

Klara ducked her chin so no one would see her face. She felt mildly ashamed. Perhaps they all did. She finished making the copy, folded the papers, and wiped her pen.

"I'll deliver this straightaway," Anton murmured and took himself off.

"Well, that's settled." Hagen looked from Klara to Josef. "I suppose now you'll wish to rest."

"I think Stark has more words for me. He was interrupted by your arrival," Josef said.

"Hmm."

Klara was always uncomfortable under Hagen's scrutiny but never more than now. "I did not like being kept in the dark, sir," she explained.

"Say what you like to him." It was a relief when the door closed behind him.

"You're done with her." Klara kept her voice low.

"Yes, but not with you." He beckoned to the place beside him with a tilt of his head. As soon as she was within reach, he took her hand and pulled her down to sit on the bed.

"Schätzen, what are you thinking?"

She tried to look at him, but her eyes were blurry. "When I think what might have happened—"

"To me or to you?"

"I don't know."

"I had to stop it, don't you see?" His smile made it impossible to speak. A clot of emotion had stopped her throat.

"I can't believe you did that." *For me,* she added silently.

He pulled again on her arm, and she toppled onto the pillows beside him. He kissed the top of her head. "I don't regret it. Try to imagine what I felt, and you'll forgive me for lying."

Any minute one of the servants might be back. They couldn't stay like this. Klara straightened and sat up. "How bad is the pain?"

"I'll drink some more of that wine." He motioned to the bedside table, and she passed him the glass. The wine had been warmed and smelled medicinal. "I'd keep you longer if I could, but conscience compels me. You must go ease the minds of Levi and your mother."

"Theresa doesn't know."

"That would surprise me. Even so, you don't want either of them to suffer."

"Don't you suffer either." Klara held up the wine, waiting for him to drink. He swallowed it, and she set aside the glass.

"Come tonight?" he asked.

Klara shook her head. "In the morning. You need rest." She smiled. "You're not fit for anything else."

He grinned. "Sadly, I think you're right. You'll have to forgive me."

Klara let herself out, sure she was losing her wits. Josef von Baeder was a rake and a liar and a spy—and she was stupidly in love with him.

CHAPTER 23

Franz von Hagen quit his nephew's house, but his nephew did not quit his thoughts so easily. Hagen was thinking of Josef when he returned to his office in the Hofburg, canceled his evening appointment, and sent for a slice of cake. He was still thinking of Josef when finally he retired to his armchair and lighted a cigar. Josef had surprised him today, and now Hagen was wondering.

Josef had made friends of Stark and Spaller. Of course, he must have felt partially responsible because he'd brought them to the ball where Stark had unexpectedly confronted Lennard von Olsberg. Still, Hagen wouldn't have thought to find the three men laughing and grinning like old friends or for Josef to allow Stark his say in private. Duels sometimes draw parties on the same side closer together; perhaps that was what had happened.

But Hagen had known Josef a long time and knew he cared more for schemes than for people. As a boy, sent to spend his summers with Hagen's own children, Josef had struggled, used to being the petted darling of his butterfly mother. He'd been teased by his older, stronger cousins, but the balance of power shifted before long. Hagen's children took after their mother—simple as bread, strong as beeches—and Josef quickly learned how to make them choose games he would win. Wrestling was for peasants. They must play at word games and archery, dignified contests more suited to their station. Josef won often enough to gain respect, and when the contests devolved into a tussle or an unsophisticated footrace, he lost with smiles and offhand grace. He knew they would not like him if he was always winning.

When Josef grew taller and stronger, he lost less often. Everyone noticed, especially women. It should not have surprised anyone when Josef matched, then exceeded, his mother's propensity for taking lovers. Hagen's wife pitied the boy, for she had never cared for her husband's sister. *Her* sons were not going to fornicate until they were in university, when she'd have no hope of preventing them, though she fully intended to try.

Hagen only watched, impressed by how skillfully the boy handled his secrets. Josef was tolerant of his aunt's instinctive mothering and amazingly effective at ignoring the fitful attentions of his own. Both ladies always ended up doing just as he wanted without suspecting a thing.

When he embarked on his army career, Josef was already well-versed in Hagen's interests. He was a good agent because he wasn't an idealist, another thing Hagen liked about him. Certainly, he respected his nephew's talents.

Hagen thought back over their conversation again. Of course Josef was in considerable pain, and Stark felt guilty over it. But their expressions today were different, and altruism wasn't a quality Hagen expected from Josef. He wasn't satisfied with the reasons he'd been given explaining why his nephew had fought in place of Kasper Stark.

Perhaps it was time he put a watcher on his secretary.

LULLED BY WARM WINE, Josef slept until midafternoon when pain woke him. Unfortunately, he couldn't swallow another dose and go back to sleep. He had a call to make, and luckily his valet had secured him a pair of crutches. Josef did not like them or what they did to the set of his coat, but he knew better than to try tottering about on his own. It would not help matters if he pitched onto his nose.

Walking with crutches wasn't as excruciating as donning his trousers or climbing into the carriage. That torment almost made him give up, but there were certain courtesies he must observe, and the sooner these were completed the better. He'd made himself plain to Stark, and he must be equally clear with Sonia von Olsberg.

When the carriage reached Am Hof platz, Josef motioned for the footman to help him alight, wishing he could somehow fly up the house's long flight of stairs. Leaning on his servant's arm, Josef made it to the second floor without coming to grief. He only cursed once.

He'd sent his card up ahead, so Sonia von Olsberg was not surprised to see him. She was beautifully dressed and perfectly composed.

"Forgive me," Josef said, for it was impossible to bow. "It's very good of you to receive me." He did not know what her eyes said, but the motion of her hand was clear. He shook his head, declining the offered chair. In spite of his injury, on this kind of errand, it was always better to stand. He'd ended many affairs, but never with the news that he'd killed one of the lady's family before. "You've heard?"

"His seconds called on me. A man from the police came by with a report."

Thank heaven for that. Josef held back a sigh. "Then you understand why I've come." He wasn't sure she did, but this would come off better if he treated it as a foregone conclusion.

"Did Lennard kill Marius?" No sign of tears on her face, but she was suspiciously pale.

"That's what we believe. I'm terribly sorry."

"Are you badly hurt?"

Josef shook his head. "I'll soon recover. But I'm sure you understand it's best we not see each other anymore."

She studied her fingers for a long time. "I understand."

"This is not how I wished it." Difficult things were best smoothed with a lie. Josef was sufficiently practiced that it did not sound like one.

She gave an unhappy smile. "It is not how I— Well, there is nothing more we can say. Perhaps it will be easier if I leave Vienna for a while."

"Where will you go?"

She pleated her skirt with her fingers. "The Princess Bonaccorso has urged me to make use of a house she has in the country."

"Where?"

She told him, and Josef nodded. Hetzendorf was close, the site of a royal hunting lodge just a few miles beyond the city.

"This is no longer a happy place for me. I may leave tonight. The nurse can follow tomorrow with the children," she said.

"I'm sorry, my dear. More sorry than I can say." He'd have to leave soon. The pain in his leg grew with each moment that passed. "I believe Lennard was your husband's murderer. His death is little consolation to me, but I hope it will be to you."

She looked up. He was tired of her, true, but he had to admit she was beautiful. She wore tragedy so becomingly. "Someday it will. Not yet, I'm afraid. When they are older, I think it will be a comfort to my sons."

He nodded, as it was impossible to bow. "Then I must be content. I should have liked to help you more."

As he'd hoped, her cheeks flushed. But a lady couldn't carry on with the man who'd killed her brother, even if that brother had killed her husband. Sonia rose from her chair, signaling the conversation was done. "Thank you for calling, sir. I wish you a speedy return to health."

Not a minute too soon. His leg was trembling. Outside the sitting room, Josef accepted his servant's arm. "Wait a minute." He needed to gather his strength to make it back down the stairs.

———

KLARA WENT to her apartment and found it empty. When a half-hour wait didn't produce Levi, she picked up her hat again and walked the few streets east to her mother's rooms. She hadn't visited the house in years but remembered the prettiness of her mother's suite and the coziness of her old attic room. She remembered running here with torn stockings and skinned knees and finding Levi, who set aside his book and carried her upstairs to bandage her knees. She must have been small then.

As Klara hurried beneath the torches lighting a large door, a shadow swung out from behind her. Startled, she looked back. A hooded figure was only a few paces behind her. Tightening her grip on her sword stick, Klara stepped over the gutter running down the middle of the old street. She stopped and waited for the person to pass. With his hood up and cloak swirling wide, all she saw was a pair of stooped shoulders—assumed, for all she knew, to conceal his true height. He slowed but walked on. As he passed the corner, Klara started again. She turned left and made the rest of her way along a side street, glancing about before walking up to the house.

"Fräulein Vogl is with a visitor," the landlady said when Klara presented herself at the door.

"She will see me," Klara said and held out her card. A moment later, the landlady returned to show her up. Like that long-ago day, Levi was here but not bent over a book. He and Theresa sat in front of the fire.

Klara's eyes narrowed. "Plans ready? Have you found out the name of my opponent?"

Theresa straightened. "You can't really mean to fight Lennard von Olsberg."

Klara grinned tightly. "I did, but I won't have to. He's dead already."

Theresa crossed herself, undoubtedly murmuring a prayer of thanks. Levi folded his hands together and watched Klara steadily. "One of my seconds fought him," she explained.

"Was it Josef von Baeder?" Levi asked.

Klara nodded. "He and Anton Spaller planned it between them."

"And what is between you?" Theresa asked. She hated arguments, but her hands tightened on her skirts, a sign she was preparing herself.

"Spaller and I are colleagues. Friends."

"You know that's not who I meant." Theresa took a breath. "He's handsome, and I daresay quite charming, but—"

"But what?" Klara asked, bristling.

"I imagine he is the one who gave her a love bite on her neck," Levi said evenly.

Theresa went white. "He knows?"

Reluctantly, Klara nodded. "He says he will keep my secret. He risked his life today to protect me."

"Today," Theresa scoffed. "A man like that only thinks of today. What about tomorrow? Next year?"

Levi laid a hand on Theresa's knee, quieting her. He invited Klara to sit down.

"Yes, darling. Sit." Theresa patted the place beside her on the sofa. She hadn't used that endearment for a good fifteen years. Klara wasn't sure she liked it anymore.

"Of course I understand," her mother said, still trying to coax her away from her place in the middle of the floor. "So handsome. But even if he knows—"

"Why not?" Klara demanded.

"Darling—"

"She doesn't want you bargaining your body. She never has. Surely you understand," Levi said quietly.

"Josef doesn't frighten me." He might not be the kind to love anyone long, but for now... "For now, he likes me. That's all."

"That's not all for you," Levi said. "Or for him. Your life is dangerous enough already. If you care for this man, you cannot invite him into it."

"I never did. He just put himself there. He's not going to hurt me. Baron von Hagen is satisfied that Lennard von Olsberg is his brother's murderer. He's stopped the investigation. We're safe."

"I don't believe it," Theresa scoffed. "And men are impossible. You know nothing of them. You can't trust Baeder. He'll change his mind."

"I know men very well," Klara said. "You both made sure of that. It's you who don't understand. Why can't you let me be happy for as little or long as I can?"

Theresa's lips fell open, but Klara didn't let her speak.

"Yes, it's risky, but I can't steal my secret back. He knows. He'll always know, but I don't think he'll tell." Klara drew in a breath. "Besides, I'm not sure, when this is over, if I want to go on as I am."

"What do you mean?" her mother asked.

Levi looked at her closely. "She wants to be a woman," he said.

Klara sought her mother's eyes. "I'd like to try it."

Theresa shook her head. "You can't."

"This life is too lonely," Klara said.

Levi didn't argue, but her mother wasn't ready to give up. "What about all your studying? What about—"

"I've spent half my life learning to be who I'm not. I want to learn who I am."

"Perhaps you should when this is over," Levi said quietly. "But there are other reasons why you cannot be with Josef von Baeder." He forestalled her with an upraised hand. "Hear me out, Klara."

She sat, waiting for Levi to choose his words.

"I was in love once." He stared down at his hands. "My family knew. They understood me, though they hated me for it. We quarreled, they cut off my allowance, and I left, vowing never to go back. We came to Vienna."

Klara shifted onto her other foot. "Was she so objectionable?"

Levi looked up and smiled. "*He* was a painter. I know things are different with you and Baeder, but appearances…"

"We are both careful."

"You think you are, but you can never be careful enough. Matthias was everything to me, my best friend, until someone began speculating about us. Matthias was furious. He challenged the other man to a duel, and because I was afraid of what people might say, I never stopped him. They fought on a spring morning out in the Prater."

Klara waited, afraid of what he'd say next.

"Both were wounded, but Matthias died. I loved him, and I killed him with whispers. Will you risk doing the same?"

She couldn't. Even if it never went so far, she must not harm Josef.

"Think on it," Levi said.

"I will." Klara swallowed. "Is there anything else you wish to say?"

Levi shook his head.

"Then I'm going home." At the door, Klara hesitated. "I'm leaving by the back door and taking the long way. You should too, Levi. On the way here, I thought I was followed."

He wanted to question her but must have seen the tiredness in her face. "I will. You go on. Take some time to be alone."

She knew how to stay out of sight. So did he. Klara walked quietly down the stairs. Levi was always too kind…and too right.

CHAPTER 24

Theresa wanted to follow her daughter and would have, if not for Levi's restraining arm. "You can't mean to send her out alone. If she was followed here—"

"That is an easy matter for her to solve," Levi said. "Give her time with her thoughts."

Theresa subsided onto the couch, biting her bottom lip.

"We can advise. We can't choose for her," Levi said.

"I don't like it." She stared at the closed door. "Josef von Baeder is not the man for her, and if Lennard von Olsberg killed Marius, then I'm a trout."

"If the police think so, why not?"

Theresa shook her head, setting her curls swaying. "It feels wrong." She'd learned to heed her suspicions. She routinely put herself in the hands of strangers, and she paid attention when hairs rose on the back of her neck, even when she couldn't explain why. "Kasper shouldn't have been followed."

The police didn't know everything they should have, and she was to blame for it. One person had been left out of everyone's calculations, and this neglect was troubling her now, like a burr caught on her clothes, scratching her skin. "You and I need to find Marius's real wife. She has something to do with this." She spoke levelly, but the certainty she felt was frightening, reminding her of old dangers and the close escape she'd once had, long years before. Theresa nodded, the decision settling on her. "I mean to know how. And why."

KLARA WAS STANDING in front of the looking glass the next morning, inspecting the shape of her cravat when she heard someone clumping up the stairs.

"Ho, Kasper!"

Josef. Klara flew to the door of her apartment, shutting it behind her so Levi wouldn't hear.

"What are you doing?" Klara asked, hurrying down to the landing where Josef was resting his leg, balanced on a pair of crutches. "Send a servant for me. Don't kill yourself on these stairs." He shouldn't be up and about, especially this early in the morning.

Josef grinned.

"You shouldn't be here," Klara said, joining him all the same. "I'll help you outside."

"You need your hat. You're coming. I've rented a window where we can watch the parade. Everyone is going. You won't find a soul in the Hofburg." He saw her hesitating. "Anton can join us, if you like."

That would be safer, unless the smile she couldn't help gave them away.

"Come on. Don't argue."

She should, but she didn't. Instead, she dashed up the stairs for her hat. "It's just the parade," she explained to Levi in passing. There wouldn't be harm in that.

LEVI STAYED at the window after Klara left, worried by her light step as she'd jumped into Josef's carriage. Such ease of movement had always been a sign, for her, of happiness. He supposed it wouldn't hurt her to have some today. At least it spared him from explaining. He looked down and saw Theresa's coach.

He hurried outside.

"Are you ready? Does Kasper—"

Levi shook his head. "Kasper doesn't know." If they found something, they would tell her. No point in troubling her otherwise. She had enough to worry about.

Even here, the streets were swollen with parade goers, anxious to secure places on the broader roads where they could watch Emperor Francis escort the tsar and Prussian emperor into the city. For weeks, Levi had heard talk of this coming spectacle—there would be cannon, regiments of dragoons, drummers, pipers, and trumpets. The emperor would ride a white charger—no, in the gilded state coach, pulled by a dozen horses.

However it happened, Levi didn't care. He was too old to care about a parade celebrating a peace he feared wouldn't last. Moreover, he was anxious to be on the road to Meidling and outside Vienna. "What makes you think his wife has anything to do with this?" he asked.

Theresa frowned. "I don't know what lies she was told. Perhaps Olsberg bribed her or she thought he was dead, but—"

"The count wouldn't have had time to contact her after receiving Kasper's letter."

"I know. Still, she's the only one with whom the police haven't spoken, and she had good reason to kill him. He'd spent months in Vienna. We don't know, in that time, what either of them could have done."

They jolted over a rut in the road. Levi shifted on the frayed seat, though the springs in this hired carriage weren't terrible. He'd endured worse. "Are you sure you aren't imagining things?"

Her lips pressed together. "Perhaps."

He wouldn't have come if he hadn't seen her play hunches before with remarkable success. Still, he wanted a fuller explanation. "Why are you so worried?"

She shrugged. "I'd pass the information to the police if I could do it without implicating myself or Kasper—if I had a hope they'd believe me or care since they decided they've found their man. I'm acting on a suspicion, nothing more, but you know—" She paused. "Well, I told you once why I changed my name when I came to Vienna."

He and Theresa shared many secrets, but this was one they didn't talk about, so Levi answered slowly, his voice soft. "You didn't want your husband to find you." He didn't see what this had to do with Olsberg's discarded wife, unless…

Theresa fixed her eyes on the windows, but Levi didn't think she saw the eager faces crowding into high windows along this broad street or the throngs jostling along the pavements, bright with sprigs of greenery and festival clothes. Her hands were knotted together, her thumb sliding across the heavy sapphire ring ornamenting her forefinger. "We'd been married only a couple of years, but for months, I'd known he no longer loved me. I was desperate and unhappy but had no reason that night to be afraid. He came home late and stood at the door of my room—something he'd done often enough before. I was angry, wondering what woman's scent would cling to him, so I pretended I was asleep until he closed the door. Listening to him walk away, I realized he'd gone the wrong way—not to his room. To Klara's. Suddenly, for no reason I could think of, I was sick with fear, trembling, unable to breathe. I leaped out of bed and waited by my bedroom door, wondering if I should rush out, ready to do it at the least sound, but I heard nothing.

"It felt like hours before he passed by again, though it couldn't have been that long. As soon as I thought it safe, I crept into Klara's room. I couldn't see her in the dark, and I was too afraid to strike a light, but she was warm when I touched her and swaddled as neatly as I had left her. Her hair was damp with sweat, as it often was when she slept, and I could feel her breathing.

"I kept a bundle of lavender tied to the cradle to ease her sleep —it hung from a ribbon. It wasn't swaying, but it made no sense to me that he would come in just to look at her. He didn't like looking at her when she was awake. More and more, I felt Klara and I were encumbrances to him.

"I sat down on the floor beside her and stayed there all night, unable to explain why I had to stay, too frightened to leave her alone. I couldn't move her to my bed. She might have woken and made a sound."

Levi had heard the outline of Theresa's story before: withered love, broken hopes, an escape from violence. He hadn't probed because he'd assumed her husband beat her, but so far in her story, no harm had come to either of them. "And in the morning?"

"I pretended nothing was wrong. He came into my room, bringing breakfast on a tray. He kissed me and said he was sorry for quarreling. I held Klara on my lap and sipped the chocolate he'd brought and broke my roll into bits. He wanted to hold her, to see if she'd take chocolate from the cup or butter from his fingers, but I wouldn't let him. She was too small for that, and for once he didn't nag at me for not getting a wet nurse for her. Eating was impossible for me, so I nursed Klara and chattered. He let me, which told me more than ever that something was wrong. I nearly wept with relief when he took himself early to the cafés of the Palais Royale.

"As soon as he left, I ransacked the house. I found scraps of a burned letter, nothing else, yet I couldn't wait, couldn't even sit still. I packed a valise, took Klara, and left."

Levi frowned. Was that all? All these years she'd been so careful of her real name. Perhaps she'd overreacted.

"I made it as far as Montmartre before I took ill," she went on, her voice level. "He'd poisoned my chocolate. I took an emetic and nearly killed myself with vomiting, but if I hadn't been so worried that morning, I'd have drunk all the chocolate and died in our rooms. And Klara—"

She turned away from the window and met his eyes. "I might be wrong today. This might just be a silly feeling."

"I hope so," Levi said. "But there's no harm in making sure."

He'd been so angry with her when she decided to blackmail Olsberg, scornful of a foolish attempt to punish another woman's faithless husband because she couldn't take revenge on her own. He'd been wrong. Oh, the blackmail had been a dangerous mistake, but she hadn't done it for herself. In a blunt, foolish way, she'd seen it as a chance to balance the scales for Klara. He'd misjudged her. He hadn't known she was still so troubled by what had gone before or that she was still afraid.

They rolled out of the city and into the woods surrounding Vienna.

CHAPTER 25

Josef had rented a first-floor window of a house fronting the route of the parade. Klara helped him out of the coach and into the house, his arm slung over her shoulder. "Wish I'd taken a window on the second floor. I could keep you here longer," he whispered, as Klara slipped away from his side.

"You still look pale," she told him, hastening across the room to the chairs the owners had set out for them. There were four, with a padded footstool in front of one of them.

"The surgeon says my wound is coming along well, but you're welcome to look later. How's your own?"

"Nearly forgotten." Her wound didn't trouble her, not as much as Josef's offer or his grimace as he lifted his leg onto the footstool. That was painful to watch, for it was her fault.

He settled back into the chair, smiling so boldly Klara had to turn her eyes to the window. Eventually, she'd have to tell him their affair was too dangerous but now didn't seem like the time.

"I ought to thank you, you know," he said, patting his thigh. "If not for this, I'd have to ride with my regiment in the parade, and it's going be slow going, even if the three monarchs finish trading compliments in under an hour and actually set out on time. Wouldn't wager any money on it."

"It will be hot," Klara said, gauging the sky, pitying the spectators on the street, who'd be standing some hours yet. The parade wasn't supposed to set out until noon. To pass the time, Josef sent for wine and cigars. Klara accepted both, earning a smile. It was absurd to feel guilt or pleasure, let alone awash in both. "You offered. I'm used to tobacco. Don't be surprised."

"You always surprise me," he said, striking a match. "It's delightful."

"Don't be ridiculous," Klara said. "When you know me better, you'll be bored." She exhaled a stream of smoke, hoping it would steady her. "I give you a week."

"I'll take that week. I'll take as many days as you'll give me, once I'm in better health. It would be a sad waste now."

Klara stared at the ash on the end of her cigar. "Is Spaller coming?" she asked, wanting a distraction. Their conversation was pitched too low for any ears but their own, but someone in the street might notice him staring, and she felt a blush creeping over her ears.

"Any minute." He sighed. "Don't worry. I'll behave myself."

He did, perfectly, except for the occasional aside only she could catch. Anton didn't notice, nor did the newly arrived occupant of the fourth chair, a colonel in Josef's regiment. He also was excused from parade duty on account of an injury, though his had been taken in the spring. He listened with interest to Anton recounting the duel, snorting when Josef downplayed the events.

"It was very high-handed," Klara said for Anton and the colonel's benefit. "I haven't forgiven him."

"Don't. He's insufferable enough already. There was a time in Italy—"

Klara didn't want to hear about Josef's troubles in Italy, which all revolved around women. Josef wasn't eager for them either.

"Not today, Reuter. Spaller here thinks I'm a decent sort, and I like it enough to give it a try," he said.

Colonel Reuter snorted but was distracted by Josef mentioning the reception that was to follow the parade at the Hofburg.

Closer to midafternoon than midday, the sound of distant cannon roused the wilting crowd. Heads turned, shoulders jostled, and people stood on tiptoe, straining for a look, but as yet there was nothing but a tremor in the air, a quiver of excitement. At last, the procession appeared. Cheers swelled, blotting out the sound of the drums and the trumpets. At the head of a troop of Hungarian hussars rode Prince Esterhazy, his great helmet lost within a fall of white plumes, the enormous jewel on his chest blinding in the sunlight. His boots were adorned with pearls.

Behind him came rank upon rank of silent, bearlike hussars, their shoulders square, their sabers bright. Next a flotilla of generals in rainbow colors, bristling with medals and arms, then an unending sea of Austrian regiments. When at last they came, the monarchs seemed few and small, in spite of their horses and plumes and uniforms, unquestionably the finest of all. But the crowd screamed approval, and the three rulers smiled wise benisons.

"They might not like each other so much in three weeks," Josef said, but Klara barely heard him.

It was something of an anticlimax to feel the drums fade and see the disorganized mill of the crowd spilling into the empty street.

"I can't go to the reception," Josef said. "Much as I hate to admit it, I must rest my leg. Spaller, will you take my invitation? You could go with Reuter."

Anton accepted gladly and the two headed off, leaving Klara and Josef alone.

"I should go." She could walk from here. It wasn't far, and Josef looked pained and tired.

"Not yet." Climbing stiffly from his seat, he fumbled with his waistcoat pocket. "I have something for you." He brought out his hand and dropped something into Klara's outstretched palm. A key. "So you can come and go without anyone knowing," he said.

It was time to tell him, to at least hint that things couldn't go on as they'd begun. "Josef—"

He glanced at her, then at the window. "Come with me."

She shouldn't. The longer she put off telling him the harder it would be, but speaking now was too much for her. Better to leave as soon as she'd helped him down the stairs.

Klara went with him into the street, fighting herself and losing. She stayed to see him into the carriage, and then she was climbing inside and sitting beside him. When they reached his house, she offered her arm, which he took, bringing her up the steps and inside.

To hell with it. Klara removed her hat and followed Josef into the drawing room, where her mother stood facing the fire.

KLARA WAS SPEECHLESS, but Josef only missed a step before he recovered. "Fräulein Vogl, what a surprise."

Theresa grimaced. "Forgive me for coming uninvited," she said. "I hate to intrude."

"Why are you here?" Klara demanded, her face hot.

"I imagine, schätzen, she has something to say to me." Josef crossed the room and arranged himself in a chair, stretching out his injured leg. "It would lessen the theatrics, perhaps, if we all sat down."

Theresa tossed her curls over her shoulder and sat, taking the time to arrange her skirts more becomingly. Klara took the chair beside Josef, fists tight, hating her mother. Josef, damn him, looked amused.

"Can this wait?" Klara growled.

"No. I've been looking everywhere for you."

Josef steepled his fingers. "How can I help you, Fräulein?"

"Don't. You know why she's come," Klara said.

"Not at all." He sounded as if he was trying to suppress a laugh. "I've certainly never been in a situation like this before."

Theresa glared at him. "I haven't come about you. I've just returned from Meidling. Levi and I went, but when we came back, we couldn't find you at home. He stayed, and I came searching."

"And found her. Well done, madam."

Klara quieted him with a look. She felt uneasy. "Why were you in Meidling?"

"To see Marius von Olsberg's wife."

"The countess is in Hetzendorf," Josef said. "Close, I grant you, but—"

Theresa clapped a hand over her mouth.

"What is it?" Klara asked. She glanced at Josef, wondering if she could ask him to leave.

"I'm not going," he warned.

Theresa's eyes were huge. "Sonia von Olsberg is there?"

"She told me she was leaving Vienna yesterday. What of it?"

"I didn't say *she* was in Meidling," Theresa said at last. "I said I was looking for Marius's wife."

Josef turned to Klara. "What haven't you told me?" When all she gave him was a panicked look, he asked again, his voice hard.

It was difficult to breathe, let alone speak. Klara unbuttoned her waistcoat and tugged out her shirt.

"I prefer you in as little clothing as possible, but intimacies in front of your mother are too much for me," Josef said.

"I've something to show you. Not me," Klara added hastily, fumbling beneath her corset for the packet hidden next to her blade. She drew it out and tore open the stitches, unfolding the creased sheet. It was warm from being so close to her skin. "He married two women, but—"

"Only the first one matters." Josef snatched the paper from her outstretched hand. "Where did you find this?"

"I did," Theresa said and told him how, until she got to the part Klara dreaded. Alerted by her tension, Theresa stopped.

"I was blackmailing Marius von Olsberg," Klara confessed quietly. "Not the other way around. That's why he met me at St. Stephen's."

"You knew about this woman—this other wife!—and said nothing?" Josef's lips had gone white.

"I couldn't admit it without giving myself away. I didn't think it mattered. You said Sonia couldn't have killed him."

"But this woman could have," he snapped. He thrust the paper at her, then changed his mind and crammed it into his coat pocket, moving as jerkily as a puppet.

"She didn't," Theresa said. "I found her in Meidling. Dead."

"When? How?"

"This morning." Theresa took a breath. "She was garroted in her chair. The man who believed himself her husband was working in the shop downstairs. A nice man. When I arrived, he'd remarked how pleasant it must be for his wife to have so many visitors. I didn't think—" She gathered herself again. "Another woman had called before me. She left scarcely half an hour before I came. I didn't recognize the name she gave, but—"

"It was a false one."

Theresa nodded. "The man said she was well dressed. Brown hair. Beautiful."

Josef raised a hand to his forehead, shielding his eyes. Theresa's description could fit many women, but because it suited Sonia von Olsberg, why would it be anyone else?

"Could she have killed Marius?' Klara asked.

"I don't know." Josef paced the room. Klara said nothing, remembering how she'd slipped from his bed while he was sleeping. Josef had noticed her absence before long. Sonia von Olsberg wouldn't have had much time, but perhaps it had been enough. "You should have told me," Josef said. "If I'd known…"

Klara looked away. It hurt to meet his eyes. "We might have stopped her."

If she'd told, the woman in Meidling might still be alive. Maybe. Perhaps. Klara shut her eyes, hating such indeterminate words, weak and wispy against death, the surest word of all.

"I don't know if she killed them, but it's possible. We have to find her." Josef picked up his hat and started for the hall.

She hurried after him. "Sonia? In Hetzendorf?" A clever woman would be on her way out of the country by now. "She could be anywhere."

Josef shook his head. "She'll come to us if we have her children." In spite of his limp, he sped down the hall, calling for his servants to summon his coach. "I want at least two of you with me—yes, I'll take Peter and Jacob. Quickly."

She couldn't tell if he was too busy to look at her of if he simply didn't want to.

"Wait, Josef! I'm coming." Klara rushed after him, through the door, and into the carriage. She turned around to offer Josef her arm. His face was set. Ignoring her hand, he reached for the strap and climbed aboard the carriage without a wince or a mutter—as if he felt nothing at all.

CHAPTER 26

Alone in Josef von Baeder's drawing room, Theresa wasn't sure what she should do. She almost thought they'd forgotten her.

At least the problems of Elke Fechter, the dead woman, and Sonia von Olsberg were now in the hands of the police. Theresa was more worried about Klara and Josef von Baeder. She'd prayed and prayed not to find her daughter here, knowing it was the only place to look.

Klara hated her now and was more in love with Baeder than any sensible creature should be. Where that man was concerned, naturally women found it impossible to be sensible, but it was incomprehensible to Theresa that her quick-thinking daughter could have made such a catastrophic mistake. They would have to leave and start over someplace new. It was the only thing to do in these circumstances, and the sooner the better.

With a regal nod, Theresa accepted the offer of Baeder's servant to call her a coach. She left the house, her mind too far away to notice the small boy who dropped out of the shadows behind the front steps and took off running.

He was quick. By the time Theresa returned home, the boy's master was in her boudoir, waiting for her.

Though startled, Theresa hid it well. "What a delightful surprise!" She walked into the room, stripping off her gloves, and bent to kiss Baron von Hagen. "I didn't expect to see you after you canceled our meeting last night. How nice you've found time today. Were you waiting long?"

"I only just arrived."

In fact, he sounded slightly breathless, and though it was tempting to ascribe that to her presence, Theresa suspected it was from hurrying up the stairs. She sat down on the carpet next to his knees and reached up for his hands. "I missed you."

He smiled at her. "Have you? I'd have thought you were too busy."

The remark was sharp enough to alarm her. So far, Baron von Hagen had proven a considerate lover: frequent and punctual with his appointments, unselfish in bed, witty in his conversation. He was attentive, in his own methodical way, and unexpectedly romantic. In the span of a week, he'd given her a beautiful bracelet and some poetry. The pedantic meter and valiantly striving lines convinced her he'd written it himself. If he was not so careless with his secrets as she'd hoped, she couldn't blame him.

She'd never expected Franz to be jealous—indeed, she'd hardly seen anyone else since he'd responded to her invitation that day in the Prater, so he had little cause to be. "I don't understand you," she said.

"You called on my nephew this afternoon."

Careful now. Theresa straightened her shoulders. "You were following me?"

"Not at all. I was following Kasper Stark."

"I don't know him." Theresa tossed her head.

"I think you must, because I'm certain you don't know my nephew."

Theresa was confident that Franz liked her, but if she was forced to plead for her daughter's life, she knew he wouldn't listen. No concern could ever surmount the interests and security of the House of Habsburg. The skin on her arms prickled.

Hagen noticed, gently caressing her. Typically, Theresa enjoyed his patience, his focused attention, the slowly mounting heat. It was tiresome having to pretend enthusiasm, and with Hagen, she never had to. This was different. He wanted answers she could never give. "Are you interrogating me?" She laughed, sure now what to do. She must turn this into a game.

"You're a clever and beautiful woman, leibchen. Don't ignore your instincts. I never do."

"Never?" She pushed herself close, and he enveloped her, as she intended. Before she captured the reassurance she sought with skin, hands, and mouth, he pulled away.

"You are an artist," he said, sweeping a careless hand through her hair. "And I'm a man with a job."

Theresa focused on his eyes, patient within the weary lines, and today, almost terrifying.

"Comets don't circle moons, leibchen. I limp. I don't scintillate at parties with my clever *bon mots*. You could do better."

"Don't be absurd, Franz." She trailed a hand down his cheek and leaned forward to kiss him. He stopped her.

"You could do better if you wanted to."

Theresa smiled. "Clearly, I don't."

"I'm a careful man. I have to be. I laid all kinds of traps for you," he said. "Don't look so alarmed. What did you expect?"

"Too much, obviously." She pushed herself away, but he caught her by the arm.

"Everyone works for someone, even if it's only themselves," Hagen said. "I hid the most wonderful forgeries for you to find—letters designed for Bonapartist sympathizers, for Russian radicals, for the beleaguered allies of the King of Saxony. You looked at some of them, didn't you?" He tapped a finger on her nose.

"But you never stole a single one or whispered my beautiful lies anywhere. It is truly remarkable."

One of the hazards of an opera career was acquiring the habit of wringing your hands. Theresa forced hers to keep still. "Some games I don't play," she said.

"Then why step into a trap for Kasper Stark? What does he mean to you? What is so urgent that you would expose yourself to contact him? He is involved in something, and I know it is important because you will not say. I will find out, leibchen. Someone is following them."

"You'll know soon enough, then, but not from me." Theresa sat back on her heels. This time, he let her slip from his grasp.

"I haven't told you what I'm willing to pay yet. I'm sure we can negotiate something." His fingers fitted together, the light gleaming off his heavy gold ring.

Theresa shook her head. She would say nothing.

"You have so many gifts. I would hate to send you to prison. I could offer you a kind of security working for me, but I would need your allegiance, your entire confidence."

"I cannot."

"Why? Is someone threatening you?"

"Just you."

He smiled. "I respect your intelligence."

"I have nothing to tell."

"Nothing?" He leaned back on the sofa, watching her over his steepled fingers. "Then I have a story for you. There once was a vixen, a very clever one, but one day she got caught in a trap. The farmer who'd set it promised he'd release her if she'd show him her den. But the vixen wouldn't, and that told him all along what he wanted to know." He smiled. "The den had pups in it. It took the farmer some time, but he found the den and caught the pups, every one. The mother could do nothing, because she was caught in his trap. There is only one kind of person, Theresa, for whom I can imagine you being so reckless."

Theresa refused to blink. She only stared at him and pressed her lips together.

"Do you still not want to tell me?" When she didn't answer, he sighed. "You'll have to come with me."

Theresa went, meek-faced and silent, reminding herself he hadn't won. If he had proof, he'd have used it. He didn't know about the poison she kept hidden inside the ring on the forefinger of her left hand. This match was hers if she took herself out of it. He didn't have Klara yet.

Levi Braun paced anxiously through the familiar rooms of the apartment near the Fleischmarkt. Everything was ready if he and Klara needed to run. His savings, an old ring, and his watch were safely tucked away in his coat pockets; the forged passports were next to an old but lovingly tended pistol inside a battered valise. The pistol was loaded. He'd been ready almost an hour and a half, but Klara didn't come, and he'd heard nothing from Theresa.

He picked up a jug of water and moistened the soil of the plants he kept on the windowsill, not liking the gray tinge in his hands. They were old hands, wrinkled and prone to cold. He had aches in his back now and in his knees. He set down the jug and picked off a few dead leaves.

A soft thud and a stir in the air made him pause. He didn't turn around. Only Klara was that quiet. His mouth softened into a smile. "You're back. Did your mother find you?"

He heard her crossing the room, but she said nothing—no quip, no curses, not even a resigned sigh. Levi turned around. The dead leaf fell from his nerveless hand.

The muffled sounds that followed disturbed no one, not even the mice who lived beneath the floors.

CHAPTER 27

Josef wouldn't speak. He wouldn't even look at her, staring instead at the parade goers still filling the streets. It was growing dark.

"I should have told you," she said in a low voice.

He didn't answer.

"Are you angry with me?"

His chin sank and rose a fraction of an inch. "And with myself. I should have seen. But why didn't I wake? I never felt her leave. I—"

"If she was listening for his return, it wouldn't have taken her long." Klara swallowed. "Is she strong?"

"She's not like you, trained to fight. *You* could have killed him."

"He nearly killed me," Klara countered.

He laughed. "So you say."

"It's true."

A muscle jumped in his cheek. "How many times have you lied to me?"

"Everything I am is lies," Klara retorted. "If you didn't guess after what you knew—"

"I'm a fool, as you've abundantly proved. We needn't argue that." He folded his arms. "Sonia's more like you than I thought."

"I'm not a killer," Klara said.

"She wasn't either, until you began dealing in secrets."

"This is my fault?"

He was still talking, not heeding her. "It wouldn't have needed much strength to kill her husband if she took him by surprise. Sonia could have done it, if she was desperate enough."

"Isn't she? To save herself and her sons?"

"Yes, if only I'd known it."

Klara looked down at her lap.

"Your mother stole those marriage lines from Mariahilfer kirche," Josef said. "I found Sonia there, you know, talking to the priest. I didn't even think why. She came at me, all breathless kisses and sweetness—she was trying to distract me, and she did." He scowled. "And that gravedigger—Gunter Kissling—she must have killed him too. She had watchers on her, but the same day Hagen went to see her, she visited St. Stephen's. To pray, she said. I don't know how she managed it, but I intend to find out."

"She had to keep the secret," Klara said, imagining Sonia arranging a meeting, then creeping up on Gunter in the dark.

Josef's eyes swiveled to hers. His gaze was as threatening as the mouth of a gun. "Like you."

Retreating into herself, Klara bore the accusation in silence. There was nothing she could say.

AT THE HOUSE, Josef disembarked without saying anything and charged up the stairs. Though it was late in the day, he pounded on the door of the house an unusually long time.

"Sir?" A breathless maid came to the door, not a manservant. There was no sign of the landlady.

"Is the countess at home?" Klara asked.

The maid shook her head.

"Her children?"

"Sir, I—"

Josef shouldered past. Grabbing the railing, he limped grimly up the stairs.

"Sir!"

"Leave him alone," Klara said, and the maid shrank away, trying to fade into the wallpaper. Klara started up the stairs, motioning Josef's two footmen to follow. Somehow, she must quiet Josef or calm him. If the children were here, they'd be frightened.

Josef strode down the corridor, flinging open doors. "Sonia!"

"She's not here," Klara reminded him, but he only swore under his breath.

The children were behind the second to last door, cowering in the arms of their nurse, beside their corded trunks.

"Where is their mother?" Josef asked.

"W-We are to join her tomorrow. When she leaves Hetzendorf," the nurse answered.

Josef swore again. "Stay here," he ordered the footmen. "Don't let them leave the house. When they do not arrive as planned, she'll come back to find out what's wrong. Don't let her escape." He stormed from the room, ignoring the whispers that rolled like distant thunder behind him.

"We'll find her," Josef vowed, once he and Klara were back in the carriage.

Klara drew in a breath. "We'll have to alert the tollkeepers and the police."

"And my uncle." He stared levelly at her.

"I know." Klara slid her hands over her knees to take the sweat off her palms. "Josef—"

He flinched at the sound of his name. Klara tried again, without it this time. "He'll want to know how you came by the church register and why it wasn't discovered by now. He'll have to know about Elke Fechter and me, but he doesn't need to know about my mother." She swallowed. "What will you tell him?"

"I don't know. As little as I can."

Klara's grip tightened on the strap hanging from the roof of the carriage. They would bounce right off the road at this pace. "Thank you."

"What will you do?"

Run, if he wasn't going to drag her in front of Baron von Hagen. "I must leave Vienna." Everything had crumbled, but if she started now, there was time to escape. "Will you let me out here?" She didn't know where she was, but it hardly mattered.

"What about your mother and Levi?"

"I'll tell Levi. Will you get word to my mother? She'll know how to find me once it is safe."

"Do you have money?"

She shrugged. "Some." Enough to get her a little distance away, but she'd go farther if she stopped at home. "Please stop the coach."

"I can't." He stared at her with a look she couldn't understand. "Don't run. Not yet. Once you do, you can't come back."

"Your uncle will know! This story won't hold if I'm not in it."

"I'll tell him something else, make up some story, cast Gunter Kissling as the blackmailer. At least let me try. Please, schätzen."

It was hard to think. The air was so thick and she felt so cold. Josef's coat buttons moved with the force of his breathing. "You want to keep me? After all this?" Her voice threatened to break, but she made herself meet his eyes. They didn't turn away.

"Yes, God help me. Please let me try."

"You're mad."

"I know." He crossed the space between them to kiss her, though she still wore her mustache.

It was dark when Josef thumped on the roof and ordered the carriage to stop. "Stay hidden," he whispered. "Give me time to speak to my uncle. I'll know soon if it's safe."

"And if it isn't?"

"Just watch for my sign." He hesitated. "If you don't see it within the next two days, find a safe place somewhere. And don't forget me."

"You know I'll never do that." She blinked at him, hoping the shine in her eyes wasn't visible in the dim light of the lamps. She pressed his hands and climbed from the carriage, lifting a hand in farewell as it rolled away.

CHAPTER 28

Klara was halfway home when she remembered that yesterday she might have been followed. She glanced back, but there was nothing to learn from the shifting, faceless crowd. Still, she'd be careful. Darting into the nearest alley, she trekked aimlessly through the maze of streets until she was certain no one was on her trail. Then she took a zigzag route to her rooms.

Gripped by the need for caution, she waited almost a quarter hour in the street. The house was quiet, save for the lights upstairs. Levi was home. Everyone else must have gone to the celebrations after the parade. It was dark. Soon, the palaces would be lit up with fireworks. There would be cannon and music.

Once she had her things, it wouldn't be hard to lose herself amid such excitement. Glancing sideways to make sure the narrow street was empty, Klara darted inside the house. The only sounds were purposeful, and they came from upstairs. Levi must be busy with something. Klara hurried up the stairs and nudged aside the door.

She almost stepped back into the hall. This couldn't be her apartment. Torn-up boards littered what remained of the floor. The few pictures were ripped from the walls, the canvases slashed. The wooden chairs were kindling and—

That couldn't be a shoe, sticking out from behind the overturned table.

It was. It was Levi's. She knew that sensible buckle and bright black shine, knew the heel that was worn on the inside. Klara's breath left her like she'd been punched. She picked her way over the rubble, not looking at anything save the shoe, though there was a stocking too and the atrophying muscle of a sixty-seven-year-old within it.

Her hand caught at the back of the disemboweled armchair that was no longer blocking her view. She didn't want to see. Her fingers clenched and her legs threatened to buckle as she tried to deny the livid purple swelling that disfigured Levi's face. The clever, kind man she loved, who'd used this body to think, talk, and laugh, was gone. Klara whimpered and dropped to her knees, ducking to the ground when something moved behind her. She rolled instinctively, just in time to see something bright and blue whisk past her. It was a silk cord, the kind used to fasten a cloak.

Scrambling backward, closer to Levi, she looked up as Sonia von Olsberg lunged for her. Klara struck out with a foot, and the countess doubled over. Her face contorted with pain, but she straightened again before Klara had time to stand. Klara didn't want to tread on Levi's slack arm, though she knew he was beyond pain. She didn't want this woman any closer to him either. Klara's empty hands curled, and her lips drew back in a snarl.

Then the countess drew something from the pocket of her traveling skirts: a pistol. The barrel leveled with Klara's eyes only a few yards away, terrifyingly steady. Klara's surge of ferocity fled like it had never been. "You killed him." Her voice trembled like a child's.

"He saw me. I had to search because you weren't here to tell me." Her head tilted to one side. "Give me the page from the register."

Klara stared dumbly.

"I know you have it." The countess drew something from her bodice. It was the note Klara had long ago given up hope of finding. "This is your writing. It matches the report I received yesterday. I asked Herr Spaller who had written it. He told me it was you."

Klara watched the countess fold the paper one-handed and tuck it away. The gun never wavered. "How did you get that?"

"Marius received it at the opera. I could tell it upset him. I took it from his pocket before he left. Now give me the page from the register. I won't ask again."

Klara was fumbling beneath her shirt before reason caught up with her. By then, it was too late to compose her face.

The countess exhaled, a long hiss. "You don't have it."

There was no point in lying. "Josef von Baeder does. He'll have shown it to Herr Hagen by now." Klara looked her square in the eye. Sonia von Olsberg could kill her and probably would, but it wouldn't save her. "You're too late. You won't escape Vienna," Klara told her. "And your sons—"

The countess cocked the pistol.

Klara closed her eyes. She should have lied, pretended the paper was hidden somewhere. Then she could—

An explosion shook the walls. Klara cowered behind arms she couldn't recall raising, waiting for pain to knock her to the ruined floor. It didn't happen, so she opened her eyes. The countess had taken a step closer. She still held the gun.

Another crackle of thunder. Fireworks, Klara realized. The countess came closer, unwilling to miss. Three more steps, and the gun would be right at Klara's forehead. Klara caved in on herself like someone broken by fear. Most of her was, but above the jittery, impossible tremors, a piece of her mind was clear. The countess had only one shot.

Klara slumped in defeat, the movement covering her tensing muscles. She fixed her eyes on the countess's riding boots. She couldn't see the pistol or know how quick the countess was with it, but that hardly mattered. She had one chance and would take it, no matter the odds. The countess's wine-colored skirts swayed as her feet braced on an intact patch of floor, within reach at last.

Klara sprung, her breath so loud she almost didn't hear the shot. She grappled the countess's legs, bowling her to the floor. As she crashed down and the gun skidded away, Klara smelled powder. Something had slammed into her side. Black closed around her, the edges of her vision aglitter with twinkling lights. She couldn't breathe.

Scrabbling sounds—her? No. Klara's eyes cleared. The countess was scrambling away, fumbling for her cord. Another bang made Klara shudder, but it didn't strike her with the force of a carriage wheel, only preceding another barrage of fireworks.

Don't let the sounds distract you. Sonia von Olsberg was coming for her again. Klara staggered to her feet, then realized her hands were empty. She should have grabbed something, but it would have to be with her right—the left arm wasn't obeying. Later, she could wonder why she felt only deadness there, not pain.

Klara struggled to stay upright as they circled the ruined furniture, her eyes on the cord looped around the countess's fingers. She mirrored Klara's every move, inch for inch. Blackness threatened to swallow Klara again, and she retreated, almost stumbling on Levi. The countess sprang forward, and Klara had to blunder over the upturned table, taking refuge behind the torn-up chair.

Soon, she'd succumb and faint or fall. This slow, stalking game was one she could only lose. Her strength was fading, and the countess just beginning to fight. If Klara let her get close, she'd overpower her.

Klara's good hand closed on a piece of broken floor. It was too wide and too long to wield well single-handedly, but it was something. Releasing a yell, Klara ran, swinging her bit of board like a farmer's scythe. She struck the countess on the arm and slammed her head on the backswing, forcing her back. Still shouting, Klara leaped forward, her next swipe clobbering Sonia von Olsberg in the face. The countess staggered, taking another blow on her right shoulder as she fell. Terrified, her strength leaking away, Klara advanced, planting her heel on the countess's chest, still flailing with her improvised weapon. As Klara's grunts turned to gasps, she realized the countess was no longer moving, and the blows made a terrible sound. Klara sagged, unable to lift her arm again.

Nobody moved, but it took some time before Klara could raise her eyes to stare at Sonia von Olsberg's blood-matted hair and misshapen face. She was as limp as Levi.

The board fell with a clatter as Klara turned away, struggling to breathe. She needed something to lean on—not her broken furniture, not the window next to Levi's ferns, surely the only undisturbed things in the room. She couldn't think why Sonia von Olsberg hadn't uprooted the plants and strewn them over the floor. She'd destroyed everything else.

Klara tried to swipe her left hand over her face and almost crumpled, blind with pain. Gasping, she tried again with the right and succeeded, but tears kept coming, so what was the point? A noise behind her made Klara turn wearily. She had no weapon and was incapable of fighting anymore.

All she met was her landlady's terrified stare. Blank herself, Klara watched the landlady gather herself until, with a scream, she turned and ran away, echoing down the stairs.

God help me.

She mustn't stay, but moving was nigh impossible. Half her coat was soaked with blood, and she was so inundated with pain there was no knowing exactly where it came from.

Walk, she told herself, and with the help of the wall and then the bannister, she succeeded in making her way to the bottom of the stairs.

The frantic landlady tried to head her off in the downstairs hall.

"Let me pass," Klara said, and the screams were swallowed in one frightened gulp. Shouldering past her, Klara staggered into the street.

It was a clear night with stars and fireworks that made her flinch, yet Klara's mind was clouded. A breeze ruffled her hair. She realized she was shivering. How was it possible to burn with pain yet be numb with cold?

She walked away from the river, south and west, as carefully as any of the drunks picking their way from tavern to tavern or tavern to home. Home—was that where she was going? She shook her head, trying to clear it. There was no place for her. Not anywhere.

Yet when she came to Josef's house, it did not surprise her to see his beacon in the window. She was safe. Klara closed her eyes for a moment, drew a long breath, then tottered forward and let herself inside, glad Josef had given her a key. In spite of her relief, the numbness was winning. Since she felt almost nothing, she was able to walk unaided to the library, where she saw a fire burning through the open door. Josef was leaning against the mantelpiece, his back toward her, one booted foot propped on the fender. Outlined by firelight, he looked lonely. And beautiful.

She knew he wasn't particular about his upholstery. Whisper quiet on the carpet, she came into the room and veered toward the couch. "I'm afraid I'll need to put myself in your hands for a while," she said in a hoarse whisper.

Josef gaped at her, but he didn't come, and in any case, Klara's eyes were no longer on him. Someone was turning in the tall armchair, setting down a half-filled glass next to a plate of cake.

Hagen looked at her without blinking. "So I see."

Klara looked at Josef, who licked his lips and said nothing. "You promised you wouldn't tell," she said, but in her mind, the words were different: *I thought you loved me.*

Hagen rose to his feet. "Send for a doctor."

Josef walked out.

CHAPTER 29

Hagen ate his cake while the doctor unpacked his bag and prepared to attend her. Klara endured, ignoring the catlike smile Hagen couldn't hide between bites. She could tell he already knew, but the doctor didn't, suddenly stepping away from her as he uncovered her strapping.

"Sir?" The physician was uncertain now, his hands spread wide like he feared taking blame.

Hagen waved an indifferent hand. "Carry on. Your business is with the wound, nothing else."

The doctor muttered something under his breath. Klara downed all the medicinal spirits he gave her but still fainted when he began to probe. When she woke, it was done. She was wearing something long and loose and laid out on a clean bed. Abandoning the struggle to lift her eyelids, Klara listened instead, but the whispered conference was too hard to hear.

"Your questions can wait until tomorrow," Hagen said, raising his voice suddenly. He must have noticed her eyelids fluttering. "Go back to sleep."

Klara didn't want to obey, but she couldn't help it.

LIGHT FILLED the room when she woke again. Klara stirred and realized movement was possible. Last time, it hadn't been.

"They dug the ball out of your shoulder. Nothing's broken. You'll be fit again in no time."

Klara turned her head away from the window. Hagen sat in a chair beside her bed, reading a sheaf of papers.

"Are you thirsty?" He stood and held a glass of water to her lips. Klara thought it might be drugged, but if it was, there was nothing she could do about it. She watched Hagen over the rim of the glass.

"Josef has tidied things at your apartment."

Klara let her head fall back into the pillows. She swallowed twice before she could speak. "What about Levi?"

"Your servant? He will be properly buried."

"He's Jewish," Klara said. It was important.

"That can be accommodated."

Klara closed her eyes, hoping it might make Hagen leave but knowing it wouldn't. He would speak when he was ready, and there was no point asking until then. The silence stretched until it all but sang, making her increasingly uncomfortable. Even through her eyelids, she felt his lizard-like gaze.

"You have such admirable nerve," he said. "A quality I think you get from your mother."

It was demeaning to show surprise. Klara kept her eyes shut. "Did Josef tell you?" It would be good to know how much blame to lay at his door.

"No. Nor did Fräulein Vogl. That, I was able to guess. What a person doesn't say is often more revealing than what they do, and she refused to betray you or explain your connection. Of course, I already suspected you were a woman. There's a certain look Josef reserves for his."

This time, her eyes fluttered open. "How childish of him."

"Not very. It took some time to decipher it. You were careful, but not careful enough."

The admonition reminded her of Levi. She couldn't speak.

"When you came in bleeding, he went whiter than I've ever seen," Hagen mused. "I knew what happened must have been gruesome, but—"

He might still be talking, but Klara wasn't listening. That battered face…

"Given your injury, you dispatched her with surprising efficiency." Hagen sounded pleased.

If it was a compliment, she didn't want to acknowledge it. "What becomes of the children? The countess's boys?"

He smiled. "This is the beautiful part. We reveal the proof of Olsberg's bigamous marriage. The children are illegitimate. The title devolves on a cousin—you don't need to know his name, only that he will be grateful to me and to Austria."

"But the boys?"

"Someone will look after them. They won't starve."

But they were orphaned. Alone.

"You're not concerned about the fate of Kasper Stark?" Hagen asked.

"Should I be?" She shifted her head on the pillows so she could see him better. It didn't make reading him any easier.

"You understand, of course, that we cannot allow the countess's death to go unpunished. Unfortunately, Herr Stark chose to shoot himself rather than surrender to the police. We think he might have blackmailed the lady into an affair—but that will never be more than a rumor."

Klara grimaced. "I see."

"Do you?"

"You have plans for me."

"Assuredly. But you must mend first." He poured out another glass of water. "In future, when you write threatening and incriminating letters, you will want to disguise your handwriting."

Klara wasn't sure what she was feeling, but an acid brew of emotion was rising in her throat. She couldn't bear for Hagen to see. "I knew that letter would get me in trouble," she said, trying for a smile and knowing it hadn't come off.

Hagen folded his hands over his stomach and sat back in his chair. "It was a careless mistake. Next time, you'll be more careful."

"Suppose I don't wish to."

"Well, I suppose we could arrest Kasper Stark if we had to. We have some very able men. Perhaps one was able to stop him before he pulled the trigger—or made him miss."

"You'd charge me with murder?"

"Only if I had to. You are born for this. You'll see." He grunted. "Better now than later. Josef's affairs never last long."

Klara lifted one eyelid to glare at him. He chuckled. "You're better at this than you think. He didn't realize until I was grilling him for details that he doesn't know your real name. He said he always called you—"

"Schätzen," Klara interrupted, desperate to prevent Hagen from saying it, but he repeated the endearment anyway, making it ugly in her ears.

"It's an excellent name for an agent. You are a treasure. I can put you anywhere." He was almost gloating.

Klara slid her hands farther beneath the sheet, afraid he would see the skin prickling on her arms. "You mentioned my mother."

"Yes, she's quite upset with me. When you're able to, you must pen her a letter. Tell her I have you safe and that all is well."

"Will that be the truth?"

"My dear, that's entirely up to you. Write it, and I will see it delivered."

Promises, even in the form of threats, were probably the best she could hope for. She would write the letter and hope her mother understood. In time, it might be possible to get a real message to her.

Hagen stood and bent over her glass, a paper packet in his hand. A white powder fell into the water in a long, snowy stream. Hagen rattled a spoon in the glass until the snowstorm turned invisible. "Time to sleep, schätzen. Tomorrow, I'll send you away from Vienna. Not far, never fear. I must have you trained for what lies ahead."

He held the glass to her mouth, watching her swallow every drop. There was no escape.

KLARA WOKE SLOWLY, and again the sun was warm on her face, a circumstance that took time to penetrate her bleary thoughts. When it did, her eyes flew open. She lurched upright—or tried to. Pain reminded her of her injury and all that had befallen, pushing her back into the pillows. She closed her eyes. At least for now, she had landed someplace soft, though there was no telling what the future held for her. She shut her leaking eyes—she'd been shot, so perhaps she was allowed to cry—but she doubted it would help.

Someone would come for her. Until then, she would lie here and wait, winnowing her mind of her sorrows so she would be strong when someone came.

There was no clock. She lay, listening to the sounds of the house, the muffled noise of the street. At last, she heard footsteps and the door. Two neat maids entered—one with a breakfast tray, the other with a dress lying over her outstretched arms.

Klara eyed it skeptically.

"Herr Hagen insists," the maid murmured.

"I will eat first." She was hungry. Halfway through her chocolate, she had a sudden memory of Levi smiling at her over his cup. Klara choked on a sob, slopping chocolate on the sheets. Levi was gone. No amount of silent preparation could sufficiently arm her.

"Miss!" The maid was at her side, taking away the cup, awkwardly patting her. The touch silenced Klara. The frightened maid drew back. "Is it your shoulder? Do you need something for the pain?"

Klara shook her head. This was something anodynes wouldn't help. She pressed her lips together, forcing her lungs to a rhythm that was regular and even. She couldn't allow such an outburst again. Not here.

"Shall I pour you some more?" The shorter offered, as the other blotted spilled chocolate from the bed covers.

"Thank you." She drank it all, though it was tasteless.

When she was finished, they helped her from the bed and washed her face and hands and neck. It felt strange to be waited on when she was used to partnering with Levi in constructing her meticulous facade. Klara told herself not to think of him and made herself notice other things. The soap here smelled of lavender, not spices and rum.

"We were asked to help you dress if you're ready, miss."

Klara nodded. Readiness was a fictional courtesy. If she wasn't ready, Hagen would order them to stuff her into the dress anyway.

She discovered there was a great deal of inconvenience in fashionable women's clothes. Everything fastened in back, in unreachable places she couldn't see. It took the two maids a quarter hour to dress her, and though Klara was accustomed to tight lacing, she wasn't used to bare arms, a bare neck, and barely covered shoulders. Her bandages showed, until the maids tucked a fichu into her neckline.

"And a shawl," the maid said, her touch light as she draped the silk on Klara's shoulders.

Klara would have argued against the lace ruffling around her throat and the absurdity of a six-inch fringe on the shawl—she'd trail it into the washstand or over the breakfast tray—but she was in no position to negotiate.

"I thought we could use this for your hair." The shorter one was the senior of the two maids, but she still spoke tentatively, holding up a wide silk bandeau of sky blue. Klara couldn't remember wearing such a color, but she said nothing, merely bending her head.

"And now, if you're ready..." The maid motioned for Klara to turn so she could see herself in the glass.

"I'm not sure I want to," Klara said.

The maid bit her lip, her face falling. "Is it your shoulder again?"

Klara smoothed her face. "A twinge. It will pass."

She was no beauty. Never would be, but she didn't look bad. Perhaps it was the way they'd arranged the fichu, but she had some shape after all. The wisps of hair beneath the bandeau softened her face—she and Levi had always combed it back. "I'm terribly pale."

Wordlessly, the younger maid uncapped a pot of rouge. It smelled of rose petals.

Klara tried to decline, but the maid wasn't deterred. "Just a dab. It will look so pretty."

She might as well look the part. Though she was frail as an autumn leaf, she didn't need to look like she'd blow away at the slightest gust.

They dabbed pink onto her cheeks, then her mouth.

"You look lovely, miss."

Klara looked sideways at the glass. It was too strange to look at herself straight on. Her bearing was austere, and the high-waisted dress was probably the only kind that would flatter her.

"Does Herr Hagen wish to see me?" she asked.

"When you're ready, he will join you in the carriage. Your trunk is already prepared."

Klara didn't ask where she was going. She doubted this girl could say. Her old life was gone. Hagen would use her, and because she was completely in his power, he need not trouble to be kind. She should be afraid of his silks and his chocolate.

Perhaps it was shock or lingering effects of the powder she'd taken to make her sleep. She should be afraid, but she wasn't. Wherever she was headed, it was new. She wouldn't have to go back to her apartment, to sort out the wreckage amid memories of Levi. He was gone, and Kasper Stark had died with him. There was an odd sort of comfort in that.

Klara bit down on her lip, telling herself that tears for Levi could wait. His loss was a lifetime kind of sorrow. She had no tears for Kasper, the person she'd worn like an ill-fitting coat. She didn't know who Hagen wanted her to be, but this tall, angular girl with steady eyes, short blonde hair, a blunt nose, and a scornful mouth was someone new—someone who might fit better.

She waved aside the maid's arm. "I can walk." It wasn't hard, if she kept her left arm still and leaned just a little on the railing with her right as she came down the stairs.

Josef waited at the bottom, talking to his uncle, but they broke off and watched her come down. Hagen's frown deepened as she came closer. "You were right. She looks well." Without another word, he took a banknote from his pocket and passed it to Josef, who waved it away.

"I did not mean it as a wager," he said and looked up to Klara, plainly trying to read her face. She was glad she'd worn the rouge. She stared back, unblinking, shutting him out as firmly as she did her pain for Levi.

"I had no choice, schätzen. He was waiting for me when I came home and had guessed much of it already."

She acknowledged this with a nod, remembering that ladies were not obliged to speak when they did not wish to. There was a different kind of power here; she might as well use it. She spoke to Hagen.

"Schätzen is a silly name. I'm Klara."

For a moment, neither man knew what to say.

"Klara Stark?" Hagen asked.

She shrugged. "You may decide the other half. Tell me when you're ready. For now, Klara is enough."

She'd seen Theresa do it countless times, so she thought she did a creditable job of swishing past Josef like he didn't exist on her way out the door.

"Klara—"

She pretended not to hear.

A footman helped her into the coach. She took the better seat, the forward-facing one. Climbing in after her, Hagen grunted in surprise but took the opposite seat, composing himself and donning a smile. "Are you quite comfortable, my dear?"

Klara employed the serene smile she'd discovered how to make in the hall. "Quite. Thank you." She settled back into the seat. "I look forward to an interesting journey."

Hagen folded his hands together. "Good. I shall enlighten you on the way."

He knocked on the roof. They rolled forward.

He thinks he owns me. Perhaps he does—now. Klara played with the thought, unspooling it, letting it wind and weave about her. She wouldn't hide from the truth, but she wouldn't lose hope either. Time, regular and relentless though it was, remained an unknown quantity. The future wasn't written.

She wouldn't free herself today, but sooner or later, the chance would come. There would be a way, and she would find it.

AUTHOR'S NOTE

Thank you! I hope you enjoyed this book—and that you will consider leaving an online review! It needn't be long. In this age of online retailers, your reviews are the endorsements that help my books get read.

There's more to come! Join my reader group for a sneak preview of *It Killed The Cat*, the sequel to Klara's story.

I first began jotting notes and research about Klara and 19th century Vienna back in 2013, during a stay in the B.C. mountains (that's British Columbia, for the non-Canadians out there!). Because of my commitment to the Fairchild series and some other group projects, I wasn't able to seriously tackle this book until 2017, when my husband Jeff told me I should buckle down and write it—and that I should go to Vienna. Of course the trip was amazing. I'm so grateful to my friend Cindy for keeping me company, getting me on the right trains, and helping me find the right locations for the scenes I'd sketched out in my battered blue notebook. Many thanks to Jeff and to Cindy's husband, Chris, for waving us off and keeping the home fires burning while the two of us had a wonderful time.

I can honestly say that the reading I did for this book was

every bit as entertaining as my trip to Vienna. The Vienna Congress is a fascinating juncture in history. For readers interested in exploring the period, I recommend Adam Zamoyski's *Rites of Peace: The Fall of Napoleon and the Congress of Vienna*, David King's *Vienna 1814: How the Conquerers of Napoleon Made Love, War and Peace at the Congress of Vienna*, and in the realm of fiction, Tracy Grant's excellent mystery, *Vienna Waltz*. For readers wanting to experience Vienna after the conference, Eva Ibbotson's *The Reluctant Heiress* and *The Star of Kazan* give wonderful pictures of the city.

I'm indebted to the friends, family, and other writers who generously shared their time and opinions to make this a better book. Regina Sirois, Cameron Garriepy and Jennie Goutet, thank you for rescuing me from plot snarls! Thank you, Jennifer Stevens, for your patient and exacting editing.

Last of all, thank you to my readers for your support and encouragement. My words matter so much more because of you.

Happy Reading!

ALSO BY JAIMA FIXSEN

Fairchild

Incognita

Courting Scandal

A Holiday in Bath

The Reformer

ABOUT THE AUTHOR

Jaima Fixsen is the author of the popular Fairchild regency romance series. She would rather read than sleep and though all her novels take place in the past, she couldn't live without indoor plumbing or smart phones.

When she isn't writing or child wrangling, she's a snow enthusiast. She lives with her family in Alberta, Canada, and most all just tries to keep up.

Made in the USA
Middletown, DE
19 July 2020

13130989R00168